CW00521549

Alexandre Dumas

The Works of Alexandre Dumas
Volume 6

Alexandre Dumas

The Works of Alexandre Dumas
Volume 6

1st Edition | ISBN: 978-3-75237-435-3

Place of Publication: Frankfurt am Main, Germany

Year of Publication: 2020

Outlook Verlag GmbH, Germany.

Reproduction of the original.

THE WORKS
OF
ALEXANDRE DUMAS
VOLUME SIX

THE REGENT'S DAUGHTER.

CHAPTER I.

AN ABBESS OF THE EIGHTEENTH CENTURY.

On the 8th February, 1719, a carriage, bearing the fleur-de-lis of France, with the motto of Orleans, preceded by two outriders and a page, entered the porch of the Abbey of Chelles, precisely as the clock struck ten, and, the door having been quickly opened, its two occupants stepped out.

The first was a man of from forty-five to forty-six years of age, short, and rather stout, with a high color, easy in his movements, and displaying in every gesture a certain air of high breeding and command.

The second, who followed slowly, was short, and remarkably thin. His face, though not precisely ugly, was very disagreeable, although bearing the evidences of a keen intellect. He seemed to feel the cold, and followed his companion, wrapped up in an ample cloak.

The first of these two made his way up the staircase with the air of a man well acquainted with the locality. Passing through a large antechamber containing several nuns, who bowed to the ground as he passed, he ran rather than walked to a reception-room, which, it must be confessed, bore but little trace of that austerity which is ordinarily ascribed to the interior of a cloister.

The other, who followed leisurely, was saluted almost as humbly by the nuns.

"And now," said the first, "wait here and warm yourself, while I go to her, and in ten minutes I will make an end of all these abuses you mention: if she deny, and I want proof, I will call you."

"Ten minutes, monseigneur," replied the man in the cloak; "in two hours your highness will not have even broached the subject of your visit. Oh! the Abbess de Chelles is a clever woman!"

So saying, he stretched himself out in an easy chair, which he had drawn near the fire, and rested his thin legs on the fender.

"Yes, yes," replied he who had been addressed as "your highness;" "I know, and if I could forget it, you take care to remind me of it often enough. Why did you bring me here to-day through all this wind and snow?"

"Because you would not come yesterday, monseigneur."

"Yesterday, it was impossible; I had an appointment with Lord Stair at five o'clock."

"In a house in the Rue des Bons Enfants. My lord does not live any longer, then, at the English embassy?"

"Abbe, I had forbidden you to follow me."

"Monseigneur, it is my duty to disobey you."

"Well, then, disobey; but let me tell stories at my pleasure, without your having the impertinence to show me that you know it, just for the sake of proving the efficiency of your police."

"Monseigneur may rest easy in future—I will believe anything!"

"I will not promise as much in return, abbe, for here I think you have made a mistake."

"Monseigneur, I know what I said, and I repeat it."

"But look! no noise, no light, perfect quiet, your account is incorrect; it is evident that we are late."

"Yesterday, monseigneur, where you stand, there was an orchestra of fifty musicians; there, where that young sister kneels so devoutly, was a buffet: what was upon it I cannot tell, but I know it was there, and in the gallery on the left, where a modest supper of lentils and cream cheese is now preparing for the holy sisters, were two hundred people, drinking, dancing, and making —"

"Well, making what?"

"Making love, monseigneur."

"Diable! are you sure of this?"

"Rather more sure than if I had seen it, and that is why you do well in coming to-day, and would have done better in coming yesterday. This sort of life does not become an abbess, monseigneur."

"No, it is only fit for an abbe. Ha!"

"I am a politician, monseigneur."

"Well, my daughter is a political abbess, that is all."

"Oh, let it be so, if it suits you, monseigneur; I am not so particular in point of morals, you know. To-morrow there will be another song or two out, but what does that matter?"——"Well, well, wait for me, and I will go and scold."

"Take my word for it, monseigneur, if you wish to scold properly you had better do it here, before me; if you fail in memory or arguments, sign to me,

3

and I will come to the rescue."

"Yes, yes, you are right," said the person who had undertaken to redress wrongs, and in whom we hope the reader has recognized Philippe d'Orleans. "Yes, this scandal must be quieted a little, at any rate: the abbess must not receive more than twice a week. There must be none of these dances and assemblies, and the cloisters must be re-established. Mademoiselle d'Orleans passed from gayety to a religious life; she left the Palais Royal for Chelles in spite of all I could do to prevent her; now, for five days in the week she must be the abbess, and that will leave her two to play the great lady."

"Ah, monseigneur, you are beginning to see the thing in its true light."

"Is not this what you wish?"

"It is what is necessary. It seems to me that an abbess who has thirty valets, fifteen footmen, ten cooks, eight grooms, and a mute—who fences, plays the horn, and the violincello—who is a surgeon and a hairdresser—who shoots and makes fireworks—cannot be very dull."

"Has not my daughter been told of my arrival," said the duke to an old nun who crossed the room with a bunch of keys in her hand; "I wish to know whether I shall go to her, or whether she is coming to me."

"Madame is coming, monseigneur," replied the sister, respectfully.

"It is well," murmured the regent, somewhat impatiently.

"Monseigneur, remember the parable of Jesus driving out the money-changers from the temple; you know it, or ought to know it, for I taught it you when I was your preceptor. Now, drive out these musicians, these Pharisees, these comedians and anatomists; three only of each profession will make a nice escort for our return."

"Do not fear, I am in a preaching vein."

"Then," replied Dubois, rising, "that is most fortunate, for here she is."

At this moment a door, leading to the interior of the convent, was opened, and the person so impatiently expected appeared.

Let us explain who was this worthy person who had succeeded, by repeated follies, in rousing the anger of Philippe d'Orleans, the most indulgent man and father in France.

Mademoiselle de Chartres, Louise-Adelaide-d'Orleans, was the second and prettiest of the regent's daughters. She had a beautiful complexion, fine eyes, a good figure, and well-shaped hands. Her teeth were splendid, and her grandmother, the princess palatine, compared them to a string of pearls in a coral casket. She danced well, sang better, and played at sight. She had learned of Cauchereau, one of the first artists at the opera, with whom she had made much more progress than is common with ladies, and especially with princesses. It is true that she was most assiduous; the secret of that assiduity will be shortly revealed.

All her tastes were masculine. She appeared to have changed sex with her brother Louis. She loved dogs and horses; amused herself with pistols and foils, but cared little for any feminine occupations.

Her chief predilection, however, was for music; she seldom missed a night at the opera when her master Cauchereau performed; and once, when he surpassed himself in an air, she exclaimed, "Bravo, bravo, my dear Cauchereau!" in a voice audible to the whole house.

The Duchesse d'Orleans judged that the exclamation was somewhat indiscreet for a princess of the blood, and decided that Mademoiselle Chartres knew enough of music. Cauchereau was well paid, and desired not to return to the Palais Royal. The duchess also begged her daughter to spend a fortnight at the convent of Chelles, the abbess of which, a sister of Marechal de Villars, was a friend of hers.

It was doubtless during this retreat that mademoiselle—who did everything by fits and starts—resolved to renounce the world. Toward the end of the holy week of 1718, she asked and obtained her father's permission to spend Easter at Chelles; but at the end of that time, instead of returning to the palais, she expressed a wish to remain as a nun.

The duke tried to oppose this, but Mademoiselle de Chartres was obstinate, and on the 23d of April she took the vows. Then the duke treated with Mademoiselle de Villars for the abbey, and, on the promise of twelve thousand francs, Mademoiselle de Chartres was named abbess in her stead, and she had occupied the post about a year.

This, then, was the abbess of Chelles, who appeared before her father, not surrounded by an elegant and profane court, but followed by six nuns dressed in black and holding torches. There was no sign of frivolity or of pleasure; nothing but the most somber apparel and the most severe aspect. The regent, however, suspected that he had been kept waiting while all this was preparing.

"I do not like hypocrisy," said he, sharply, "and can forgive vices which are not hidden under the garb of virtues. All these lights, madame, are doubtless the remains of yesterday's illumination. Are all your flowers so faded, and all your guests so fatigued, that you cannot show me a single bouquet nor a single dancer?"

"Monsieur," said the abbess in a grave tone, "this is not the place for fetes and amusements."——"Yes," answered the regent, "I see, that if you feasted yesterday, you fast to-day."

"Did you come here, monsieur, to catechise? At least what you see should reply to any accusations against me."

"I came to tell you, madame," replied the regent, annoyed at being supposed to have been duped, "that the life you lead displeases me; your conduct yesterday was unbecoming an abbess; your austerities to-day are unbecoming a princess of the blood; decide, once for all, between the nun and the court lady. People begin to speak ill of you, and I have enemies enough of my own, without your saddling me with others from the depth of your convent."

"Alas, monsieur, in giving entertainments, balls, and concerts, which have been quoted as the best in Paris, I have neither pleased those enemies, nor you, nor myself. Yesterday was my last interview with the world; this morning I have taken leave of it forever; and to-day, while still ignorant of your visit, I had adopted a determination from which I will never depart."

"And what is it?" asked the regent, suspecting that this was only a new specimen of his daughter's ordinary follies.

"Come to this window and look out," said the abbess.

The regent, in compliance with the invitation, approached the window, and saw a large fire blazing in the middle of the courtyard. Dubois—who was as curious as if he had really been an abbe—slipped up beside him.

Several people were rapidly passing and repassing before the fire, and throwing various singular-shaped objects into the flames.

"But what is that?" asked the regent of Dubois, who seemed as much surprised as himself.

"That which is burning now?" asked the abbe.——"Yes," replied the regent.

"Ma foi, monseigneur, it looks to me very much like a violincello."

"It is mine," said the abbess, "an excellent violincello by Valeri."

"And you are burning it!" exclaimed the duke.

"All instruments are sources of perdition," said the abbess, in a tone which betrayed the most profound remorse.

"Eh, but here is a harpsichord," interrupted the duke.

"My harpsichord, monsieur; it was so perfect that it enticed me toward earthly things; I condemned it this morning."

"And what are those chests of papers with which they are feeding the fire?" asked Dubois, whom the spectacle seemed to interest immensely.

"My music, which I am having burned."

"Your music?" demanded the regent.

"Yes, and even yours," answered the abbess; "look carefully and you will see your opera of 'Panthée' follow in its turn. You will understand that my resolution once taken, its execution was necessarily general."

"Well, madame, this time you are really mad! To light the fire with music, and then feed it with bass-viols and harpsichords is really a little too luxurious."

"I am doing penance, monsieur."

"Hum, say rather that you are refitting your house, and that this is an excuse for buying new furniture, since you are doubtless tired of the old."

"No, monseigneur, it is no such thing."

"Well, then, what is it? Tell me frankly."

"In truth, I am weary of amusing myself, and, indeed, I intend to act differently."

"And what are you going to do?"

"I am going with my nuns to visit my tomb."

"Diable, monseigneur!" exclaimed the abbe, "her wits are gone at last."

"It will be truly edifying, will it not, monsieur?" continued the abbess, gravely.

"Indeed," answered the regent, "if you really do this, I doubt not but people will laugh at it twice as much as they did at your suppers."

"Will you accompany me, messieurs?" continued the abbess; "I am going to spend a few minutes in my coffin; it is a fancy I have had a long time."

"You will have plenty of time for that," said the regent; "moreover, you have not even invented this amusement; for Charles the Fifth, who became a monk as you became a nun, without exactly knowing why, thought of it before you."

"Then you will not go with me, monsieur?" said the abbess.

"I," answered the duke, who had not the least sympathy with somber ideas, "I go to see tombs! I go to hear the De Profundis! No, pardieu! and the only thing which consoles me for not being able to escape them some day, is, that I shall neither see the one nor the other."

"Ah, monsieur," answered the abbess, in a scandalized tone, "you do not, then, believe in the immortality of the soul?"

"I believe that you are raving mad. Confound this abbe, who promises me a feast, and brings me to a funeral."

"By my faith, monseigneur," said Dubois, "I think I prefer the extravagance of yesterday; it was more attractive."

The abbess bowed, and made a few steps toward the door. The duke and Dubois remained staring at each other, uncertain whether to laugh or cry.

"One word more," said the duke; "are you decided this time, or is it not some fever which you have caught from your confessor? If it be real, I have nothing to say; but if it be a fever, I desire that they cure you of it. I have Morceau and Chirac, whom I pay for attending on me and mine."

"Monseigneur," answered the abbess, "you forget that I know sufficient of medicine to undertake my own cure, if I were ill: I can, therefore, assure you that I am not. I am a Jansenist; that is all."

"Ah," cried the duke, "this is more of Father le Doux's work, that execrable Benedictine! At least I know a treatment which will cure him."

"What is that?" asked the abbess.

"The Bastille."

And he went out in a rage, followed by Dubois, who was laughing heartily.

"You see," said the regent, after a long silence, and when they were nearing Paris, "I preached with a good grace; it seems it was I who needed the sermon."

"Well, you are a happy father, that is all; I compliment you on your younger daughter, Mademoiselle de Chartres. Unluckily your elder daughter, the Duchesse de Berry—"

"Oh, do not talk of her; she is my ulcer, particularly when I am in a bad temper."

"Well?"

"I have a great mind to make use of it by finishing with her at one blow."

"She is at the Luxembourg?"

"I believe so."

"Let us go to the Luxembourg, monseigneur."

"You go with me?"

"I shall not leave you to-night."

"Well, drive to the Luxembourg."

CHAPTER II.

DECIDEDLY THE FAMILY BEGINS TO SETTLE DOWN.

Whatever the regent might say, the Duchesse de Berry was his favorite daughter. At seven years of age she had been seized with a disease which all the doctors declared to be fatal, and when they had abandoned her, her father, who had studied medicine, took her in hand himself, and succeeded in saving her.

From that time the regent's affection for his daughter became almost a weakness. He allowed the haughty and self-willed child the most perfect liberty; her education was neglected, but this did not prevent Louis XIV. from choosing her as a wife for his grandson the Duc de Berry.

It is well known how death at once struck a triple blow at the royal posterity, and within a few years carried off the dauphin, the Duc and Duchesse de Bourgoyne and the Duc de Berry.

Left a widow at twenty years of age, loving her father almost as tenderly as he loved her, and having to choose between the society of Versailles and that of the Palais Royal, the Duchesse de Berry, young, beautiful, and fond of pleasure, had quickly decided. She took part in all the fetes, the pleasures and follies of her father.

The Duc d'Orleans, in his increasing fondness for his daughter—who already had six hundred thousand francs a year—allowed her four hundred thousand francs more from his private fortune. He gave up the Luxembourg to her, gave her a bodyguard, and at length, to the scandal of those who advocated the old forms of etiquette, he merely shrugged his shoulders when the Duchesse de Berry passed through Paris preceded by cymbals and trumpets, and only laughed when she received the Venetian ambassador on a throne, raised on three steps, which nearly embroiled France with the republic of Venice.

About this time the Duchesse de Berry took a fancy to fall in love with the Chevalier de Riom.

The Chevalier de Riom was a nephew or grand-nephew of the Duc de Lauzun, who came to Paris in 1715 to seek his fortune, and found it at the Luxembourg. Introduced to the princess by Madame de Mouchy, he soon established the same influence over her as his uncle, the Duc de Lauzun, had exercised over La Grande Mademoiselle fifty years before, and was soon established as her lover, supplanting Lahaie, who was sent on an embassy to Denmark.

The duchess had the singular moderation of never having had more than two lovers; Lahaie, whom she had never avowed, and Riom, whom she proclaimed aloud.

This was not the true cause of the malice with which the princess was pursued; it arose rather from the previous offenses of her passage through Paris, the reception of the ambassadors, her bodyguard, and her assumptions. The duke himself was indignant at Riom's influence over his daughter. Riom had been brought up by the Duc de Lauzun, who in the morning had crushed the hand of the Princesse de Monaco with the heel of the boot which, in the evening, he made the daughter of Gaston d'Orleans pull off, and who had given his nephew the following instruction, which Riom had fully carried out.

"The daughters of France," said he, "must be treated with a high hand;" and Riom, trusting to his uncle's experience, had so well schooled the Duchesse de Berry that she scarcely dared to give a fete without his permission.

The duke took as strong a dislike to Riom as his careless character allowed him to take to any one, and, under pretext of serving the duchess, had given him a regiment, then the government of Cognac, then the order to retire to his government, which almost made his favors look like disfavors and disgrace.

The duchess was not deceived; she went to her father, begged, prayed, and scolded, but in vain; and she went away threatening the duke with her anger, and declaring that Riom should not go.

The duke's only reply was to repeat his orders for Riom's departure the next day, and Riom had respectfully promised to obey.

The same day, which was the one preceding that on which our story opens, Riom had ostensibly set out, and Dubois himself had told the duke that he had left for Cognac at nine o'clock.

Meanwhile the duke had not again seen his daughter; thus, when he spoke of going to finish with her, it was rather a pardon than a quarrel that he went to seek. Dubois had not been duped by this pretended resolution; but Riom was gone, and that was all he wanted; he hoped to slip in some new personage who should efface all memory of Riom, who was to be sent to join the Maréchal de Berwick in Spain.

The carriage stopped before the Luxembourg, which was lighted as usual.

The duke ascended the steps with his usual celerity, Dubois remained in a corner of the carriage. Presently the duke appeared at the door with a disappointed air.

"Ah, monseigneur," said Dubois, "are you refused admittance?"

"No, the duchesse is not here."

"Where, then—at the Carmelites?"

"No, at Meudon."

"At Meudon, in February, and in such weather; what can she be doing there?"

"It is easy to know."

"How?"

"Let us go to Meudon."

"To Meudon!" said the regent, jumping into the carriage; "I allow you five-and-twenty minutes to get there."

"I would humbly beg to remind monseigneur," said the coachman, "that the horses have already gone ten leagues."

"Kill them, but be at Meudon in five-and-twenty minutes."

There was no reply to be made to such an order; the coachman whipped his horses, and the noble animals set out at as brisk a pace as if they had just left the stable.

Throughout the drive Dubois was silent, and the regent thoughtful; there was nothing on the route to arrest the attention of either, and they arrived at Meudon full of contradictory reflections.

This time both alighted; Dubois, thinking the interview might be long, was anxious to find a more comfortable waiting-place than a carriage.

At the door they found a Swiss in full livery—he stopped them—the duke made himself known.

"Pardon," said the Swiss, "I did not know that monseigneur was expected."

"Expected or not, I am here; send word to the princess."

"Monseigneur is to be at the ceremony?" asked the Swiss, who seemed embarrassed.

"Yes, of course," put in Dubois, stopping the duke, who was about to ask what ceremony; "and I also."

"Then shall I lead monseigneur at once to the chapel?"

"To the chapel?" asked the duke.

"Yes; for the ceremony is already commenced."

"Ah, Dubois," said the duke, "is she also going to take the veil?"

"Monseigneur," said Dubois, "I should rather say she is going to be married."

"Pardieu!" exclaimed the regent, "that would crown all;" and he darted toward the staircase, followed by Dubois.

"Does not monseigneur wish me to guide him?" asked the Swiss.

"It is needless," cried the regent; "I know the way."

Indeed—with an agility surprising in so corpulent a man—the regent darted through the rooms and corridors, and arrived at the door of the chapel, which appeared to be closed, but yielded to the first touch. Dubois was right.

Riom, who had returned secretly, was on his knees with the princess, before the private chaplain of the Luxembourg, while M. de Pons, Riom's relative, and the Marquis de la Rochefoucauld, captain of the princess's guard, held the canopy over their heads; Messrs. de Mouchy and de Lauzun stood, one by the duchess and the other by Riom.

"Certainly fortune is against us, monseigneur," said Dubois; "we are five minutes too late."

"Mordieu!" cried the duke, exasperated, "we will see."

"Chut," said Dubois; "I cannot permit sacrilege. If it were any use, I do not say; but this would be mere folly."

"Are they married, then?" asked the duke, drawing back.

"So much married, monseigneur, that the devil himself cannot unmarry them, without the assistance of the pope."

"I will write to Rome!"

"Take care, monseigneur; do not waste your influence; you will want it all, so get me made a cardinal."

"But," exclaimed the regent, "such a marriage is intolerable."

"Mésalliances are in fashion," said Dubois; "there is nothing else talked of—Louis XIV. made a mésalliance in marrying Madame de Maintenon, to whom you pay a pension as his widow—La Grande Mademoiselle made a mésalliance in marrying the Duc de Lauzun—you did so in marrying Mademoiselle de Blois, so much so, indeed, that when you announced the marriage to your mother, the princess palatine, she replied by a blow. Did not I do the same when I married the daughter of a village schoolmaster? After such good examples, why should not your daughter do so in her turn?"

13

"Silence, demon," said the regent.

"Besides," continued Dubois, "the Duchesse de Berry's passion began to be talked about, and this will quiet the talk; for it will be known all through Paris to-morrow. Decidedly, monseigneur, your family begins to settle down."

The Duc d'Orleans uttered an oath, to which Dubois replied by a laugh, which Mephistopheles might have envied.

"Silence!" cried a Swiss, who did not know who it was that was making a noise, and did not wish the pious exhortation of the chaplain to be lost.

"Silence, monseigneur," repeated Dubois; "you are disturbing the ceremony."

"If we are not silent," replied the duke, "the next thing they will do will be to turn us out."

"Silence!" repeated the Swiss, striking the flagstone with his halberd, while the Duchesse de Berry sent M. de Mouchy to learn who was causing the disturbance.

M. de Mouchy obeyed the orders of the duchess, and perceiving two persons who appeared to be concealing themselves in the shade, he approached them.

"Who is making this noise?" said he; "and who gave you permission to enter this chapel?"

"One who has a great mind to send you all out by the window," replied the regent, "but who will content himself at present with begging you to order M. de Riom to set out at once for Cognac, and to intimate to the Duchesse de Berry that she had better absent herself from the Palais Royal."

The regent went out, signing to Dubois to follow; and, leaving M. de Mouchy bewildered at his appearance, returned to the Palais Royal.

That evening the regent wrote a letter, and ringing for a valet:

"Take care that this letter is dispatched by an express courier to-morrow morning, and is delivered only to the person to whom it is addressed."

That person was Madame Ursule, Superior of the Ursuline Convent at Clisson.

CHAPTER III.

WHAT PASSED THREE NIGHTS LATER AT EIGHT HUNDRED LEAGUES FROM THE PALAIS ROYAL.

Three nights after that on which we have seen the regent, first at Chelles and then at Meudon, a scene passed in the environs of Nantes which cannot be omitted in this history; we will therefore exercise our privilege of transporting the reader to that place.

On the road to Clisson, two or three miles from Nantes—near the convent known as the residence of Abelard—was a large dark house, surrounded by thick stunted trees; hedges everywhere surrounded the inclosure outside the walls, hedges impervious to the sight, and only interrupted by a wicket gate.

This gate led into a garden, at the end of which was a wall, having a small, massive, and closed door. From a distance this grave and dismal residence appeared like a prison; it was, however, a convent, full of young Augustines, subject to a rule lenient as compared with provincial customs, but rigid as compared with those of Paris.

The house was inaccessible on three sides, but the fourth, which did not face the road, abutted on a large sheet of water; and ten feet above its surface were the windows of the refectory.

This little lake was carefully guarded, and was surrounded by high wooden palisades. A single iron gate opened into it, and at the same time gave a passage to the waters of a small rivulet which fed the lake, and the water had egress at the opposite end.

In the summer, a small boat belonging to the garden was seen on the water, and was used for fishing.

Sometimes, also, in summer, on dark nights, the river-gate was mysteriously opened, and a man, wrapped in a large brown cloak, silently dropped into the little boat, which appeared to detach itself from its fastenings, then glided quietly along, and stopped under one of the barred windows of the refectory.

Soon a sound was heard, imitating the croaking of a frog or the cry of the owl so common there, and then a young girl would appear at the window, and pass her head through the opening between the bars, which were, however, too high for the man to reach. A low and tender conversation was then carried on, and at length, after a different hour and a different signal had been agreed upon for their next interview, they separated, the boat disappeared, the gate shut gently, and the young girl closed the window with a sigh.

But now it was the month of February, and in the terrible winter of 1719. The trees were powdered with hoar frost, and it was at this time impossible to glide quietly along in the little boat, for the lake was covered with ice. And yet, in this biting cold, in this dark, starless night, a cavalier ventured alone into the open country, and along a cross-road which led to Clisson. He threw the reins on the neck of his horse, which proceeded at a slow and careful pace.

Soon, however, in spite of his instinctive precaution, the poor animal, which had no light to guide him, struck against a stone and nearly fell. The rider soon perceived that his horse was lamed, and on seeing a trail of blood upon the snow, discovered that it was wounded.

The young man appeared seriously annoyed at the accident, and while deliberating what course to take, he heard a sound of horses' feet on the same road; and, feeling sure that if they were pursuing him he could not escape them, he remounted his horse, drew aside behind some fallen trees, put his sword under his arm, drew out a pistol, and waited.

The cavalcade soon appeared; they were four in number, and rode silently along, passing the group of trees which hid the cavalier, when suddenly they stopped. One who appeared the chief alighted, took out a dark lantern, and examined the road.

As they could not see far, they returned some steps, and, by the light of their lantern, perceived the cavalier.

The sound of cocking pistols was now heard.

"Hola!" said the cavalier with the wounded horse, taking the initiative; "who are you, and what do you want?"

"It is he," murmured two or three voices.

The man with the lantern advanced toward the cavalier.

"Advance one step further and you are a dead man," said the cavalier. "Declare your name at once, that I may know with whom I have to deal."

"Shoot no one, Gaston de Chanlay," replied the man with the lantern, calmly; "and put up your pistols."

"Ah! it is the Marquis de Pontcalec."

"Yes; it is I."

"And what do you come here for, may I ask?"

16

"To demand some explanation of your conduct. Approach and reply, if you please."

"The invitation is singular, marquis. If you wish for an answer, could you not ask it in other terms?"

"Approach, Gaston," said another voice; "we really wish to speak with you."

"A la bonne heure," said Chanlay, "I recognize you there, Montlouis; but I confess I am not accustomed to M. de Pontcalec's manner of proceeding."

"My manners are those of a frank and open Breton, monsieur," replied the marquis, "of one who has nothing to hide from his friends, and is willing to be questioned as freely as he questions others."

"I join Montlouis," said another voice, "in begging Gaston to explain amicably. Surely it is not our interest to quarrel among ourselves."

"Thanks, Du Couëdic," said De Chanlay, "I am of the same opinion; so here I am"—and sheathing his sword at these words, the young man issued from his retreat and approached the group.

"M. de Talhouet," said Pontcalec, in the tone of a man who has a right to issue commands, "watch that no one approaches."

M. de Talhouet obeyed, and rode round in a circle, keeping both eyes and ears open.

"And now," said the marquis, "let us put out our lantern, since we have found our man!"

"Messieurs," said De Chanlay, "all this seems to me somewhat strange. It appears that you were following me—that you were seeking for me, now you have found me, and may put out your lantern. What does it mean? If it is a joke, I confess I think both time and place ill-chosen."

"No, monsieur," replied Pontcalec, in his hard, dry voice, "it is not a joke; it is an interrogatory."

"An interrogatory?" said DeChanlay, frowning.

"An explanation, rather," said Montlouis.

"Interrogatory or explanation, it matters not," said Pontcalec, "the thing is too serious to argue about words. M. de Chanlay, I repeat, reply to our questions."

"You speak roughly, Marquis de Pontcalec," replied the chevalier.

"If I command, it is because I have the right to do so. Am I, or am I not, your chief?"

"Certainly you are; but that is no reason for forgetting the consideration which one gentleman owes to another."

"Monsieur de Chanlay, all these objections seem to me like shuffling. You have sworn to obey—do so now."

"I swore to obey," replied the chevalier, "but not as a servant."

"You swore to obey as a slave. Obey, then, or submit to the consequences of your disobedience!"

"Monsieur le Marquis—!"

"My dear Gaston," cried Montlouis, "speak, I beg, as soon as possible: by a word you can remove all suspicion."

"Suspicion!" cried Gaston, pale with anger, "am *I* suspected, then?"

"Certainly you are," said Pontcalec, with his ordinary roughness. "Do you think if we did not suspect you we should amuse ourselves by following you on such a night as this?"

"Oh, that is quite another matter!" said Gaston, coldly; "tell me your suspicions—I listen."

"Chevalier, remember the facts; we four were conspiring together, and we did not seek your aid; you offered it, saying, that besides being willing to aid in the public good, you had a private revenge to serve in this. Am I not right?"

"You are."

"We received you—welcomed you as a friend, as a brother; we told you all our hopes, all our plans; nay, more—you were elected, by chance, the one to strike the glorious blow. Each one of us offered to take your part, but you refused. Is it not so?"

"You have spoken the strictest truth, marquis."

"This very morning we drew the lots; this evening you should be on the road to Paris. Instead of that, where do we find you? on the road to Clisson, where are lodged the mortal enemies of Breton independence, where lives your sworn foe—the Marechal de Montesquieu."

"Ah! monsieur," said Gaston, scornfully.

"Reply by open words, and not by sneers: reply, M. de Chanlay, and quickly."

"Reply, Gaston," said Du Couëdic and Montlouis, imploringly.

"And to what am I to reply?"

"You are to account for your frequent absence during the last two months—

for the mystery which surrounds you—for refusing, as you do, once or twice weekly, to join our nightly meetings. We confess, Gaston, all this has made us uneasy; by a word you can reassure us."

"You see, monsieur, that you are proved guilty by hiding, instead of pursuing your course."

"I did not pursue my course, because my horse was wounded; you may see the stains of blood upon the road."

"But why did you hide?"

"Because I wished to know first who was pursuing me. Have I not the fear of being arrested, as well as yourselves?"

"And where are you going?"

"If you had followed my steps as you have done hitherto, you would have found that my path did not lead to Clisson."

"Nor to Paris."

"I beg," said De Chanlay, "that you will trust me, and respect my secret—a secret in which not only my own honor, but that of another, is concerned. You do not know, perhaps—it may be exaggerated—how extreme is my delicacy on this point."

"Then it is a love-secret," said Montlouis.——"Yes, and the secret of a first love," replied Gaston.

"All evasions," cried Pontcalec.

"Marquis!" said Gaston, haughtily.

"This is not saying enough, my friend," replied Du Couëdic. "How can we believe that you are going to a rendezvous in such weather, and that this rendezvous is not at Clisson—where, except the Augustine Convent, there is not a single house for two miles around."

"M. de Chanlay," said the Marquis de Pontcalec, in an agitated voice, "you swore to obey me as your chief, and to devote soul and body to our holy cause. Monsieur, our undertaking is serious—our property, our liberties, our lives and our honor are at stake;—will you reply clearly and freely to the questions which I put to you in the name of all, so as to remove all doubts? If not, Gaston de Chanlay—by virtue of that right which you gave me, of your own free will, over your life—if not, I declare, on my honor, I will blow your brains out with my own hand!"

A solemn silence followed these words; not one voice was raised to defend Gaston; he looked at each one in turn, and each one turned away from him.

"Marquis," said the chevalier at length, in a tone of deep feeling, "not only do you insult me by suspicions, but you grieve me by saying that I can only remove those suspicions by declaring my secret. Stay," added he, drawing a pocketbook from his coat, and hastily penciling a few words on a leaf which he tore out; "stay, here is the secret you wish to know; I hold it in one hand, and in the other I hold a loaded pistol. Will you make me reparation for the insult you have offered me? or, in my turn, I give you my word as a gentleman that I will blow my brains out. When I am dead, open my hand and read this paper; you will then see if I deserved your suspicions."

And Gaston held the pistol to his head with the calm resolution which showed that he would keep his word.

"Gaston! Gaston!" cried Montlouis, while Du Couëdic held his arm; "stop, in Heaven's name! Marquis, he would do as he said; pardon him, and he will tell us all. Is it not so, Gaston? You will not have a secret from your brothers, who beg you, in the names of their wives and children, to tell it them."

"Certainly," said the marquis, "I not only pardon but love him; he knows it well. Let him but prove his innocence, and I will make him every reparation, but, before that, nothing: he is young, and alone in the world. He has not, like us, wives and children, whose happiness and whose fortune he is risking; he stakes only his own life, and he holds that as cheaply as is usual at twenty years of age; but with his life he risks ours; and yet, let him say but one word showing a justification, and I will be the first to open my arms to him."

"Well, marquis," said Gaston, after a few moments' silence, "follow me, and you shall be satisfied."

"And we?" asked Montlouis and Du Couëdic.

"Come, also, you are all gentlemen; I risk no more in confiding my secret to all than to one."

The marquis called Talhouet, who had kept good watch, and now rejoined the group, and followed without asking what had passed.

All five went on but slowly, for Gaston's horse was lame; the chevalier guided them toward the convent, then to the little rivulet, and at ten paces from the iron gate he stopped.

"It is here," said he.

"Here?"

"At the convent?"

"Yes, my friends; there is here, at this moment, a young girl whom I have loved since I saw her a year ago in the procession at the Fete Dieu at Nantes;

she observed me also—I followed her, and sent her a letter."

"But how do you see her?" asked the marquis.

"A hundred louis won the gardener over to my interest; he has given me a key to this gate; in the summer I come in a boat to the convent wall; ten feet above the water is a window, where she awaits me. If it were lighter, you could see it from this spot—and, in spite of the darkness, I see it now."

"Yes, I understand how you manage in summer, but you cannot use the boat now."

"True; but, instead, there is a coating of ice, on which I shall go this evening; perhaps it will break and engulf me; so much the better, for then, I hope, your suspicions would die with me."

"You have taken a load from my breast," said Montlouis.

"Ah! my poor Gaston, how happy you make me; for, remember, Du Couëdic and I answered for you."

"Chevalier," said the marquis, "pardon and embrace us."

"Willingly, marquis; but you have destroyed a portion of my happiness."

"How so?"

"I wished my love to have been known to no one. I have so much need of strength and courage! Am I not to leave her to-night forever?"

"Who knows, chevalier? You look gloomily at the future."

"I know what I am saying, Montlouis."

"If you succeed—and with your courage and sang-froid you ought to succeed —France is free: then she will owe her liberty to you, and you will be master of your own fate."

"Ah! marquis, if I succeed, it will be for you; my own fate is fixed."

"Courage, chevalier; meanwhile, let us see how you manage these love affairs."

"Still mistrust, marquis?"

"Still; my dear Gaston, I mistrust myself: and, naturally enough; after being named your chief, all the responsibility rests on me, and I must watch over you all."

"At least, marquis, I am as anxious to reach the foot of that wall as you can be to see me, so I shall not keep you waiting long."

Gaston tied his horse to a tree; by means of a plank thrown across, he passed the stream, opened the gate, and then, following the palisades so as to get away from the stream, he stepped upon the ice, which cracked under his feet.

"In Heaven's name," cried Montlouis, "be prudent."

"Look, marquis," said Gaston.

"I believe you; I believe you, Gaston."

"You give me fresh courage," replied the chevalier.

"And now, Gaston, one word more. When shall you leave?"

"To-morrow at this time, marquis, I shall probably be thirty leagues on the way to Paris."

"Come back and let us embrace, and say adieu."——"With pleasure."

Gaston retraced his steps, and was embraced cordially by each of the chevaliers, who did not turn away till they saw that he had arrived safely at the end of his perilous journey.

CHAPTER IV.

SHOWING HOW CHANCE ARRANGES SOME MATTERS BETTER THAN PROVIDENCE.

In spite of the cracking of the ice, Gaston pursued his way boldly, and perceived, with a beating heart, that the winter rains had raised the waters of the little lake, so that he might possibly be able to reach the window.

He was not mistaken; on giving the signal, the window was opened, then a head appeared nearly at the level of his own, and a hand touched his; it was the first time. Gaston seized it, and covered it with kisses.

"Gaston, you have come, in spite of the cold, and on the ice; I told you in my letter not to do so."

"With your letter on my heart, Helene, I think I can run no danger; but what have you to tell me? You have been crying!"

"Alas, since this morning I have done little else."

"Since this morning," said Gaston, with a sad smile, "that is strange; if I were not a man, I too should have cried since this morning."

"What do you say, Gaston?"

"Nothing, nothing; tell me, what are your griefs, Helene?"

"Alas! you know I am not my own mistress. I am a poor orphan, brought up here, having no other world than the convent. I have never seen any one to whom I can give the names of father or mother—my mother I believe to be dead, and my father is absent; I depend upon an invisible power, revealed only to our superior. This morning the good mother sent for me, and announced, with tears in her eyes, that I was to leave."

"To leave the convent, Helene?"

"Yes; my family reclaims me, Gaston."

"Your family? Alas! what new misfortune awaits us?"

"Yes, it is a misfortune, Gaston. Our good mother at first congratulated me, as if it were a pleasure; but I was happy here, and wished to remain till I became your wife. I am otherwise disposed of, but how?"

"And this order to remove you?"

"Admits of neither dispute nor delay. Alas! it seems that I belong to a powerful family, and that I am the daughter of some great nobleman. When the good mother told me I must leave, I burst into tears, and fell on my knees, and said I would not leave her; then, suspecting that I had some hidden motive, she pressed me, questioned me, and—forgive me, Gaston—I wanted to confide in some one; I felt the want of pity and consolation, and I told her all—that we loved each other—all except the manner in which we meet. I was afraid if I told her that, that she would prevent my seeing you this last time to say adieu."

"But did you not tell, Helene, what were my plans; that, bound to an association myself for six months, perhaps for a year, at the end of that time, the very day I should be free, my name, my fortune, my very life, was yours?"

"I told her, Gaston; and this is what makes me think I am the daughter of some powerful nobleman, for then Mother Ursula replied: 'You must forget the chevalier, my child, for who knows that your new family would consent to your marrying him?'"

"But do not I belong to one of the oldest families in Brittany? and, though I am not rich, my fortune is independent. Did you say this, Helene?"

"Yes; I said to her, 'Gaston chose me, an orphan, without name and without fortune. I may be separated from him, but it would be cruel ingratitude to forget him, and I shall never do so.'"

"Helene, you are an angel. And you cannot then imagine who are your parents, or to what you are destined?"

"No; it seems that it is a secret on which all my future happiness depends; only, Gaston, I fear they are high in station, for it almost appeared as if our superior spoke to me with deference."

"To you, Helene?"

"Yes."

"So much the better," said Gaston, sighing.

"Do you rejoice at our separation, Gaston?"

"No, Helene; but I rejoice that you should find a family when you are about to lose a friend."

"Lose a friend, Gaston! I have none but you; whom then should I lose?"

"At least, I must leave you for some time, Helene."

"What do you mean?"

"I mean that Fate has endeavored to make our lots similar, and that you are not the only one who does not know what the morrow may bring forth."

"Gaston! Gaston! what does this strange language mean?"

"That I also am subject to a fatality which I must obey—that I also am governed by an irresistible and superior power."

"You! oh heavens!"

"To a power which may condemn me to leave you in a week—in a fortnight —in a month; and not only to leave you, but to leave France."

"Ah, Gaston! what do you tell me?"

"What in my love, or rather in my egotism, I have dreaded to tell you before. I shut my eyes to this hour, and yet I knew that it must come; this morning they were opened. I must leave you, Helene."

"But why? What have you undertaken? what will become of you?"

"Alas! Helene, we each have our secret," said the chevalier, sorrowfully; "I pray that yours may be less terrible than mine."

"Gaston!"

"Were you not the first to say that we must part, Helene? Had not you first the courage to renounce me? Well; blessings on you for that courage—for I, Helene, had it not."

And at these last words the young man again pressed his lips to her hand, and Helene could see that tears stood in his eyes.

"Oh, mon Dieu!" murmured she, "how have we deserved this misery?"

At this exclamation Gaston raised his head. "Come," said he, as if to himself, "courage! It is useless to struggle against these necessities; let us obey without a murmur, and perhaps our resignation may disarm our fate. Can I see you again?"

"I fear not—I leave to-morrow."

"And on what road?"

"To Paris."

"Good heavens!" cried Gaston; "and I also."

"You, also, Gaston?"

"Yes, Helene; we were mistaken, we need not part."

"Oh, Gaston; is it true?"

25

"Helene, we had no right to accuse Providence; not only can we see each other on the journey, but at Paris we will not be separated. How do you travel?"

"In the convent carriage, with post horses and by short stages."

"Who goes with you?"

"A nun, who will return to the convent when she has delivered me over to those who await me."

"All is for the best, Helene. I shall go on horseback, as a stranger, unknown to you; each evening I may speak to you, or, if I cannot do so, I shall at least see you—it will be but a half separation."

And the two lovers, with the buoyant hopes of youth, after meeting with tears and sadness, parted with smiles and joyous confidence in the future. Gaston recrossed the frozen lake, and found, instead of his own wounded horse, that of Montlouis, and, thanks to this kindness, reached Nantes safely in less than three quarters of an hour.

CHAPTER V.

THE JOURNEY.

That very night Gaston made his will, and deposited it with a notary at Nantes.

He left everything to Helene de Chaverny; begged her, if he died, not to renounce the world, but to accept the career opening to her youth and beauty; but, as he was the last of his family, he begged her, in memeory of him, to call her first son Gaston.

He next went to see each of his friends, and once more told them that he believed the enterprise would be successful. Pontcalec gave him half a piece of gold and a letter, which he was to present to a certain Captain la Jonquiere, their correspondent at Paris, who would put Gaston in communication with the important persons he went to seek. He then put all the ready money he had into a valise, and, accompanied only by an old servant named Owen, in whom he had great confidence, he set out from Nantes.

It was midday, a bright sun shone on the stream, and sparkled on the icicles which hung from the leafless trees, as Gaston made his way along the deserted road, looking in vain for anything resembling the convent carriage.

The servant appeared much more anxious to quicken their pace than Gaston himself did, for to him the journey was fraught with annoyances, and he was so anxious to arrive at that Paris of which he had heard such wonderful tales, that, had it been possible, he would willingly have added wings to their horses' feet.

Gaston, however, traveled slowly as far as Oudan, but the convent carriage proceeded more slowly still. At Oudan he halted; he chose the Char Couronne, a house which had some windows overlooking the road, and which, moreover, was the best inn in the village.

While his dinner was preparing, Gaston, in spite of the cold, remained in the balcony; but in vain he looked for the carriage he so much wished to see.

Then he thought that perhaps Helene had preceded him, and was already in the inn. He went at once to a window at the back, overlooking the courtyard, to inspect the carriages standing there.

His attention was arrested by seeing, not the carriage, but his servant, Owen, speaking earnestly to a man dressed in gray and wrapped in a sort of military cloak, who, after a short conversation, mounted his horse and rode off with the air of a man to whom speed is of the utmost importance, as Gaston heard his steps along the road to Paris.

At this moment the servant raised his eyes, and began busily brushing the snow from his boots and clothes.

Gaston signed to him to approach.

"Who were you talking with, Owen?"

"To a man, M. Gaston."

"Who is that man?"

"A traveler—a soldier, who was asking his way."

"His way; to what place?"

"To Rennes."

"But you could not tell him, for you do not know this place."

"I asked the landlord, monsieur."

"Why could not he ask himself?"

"Because he had had a quarrel with him about the price of his dinner, and did not wish to speak to him again."

"Hum," said Gaston.

Nothing was more natural than this, yet Gaston became thoughtful; but he quickly threw off his suspicions, accusing himself of becoming timid at a time when he most needed courage; his brow remained clouded, however, for the carriage did not appear.

He thought at one moment that Helene might have chosen another road in order to part from him without noise or quarrel, but he soon concluded that it was only some accident which delayed her; he sat down again to table, though he had finished his dinner, and when Owen appeared to clear away, "Some wine," said he. Owen had already removed a half empty bottle.

"Some wine?" repeated the servant in astonishment, for Gaston usually drank but little.

"Yes, some wine; is there anything surprising in that?"

"No, monsieur," replied Owen.

And he transmitted the order for a second bottle of wine to the waiter. Gaston poured out a glass, drank it, then a second.

Owen stared.

Then, thinking it both his duty and his interest to prevent his master's finishing the bottle—

"Monsieur," said he, "I have heard that if you are riding, it is bad to drink when it is very cold. You forgot that we have a long way to go, and that it will be getting still colder, and, if we wait much longer, we shall get no post-horses. It is nearly three o'clock, now, and at half-past four it will be dark."

This behavior surprised Gaston.

"You are in a very great hurry, Owen," said he; "have you a rendezvous with the man who was asking his way of you?"

"Monsieur knows that to be impossible," replied Owen, "since he is going to Rennes, and we to Paris."

However, under the scrutinizing gaze of his master, Owen turned red, when suddenly, at the sound of wheels, Gaston ran to the window. It was the dark carriage.

At this sight Gaston darted from the room.

It was then Owen's turn to run to the window to see what it was that had so much interested his master. He saw a green and black carriage stop, from which the driver alighted and opened the door; then he saw a young lady in a cloak go into the hotel, followed by an Augustine sister; the two ladies, announcing that they should only remain to dine, asked for a room.

But to reach this room they had to cross a public salon, in which Gaston stood near the fire-place; a rapid but meaning glance was exchanged between him and Helene, and, to Gaston's great satisfaction, he recognized in the driver of the carriage the convent gardener. He let him pass, however, unnoticed, but as he crossed the yard to go to the stable, he followed him.

He accosted the gardener, who told him that he was to take the two ladies to Rambouillet, where Helene would remain, and then he was to take back Sister Therese to Clisson.

Gaston, raising his eyes suddenly, saw Owen watching him, and this curiosity displeased him.

"What are you doing there?" asked he.

"Waiting for orders," said Owen.

"Do you know that fellow?" asked Gaston of the gardener.

"M. Owen, your servant? Of course I do; we are from the same place."

"So much the worse," murmured Gaston.

"Oh, Owen is an honest fellow."

"Never mind," said Gaston; "not a word of Helene, I beg."

The gardener promised; and, indeed, it was his own interest to keep the secret, for, had it been discovered that he had given Gaston the key, he would have lost his place.

After a hasty meal, the carriage was again ordered, and at the door Gaston met the ladies, and handed them in. Chanlay was not quite unknown to the sister, so she thanked him graciously as he handed her in.

"Monsieur," said Owen, behind the chevalier, "our horses are ready."

"One more glass," said Gaston, "and I shall start."

To Owen's great surprise, Gaston returned to the room and ordered a third bottle—for Owen had removed the second, of which Gaston had only drank his two glasses.

Gaston remained about a quarter of an hour, and then, having no further motive for waiting, he set out.

When they had ridden a short distance, they saw the carriage imbedded in a deep rut, where, in spite of the efforts of the horses and the gardener, it remained stationary. Gaston could not leave him in such a dilemma, and the gardener, recognizing Owen, called to him for aid. The two riders dismounted, opened the carriage door, took out the ladies, and succeeded in freeing the carriage, so that they were able to proceed.

An acquaintanceship was thus established, and the poor nun, who was very timid, inquired of Gaston if the road were safe. Gaston reassured her, and said that he and his servant would escort them, and his offer was at once accepted with thanks.

Meanwhile Helene had played her part admirably, showing that a young girl, however simple and naïve, has the instinct of dissimulation, which only requires opportunity to develop itself.

Gaston rode along close to the door, for the road was narrow, and Sister Therese asked him many questions. She learned that he was called the Chevalier de Livry, and was the brother of one of the young ladies who had been in the convent school, but who was now married to Montlouis.

They stopped, as previously arranged, at Ancenis.

The gardener confirmed what Gaston had said of his relationship to Mademoiselle de Livry, so that Sister Therese had no suspicion, and was very friendly with him.

She was, in fact, delighted, on starting the next morning, to find him already mounted, and to receive his accustomed politeness in handing them into the carriage. As he did so, he slipped a note into Helene's hand, and by a glance she told him he should receive a reply.

Gaston rode by the side of the carriage, for the road was bad, and assistance was frequently required, either to free a wheel, to assist the ladies to alight for the purpose of walking up a steep ascent, or some of the many accidents of a journey. "My dear Helene," said Sister Therese, several times, "what would have become of us without the aid of this gentleman?"

Before arriving at Angers, Gaston inquired at what hotel they were going to stay, and, finding that it was the same at which he intended to put up, he sent Owen on before to engage apartments.

When they arrived, he received a note, which Helene had written during dinner. She spoke of her love and happiness as though they were secure and everlasting.

But Gaston looked on the future in its true light. Bound by an oath to undertake a terrible mission, he foresaw sad misfortunes after their present short-lived joy. He remembered that he was about to lose happiness, just as he had tasted it for the first time, and rebelled against his fate. He did not remember that he had sought that conspiracy which now bound him, and which forced him to pursue a path leading to exile or the scaffold, while he had in sight another path which would lead him direct to happiness.

It is true that when Gaston joined the conspiracy he did not know Helene, and thought himself alone in the world. At twenty years of age he had believed that the world had no pleasure for him; then he had met Helene, and the world became full of pleasure and hope: but it was too late; he had already entered on a career from which he could not draw back.

Meanwhile, in the preoccupation of his mind, Gaston had quite forgotten his suspicions of Owen, and had not noticed that he had spoken to two cavaliers similar to the one whom he had seen the first evening; but Owen lost nothing of what passed between Gaston and Helene.

As they approached the end of their journey, Gaston became sad; and when the landlord at Chartres replied to the question of Sister Therese, "To-morrow you may, if you choose, reach Rambouillet," it was as though he had said, "To-morrow you separate forever."

Helene, who loved as women love, with the strength, or rather the weakness, to sacrifice everything to that love, could not understand Gaston's passive submission to the decrees of Providence, and she would have preferred to have seen him make some effort to combat them.

But Helene was in this unjust to Gaston; the same ideas tormented him. He knew that at a word from him Helene would follow him to the end of the world—he had plenty of gold—it would be easy for Helene one evening, instead of going to rest, to go with him into a post-chaise, and in two days they would be beyond the frontier, free and happy, not for a day or a month, but forever.

But one word, one little word, opposed itself to all this. That word was honor. He had given his oath, and he would be disgraced if he did not keep it.

The last evening Helene expected that Gaston would speak, but in vain, and she retired to rest with the conviction that Gaston did not love her as she loved him.

That night Gaston never slept, and he rose pale and despairing. They breakfasted at a little village. The nun thought that in the evening she would begin her homeward journey toward her beloved convent. Helene thought that it was now too late to act, even if Gaston should speak. Gaston thought that he was about to lose forever the woman whom he loved.

About three o'clock in the afternoon they all alighted to walk up a steep hill, from the summit of which they could see before them a steeple and a number of houses. It was Rambouillet; they did not know it, but they felt that it was.

Gaston was the first to break the silence. "There," said he, "our paths separate. Helene, I implore you preserve the recollection of me, and, whatever happens, do not condemn or curse me."

"Gaston, you only speak of the most terrible things. I need courage, and you take it from me. Have you nothing joyful to tell me? I know the present is dark, but is the future also as dreadful? Are there not many years, and therefore many hopes, to look forward to? We are young—we love one another; are there no means of struggling against the fate which threatens us? Oh, Gaston! I feel in myself a great strength, and if you but say—but no, I am mad; it is I who suffer, and yet I who console."

"I understand you, Helene—you want a promise, do you not? Well, judge if I am wretched; I dare not promise. You tell me to hope, and I can but despair. If I had ten years, five years, one year, at my own disposal, I would offer them to you, Helene, and think myself blessed, but from the moment I leave you, we lose each other. From to-morrow morning I belong no more to myself."

"Oh!" cried Helene, "unhappy that I am, did you then deceive me when you said you loved me; are you pledged to another?"

"At least, my poor Helene," said Gaston, "on this point I can reassure you. I have no other love."

"Then we may yet be happy, Gaston, if my new family will recognize you as my husband."

"Helene, do you not see that every word you utter stabs me to the heart?"

"But at least tell me what it is."

"Fate, which I cannot escape; ties which I dare not break."

"I know of none such," cried the young girl. "I am promised a family, riches, station, and a name; and yet, Gaston, say but one word and I leave them all for you. Why, then, will you not do as much for me?"

Gaston answered not; and at this moment Sister Therese rejoined them, and they again got into the carriage. When they neared the town, the nun called Gaston, told him that, perhaps, some one might come to meet Helene, and that a stranger should not be seen with them. Gaston bowed silently and sadly, and turned to leave them.

Helene was no ordinary woman; she saw Gaston's distress. "Is it adieu, or au revoir?" cried she, boldly.

"Au revoir," said Gaston, and he rode off quickly.

CHAPTER VI.

A ROOM IN THE HOTEL AT RAMBOUILLET.

Gaston went away without saying how they were to meet again; but Helene thought that he would certainty manage that, and she contented herself with watching him as long as she could. Ten minutes later the carriage stopped at the Tigre-Royal. A woman, who was waiting, came out hastily, and respectfully assisted the ladies to alight, and then guided them through the passages of the hotel, preceded by a valet carrying lights.

A door opened, Madame Desroches drew back to allow Helene and Sister Therese to pass, and they soon found themselves on a soft and easy sofa, in front of a bright fire.

The room was large and well furnished, but the taste was severe, for the style called Rococo was not yet introduced. There were four doors; the first was that by which they had entered—the second led to the dining-room, which was already lighted and warmed—the third led into a richly-appointed bedroom—the fourth did not open.

Helene admired the magnificence of all around her—the quiet and respectful manner of the servants; while Sister Therese rejoiced, when she saw the smoking supper, that it was not a fast day.

Presently Madame Desroches returned, and approaching the sister, handed her a letter. She opened it, and read as follows:

"Sister Therese may pass the night at Rambouillet, or leave again at once, according to her own wish. She will receive two hundred louis offered to the convent by Helene, and will give up her charge to the care of Madame Desroches, who is honored by the confidence of Helene's parents."

At the bottom of the letter, instead of a signature, was a cipher, which the sister compared with that on a letter which she had brought from Clisson. The identity being proved—

"My child," said she, "I leave you after supper."

"So soon!" said Helene, to whom Therese was now the only link to her past life.

"Yes, my child. It is at my option to sleep here, but I prefer to return at once; for I wish to be again at home, where the only thing wanting to my happiness will be your presence."

Helene threw herself on Therese's neck, weeping. She recalled her youth, passed so happily among affectionate companions, and she again saw the towers and steeples of her former residence.

They sat down to table, and Sister Therese hastily partook of some refreshment, then embraced Helene, who wished to accompany her to the carriage; but Madame Desroches begged her not to do so, as the hotel was full of strangers.

Helene then asked permission to see the poor gardener, who had been their escort, once more. This man had become a friend to her, and she quitted him and Therese sadly.

Madame Desroches, seeing that Helene felt vainly in her pocket, said, "Does mademoiselle want anything?"

"Yes," said Helene; "I should wish to give a souvenir to this good man."

Madame Desroches gave Helene twenty-five louis, and she, without counting them, slipped them into the gardener's hand, who overwhelmed her with tears and thanks.

At length they were forced to part, and Helene, hearing the sound of their carriage driving away, threw herself on a sofa, weeping.

Madame Desroches reminded her that she had eaten nothing. Helene insisted that she should sup with her. After her meal she showed Helene her bedroom, saying, "Will mademoiselle ring when she requires her femme-de-chambre; for this evening mademoiselle will receive a visit."

"A visit!" cried Helene.

"Yes, mademoiselle; from a relation."

"And is it the one who watches over me?"

"From your birth, mademoiselle."

"Oh, mon Dieu!" cried Helene; "and he is coming?"

"He is most anxious to know you."

"Oh," murmured Helene; "I feel as if I should faint."

Madame Desroches ran to her, and supported her.

"Do you feel so much terror," asked she, "at seeing one who loves you?"

"It is not terror, it is agitation," said Helene. "I did not know that it would be to-night; and this important news quite overcomes me."

"But I have not told you all: this person is necessarily surrounded by mystery."

"Why so?"

"I am forbidden to reply to that question, mademoiselle."

"What necessity can there be for such precautions with a poor orphan like me?"

"They are necessary, believe me."

"But in what do they consist?"

"Firstly, you may not see the face of this person; so that you may not recognize him if you meet him in the world."

"Then he will come masked?"

"No, mademoiselle: but the lights will be extinguished."

"Then we shall be in darkness?"

"Yes."

"But you will remain with me, Madame Desroches."

"No, mademoiselle; that is expressly forbidden."

"By whom?"

"By the person who is coming."

"But do you, then, owe such absolute obedience to this person?"

"More than that, mademoiselle, I owe him the deepest respect."

"Is he, then, of such high station?"

"He is of the very highest in France."

"And he is my relation?"

"The nearest."

"For Heaven's sake, Madame Desroches, do not leave me in uncertainty on this point."

"I have already told you, mademoiselle, that there are some questions to which I am expressly forbidden to reply," and she was about to retire.

"Why do you leave me?" asked Helene.

"I leave you to your toilet."

"But, madame—"

Madame Desroches made a low, ceremonious curtsey, and went out of the room, closing the door behind her.

CHAPTER VII.

A SERVANT IN THE ROYAL LIVERY.—
MONSEIGNEUR LE DUC D'ORLEANS.

While the things which we have related were passing in the parlor of the hotel Tigre-Royal, in another apartment of the same hotel, seated near a large fire, was a man shaking the snow from his boots, and untying the strings of a large portfolio. This man was dressed in the hunting livery of the house of Orleans; the coat red and silver, large boots, and a three-cornered hat, trimmed with silver. He had a quick eye, a long pointed nose, a round and open forehead, which was contradicted by thin and compressed lips.

This man murmured to himself some phrases which he interrupted by oaths and exclamations, which seemed less the result of words than thoughts.

"Come, come," said he, "M. de Montaran did not deceive me, and our Bretons are hard at the work; but for what earthly reason can he have come by such short stages? He left at noon on the 11th, and only arrived on the evening of the 21st. This probably hides some new mystery, which will be explained by the fellow recommended by Montaran, and with whom my people were in communication on the journey. Hola!"

And he rang a silver bell. A man, dressed in gray, like those we have seen on the route, appeared.

"Ah! it is you, Tapin?"

"Yes, monseigneur; the affair being important, I thought it better to come myself."

"Have you questioned the men you placed on the road?"

"Yes, monseigneur; but they know nothing but the places at which our conspirators stopped; in fact, that is all they were told to learn."

"I will try to learn from the servant. What sort of man is he?"

"Oh, a mischievous simpleton, half Norman, half Breton; a bad fellow."

"What is he about now?"

"Serving his master's supper."

"Whom, I hope, they have placed as I desired?"

"Yes, monseigneur."

"In a room without curtains?"

"Yes, monseigneur."

"And you have made a hole in the shutter?"

"Yes, monseigneur."

"Well, then, send me the servant, and remain within call."

The man in the red coat consulted his watch.

"Half-past eight," said he; "at this hour Monseigneur the Regent returns to St. Germains and asks for Dubois; as Dubois is not there, he rubs his hands and prepares for some folly. Rub your hands, Philippe d'Orleans, and amuse yourself at your pleasure, for the danger is not at Paris, but here. We shall see if you will laugh at my secret police this time. Ah! here is our man."

At this moment Tapin introduced Owen.

"Here is the person you wished to see," said he.

Owen remained standing, trembling, near the door, while Dubois wrapped himself in a large cloak, which left only the upper part of his face visible to him on whom he fixed his cat-like eyes.

"Approach, my friend," said Dubois.

In spite of the cordiality of this invitation, it was given in so harsh a voice that Owen would have preferred being at a greater distance from this man, who looked at him so strangely.

"Well, fellow," said Dubois, seeing that he did not stir, "did you not hear me?"

"Yes, monseigneur," said Owen.

"Then why do you not obey?"

"I did not know you spoke to me."

And Owen then stepped forward.

"You have received fifty louis to speak the truth to me," continued Dubois.

"Pardon, monseigneur," said Owen, who began to recover his composure; "I have not received them; they were promised to me, but—"

Dubois took a handful of gold from his pocket, counted fifty louis, and placed them in a pile on the table.

Owen looked at the pile with an expression of which one would have supposed his dull countenance incapable.

"Good," thought Dubois; "he is avaricious."

In reality, the fifty louis had always appeared very doubtful to Owen. He had betrayed his master with scarcely a hope of obtaining his reward; and now the promised gold was before his eyes.

"May I take them?" asked Owen, spreading his hand toward them.

"Wait a moment," said Dubois, who amused himself by exciting that cupidity which any but a peasant would have concealed; "we will make a bargain."

"What is it?" asked Owen.

"Here are the fifty louis."

"I see them," said Owen, passing his tongue over his lips, like a thirsty dog.

"At every answer you make to a question of mine, I either add ten louis if it is important, or take them away if it is unimportant and stupid."

Owen started; he did not like the terms.

"Now," said Dubois, "let us talk. What place have you come from?"

"Direct from Nantes."

"With whom?"

"With the Chevalier Gaston de Chanlay."

These being preliminary questions, the pile remained undisturbed.

"Listen!" said Dubois.

"I am all attention."

"Did your master travel under his own name?"

"He set out in his own name, but changed it on the journey."

"What name did he take?"

"M. de Livry."

Dubois added ten louis, but as they would not stand on the others, he commenced a second pile.

Owen uttered a joyful cry.

"Oh," said Dubois, "do not exult yet. We are not near the end. Is there a M. de Livry at Nantes?"

"No, monseigneur; but there is a Demoiselle de Livry."

"Who is she?"

"The wife of M. de Montlouis, an intimate friend of my master."

"Good," said Dubois, adding ten louis; "and what was your master doing at Nantes?"

"What most young men do; he hunted, danced, and so on."

Dubois took away ten louis. Owen shuddered.

"Stop," said he, "he did somethingelse."

"Ah! what was that?"

"I do not know," replied Owen.

Dubois held the ten louis in his hand.

"And since his departure, what has he done?"

"He passed through Oudon, Ancenis, Le Mans, Nogent, and Chartres."

Dubois stretched out his hand, and took up another ten louis.

Owen uttered a dolorous cry.

"And did he make no acquaintance on the route?"

"Yes; with a young lady from the Augustine convent at Clisson, who was traveling with a sister of the convent, named Therese."

"And what was the young lady called?"

"Mademoiselle Helene de Chaverny."

"Helene! A promising name. Doubtless, she is your master's mistress?"

"I do not know," said Owen; "he would not have told me."

"He is a shrewd fellow," said Dubois, taking ten louis from the fifty.

Owen trembled: four such answers, and he would have betrayed his master for nothing.

"And these ladies are going to Paris with him?"

"No, monseigneur; they stop at Rambouillet."

"Ah," said Dubois.

The tone of this exclamation gave Owen some hope.

"Come," said Dubois, "all this is not very important, but one must encourage beginners."

And he added ten louis to the pile.

"Sister Therese," continued Owen, "is already gone home."

"So that the young lady remains alone?"

"No," answered Owen.

"How so?"

"A lady from Paris awaited her."

"From Paris?"

"Yes."

"Do you know her name?"

"I heard Sister Therese call her Madame Desroches."

"Madame Desroches!" cried Dubois, and he began another pile with ten louis.

"Yes," replied Owen, delighted.

"Are you sure?"

"Of course I am; she is a tall, thin, yellow-looking woman."

Dubois added ten louis. Owen thought that if he had made an interval between each adjective he might have had twenty louis.

"Thin, tall, yellow," repeated Dubois; "just so."

"From forty to forty-five," added Owen.

"Exactly," said Dubois, adding ten louis.

"In a silk dress, with large flowers on it."

"Very good," said Dubois.

Owen saw that his questioner knew enough about the lady, and waited.

"And you say that your master made acquaintance with the young lady en route?"

"Yes, monsieur, but I think it was a farce."

"What do you mean?"

"I mean that they knew each other before; and I am sure of one thing, that my master waited for her three hours at Oudon."

"Bravo," said Dubois, adding ten louis; "we shall make something of you."

"You do not wish to know anything more, then?" asked Owen, extending his hand toward the two piles of gold.

"Stop," said Dubois; "is the young lady pretty?"

"Beautiful as an angel," answered Owen.

"And, no doubt, they made an appointment to meet in Paris?"

"No, monsieur, I think they said adieu forever."

"Another farce."

"I do not think so, monsieur; my master was so sad when they separated."

"And they are not to meet again?"

"Yes, once more, I think, and all will be over."

"Well, take your money; and remember that if you mention one word of this, in ten minutes you will be a dead man."

Owen snatched the money, which disappeared in his pocket instantly.

"And now," said he, "may I go?"

"No, idiot; from this moment you belong to me, for I have bought you, and you will be more useful to me at Paris than elsewhere."

"In that case I will remain, monsieur, I promise."

"There is no need to promise."

At this moment the door opened, and Tapin appeared, looking very much agitated.

"What has happened now?" asked Dubois.

"Something very important, monseigneur; but send away this man."

"Return to your master," said Dubois, "and if he writes to any one whatever, remember that I am most anxious to see his writing."

Owen went out, delighted to be set free.

"Well, Tapin," said Dubois, "what is it?"

"Monseigneur, after the hunt at St. Germains, his royal highness, instead of returning to Paris, sent away every one, and gave orders to proceed to Rambouillet."

"The regent coming to Rambouillet!"

"He will be here in half an hour, and would have been here now, if hunger had not luckily obliged him to enter the chateau and procure some refreshment."

"And what is he coming to Rambouillet for?"

"I do not know, monseigneur, unless it be for the young girl who has just arrived with a nun, and who is now in the pavilion of the hotel."

"You are right, Tapin; it is doubtless for her; and Madame Desroches, too. Did you know that Madame Desroches was here?"

"No, monseigneur, I did not."

"And are you sure that your information is correct, my dear Tapin?"

"Oh, monseigneur, it was from L'Eveille, whom I placed near his royal highness, and what he says is gospel truth."

"You are right," said Dubois, who seemed to know the qualities of this man, "if it be L'Eveille, there is no doubt."

"The poor fellow has lamed his horse, which fell near Rambouillet."

"Thirty louis for the horse; he may gain what he can of it."

Tapin took the thirty louis.

"You know the situation of the pavilion, do you not?"

"Perfectly."

"Where is it?"

"One side looks on the second courtyard; the other on a deserted lane."

"Place men in the courtyard and in the lane, disguised as stablemen, or how you please; let no one enter the pavilion but monseigneur and myself; the life of his royal highness is at stake."

"Rest easy, monseigneur."

"Do you know our Breton?"

"I saw him dismount."

"Do your men know him?"

"They all saw him on the road."

"Well, I recommend him to you."

"Shall we arrest him?"

"Certainly not; he must be allowed to go where he pleases, and act as he pleases, and he must have every opportunity to do so. If he were arrested now, he would tell nothing, and our plans would be disconcerted; no, no, these plans must hatch."

"Hatch what, monseigneur?" said Tapin, who appeared to be on confidential terms with Dubois.

"My archbishop's miter, M. Lecocq," said Dubois, "and now to your work; I go to mine."

Both left the room and descended the staircase, but separated at the door; Lecocq went along the Rue de Paris; and Dubois, slipping along by the wall, went to peep through the hole in the shutter.

CHAPTER VIII.

THE UTILITY OF A SEAL.

Gaston had just supped; for at his age, whether a man be in despair or in love, nature asserts her rights. He was leaning on the table thoughtfully. The lamp threw a light over his face, and enabled Dubois to gratify his curiosity.

He looked at him with an attention almost alarming: his quick eye darted—his lip curled with a smile, which gave one the idea of a demon smiling at the sight of one of those victims who seem to have vowed their own perdition.

While looking, he murmured, "Young, handsome, black eyes, proud lips—he is a Breton, he is not corrupted, like the conspirators of Cellamare, by the soft glances of the ladies at court;—then the other spoke of carrying off, dethroning, but this one—*diable*, this one; and yet," continued he, after a pause, "I look in vain for traces of cunning on that open brow. I see no Machiavelism in the corners of that mouth, so full of loyalty and honor; yet no doubt all is arranged to surprise the regent on his visit to this Clisson demoiselle. Who will say again that Bretons have dull brains?

"No," said Dubois, after another pause, "it cannot be so. It is impossible that this young man with his calm sad face should be ready in a quarter of an hour to kill a man, and that man the first prince of the blood. No, I cannot believe in such sang-froid; and yet the regent has kept this amourette secret even from me; he goes out to hunt at St. Germains, announces aloud that he shall sleep at the Palais Royal, then all at once gives counter orders, and drives to Rambouillet. At Rambouillet, the young girl waits, and is received by Madame Desroches; who can she be watching for, if not for the regent? and this young girl is the mistress of the chevalier—but is she?—Ah! we must learn. We must find out how far we can depend on Owen," and Dubois left his observatory and waited on the staircase—he was quite hidden in the shade, and he could see Gaston's door in the light.

The door presently opened, and Owen appeared.

He held a letter in his hands, and after hesitating a minute, he appeared to have taken his determination, and mounted the staircase.

"Good," said Dubois, "he has tasted the forbidden fruit, and he is mine."

Then, stopping Owen: "Give me the letter which you were bringing me, and wait here."

"How did you know I had a letter?" asked Owen, bewildered.

Dubois shrugged his shoulders, took the letter, and disappeared.

In his room he examined the seal; the chevalier, who had no wax, had used that on the bottle, and had sealed it with the stone of a ring.

Dubois held the letter above the candle, and the wax melted. He opened the letter and read:

"DEAR HELENE—Your courage has doubled mine; manage so that I can enter the house, and you shall know my plans."

"Oh!" said Dubois, "it seems she does not know them yet. Things are not as far advanced as I supposed."

He resealed the letter with one of the numerous rings which he wore, and which resembled that of the chevalier, and calling Owen—

"Here," said he, "is your master's letter; deliver it faithfully, bring me the answer, and you shall have ten louis."

"Ah!" thought Owen, "has this man a mine of gold?" And he went off.

Ten minutes after he returned with the reply.

It was on scented and ornamented paper, sealed with the letter H.

Dubois opened a box, took out a kind of paste in which he was about to take the impression of the seal, when he observed that from the manner in which it was folded, he could read it without opening. It was as follows:

"The person who sent for me at Bretagne is coming to meet me here instead of waiting at Paris, so impatient is he, I am told, to see me. I think he will leave again to-night. Come to-morrow morning before nine. I will tell you all that has passed, and then we can arrange how to act."

"This," said Dubois, still taking Helene for the chevalier's accomplice, "makes it clearer. If this is the way they bring up young ladies at Clisson, I congratulate them and monseigneur, who, from her age, concludes her to be simple and ingenuous. Here," said he to Owen, "here is the letter, and your ten louis."

Owen took them.

At this moment ten o'clock struck, and the rolling of a carriage was heard. Dubois went to the window, and saw it stop at the hotel door.

In the carriage was a gentleman whom Dubois at once recognized as Lafare, captain of his royal highness's guards. "Well," said he, "he is more prudent than I thought; but where is he? Ah!"

This exclamation was uttered at the sight of a man dressed in the same red livery which he himself concealed under his cloak, and who followed the carriage mounted on a superb Spanish jenet, which, however, he could not have ridden long, for while the carriage horses were covered with foam, this one was quite fresh.

Lafare at once demanded a room and supper; meanwhile the man dismounted, threw the reins to a page, and went toward the pavilion.

"Well," said Dubois, "all this is as clear as a mountain stream; but how is it that the face of the chevalier does not appear? is he too much occupied with his chicken to have heard the carriage? Let us see. As to you, monseigneur," continued Dubois, "be assured; I will not disturb your tete-à-tete. Enjoy at your pleasure this commencement of ingenuity, which promises such happy results. Ah! monseigneur, it is certain that you are short-sighted."

Dubois went down, and again took up his post at his observatory. As he approached it, Gaston rose, after putting his note in his pocket-book.

"Ah," said Dubois, "I must have that pocket-book. I would pay high for it. He is going out, he buckles on his sword, he looks for his cloak; where is he going? Let us see: to wait for his royal highness's exit? No, no, that is not the face of a man who is going to kill another; I could sooner believe he was about to spend the evening under the windows of his sweetheart.

"Ah, if he had that idea it would be a means—"

It would be difficult to render the expression which passed over the face of Dubois at this moment.

"Yes, but if I were to get a sword-thrust in the enterprise, how monseigneur would laugh; bah! there is no danger: our men are at their post, and besides, nothing venture, nothing gain."

Encouraged by this reflection, Dubois made the circuit of the hotel, in order to appear at one end of the little lane as Gaston appeared at the other.

As he had expected, at the end of the lane he found Tapin, who had placed L'Eveille in the courtyard; in two words he explained his project. Tapin pointed out to Dubois one man leaning on the step of an outer door, a second was playing a kind of Jew's harp, and seemed an itinerant musician, and there was another, too well hidden to be seen.

Dubois, thus sure of support, returned into the lane.

He soon perceived a figure at the other end, and at once recognized the chevalier, who was too thoughtful even to notice that he was passing any one.

Dubois wanted a quarrel, and he saw that he must take the initiative. He turned and stopped before the chevalier, who was trying to discover which were the windows of the room in which Helene was.

"My friend," said he roughly, "what are you doing at this hour before this house?"

Gaston was obliged to bring back his thoughts to the materialism of life.

"Did you speak to me, monsieur?" said he.

"Yes," replied Dubois, "I asked what you were doing here."

"Pass on," said the chevalier; "I do not interfere with you; do not interfere with me."

"That might be," said Dubois, "if your presence did not annoy me."

"This lane, narrow as it is, is wide enough for both, monsieur; walk on one side, and I will walk on the other."

"I wish to walk alone," said Dubois, "therefore, I beg you will choose some other window; there are plenty at Rambouillet to choose from."

"And why should I not look at these windows if I choose?" asked Chanlay.

"Because they are those of my wife," replied Dubois.——"Of your wife!"

"Yes; of my wife, who has just arrived from Paris, and of whom I am jealous, I warn you."

"Diable," murmured Gaston; "he must be the husband of the person to whom Helene has been given in charge;" and in order to conciliate a person who might be useful to him—

"Monsieur," said he politely, "in that case I am willing to leave a place where I was walking without any object in view."

"Oh," thought Dubois, "here is a polite conspirator; I must have a quarrel."

Gaston was going away.

"You are deceiving me, monsieur," said Dubois.

The chevalier turned as though he had been bitten by a serpent; however, prudent for the sake of Helene, and for the mission he had undertaken, he restrained himself.

"Is it," said he, "because I was polite that you disbelieve my word?"

"You spoke politely because you were afraid; but it is none the less true that I saw you looking at that window."

"Afraid—I afraid!" cried Chanlay, facing him; "did you say that I was afraid?"

"I did," replied Dubois.

"Do you, then, seek a quarrel?"

"It appears so. I see you come from Quimper—Corentin."

"Paques-Dieu!" said Gaston, drawing his sword, "draw!"

"And you, off with your coat," said Dubois, throwing off his cloak, and preparing to do the same with his coat.

"Why so?" asked the chevalier.

"Because I do not know you, monsieur, and because those who walk at night frequently have their coat prudently lined with a shirt of mail."

At these words the chevalier's cloak and coat were thrown aside; but, at the moment when Gaston was about to rush on his adversary, the four men appeared and seized him.

"A duel, monsieur," cried they, "in spite of the king's prohibition!" and they dragged him toward the door.

"An assassination," murmured Gaston, not daring to cry out, for fear of compromising Helene; "cowards!"

"We are betrayed, monsieur," said Dubois, rolling up Gaston's cloak and coat, and putting them under his arm; "we shall meet again to-morrow, no doubt."

And he ran toward the hotel, while they shut up Gaston in the lower room.

Dubois ran up the staircase and into his room, where he opened the precious pocket-book. He found in one pocket a broken coin and a man's name. This coin was evidently a sign of recognition, and the name was probably that of the man to whom Gaston was addressed, and who was called Captain la Jonquiere. The paper was oddly folded.

"La Jonquiere," said Dubois; "we have our eyes on *him* already."

He looked over the rest of the pocket-book—there was nothing.

"It is little," said Dubois, "but it is enough."

He folded a paper like the other, took the name, and rang the bell.

Some one knocked; the door was fastened inside. "I forgot," said Dubois, opening it, and giving entrance to Monsieur Tapin.

"What have you done with him?"

"He is in the lower room, and watched."

"Take back his cloak and coat to the place where he threw them; make your excuses, and set him free. Take care that everything is in his pockets, so that he may suspect nothing. Bring me my coat and cloak."

Monsieur Tapin bowed low, and went to obey his orders.

CHAPTER IX.

THE VISIT.

All this passed, as we have said, in the lane under Helene's windows. She had heard the noise; and, as among the voices she thought she distinguished that of the chevalier, she ran anxiously to the window, when, at the same moment, Madame Desroches appeared.

She came to beg Helene to go into the drawing-room, as the visitor had arrived.

Helene started, and nearly fell; her voice failed her, and she followed, silent and trembling.

The room into which Madame Desroches led her was without any light, except what was thrown on the carpet by the last remains of a fire. Madame Desroches threw some water over the flame, and left the room entirely dark.

Begging Helene to have no fear, Madame Desroches withdrew. The instant after, Helene heard a voice behind the fourth door, which had not yet opened.

She started at the sound, and involuntarily made a few steps toward the door.

"Is she ready?" said the voice.

"Yes, monseigneur," was the reply.

"Monseigneur!" murmured Helene; "who is coming, then?"

"Is she alone?"

"Yes, monseigneur."

"Is she aware of my arrival?"

"Yes, monseigneur."

"We shall not be interrupted?"

"Monseigneur may rely upon me."

"And no light?"

"None whatever."

The steps approached, then stopped.

"Speak frankly, Madame Desroches," said the voice. "Is she as pretty as they said?"

"More beautiful than your highness can imagine."

"Your highness! who can he be?" thought Helene, much agitated.

At this moment the door creaked on its hinges and a heavy step approached.

"Mademoiselle," said the voice, "I beg you to receive and hear me."

"I am here," said Helene, faintly.

"Are you frightened?"

"I confess it, mon—Shall I say 'monsieur' or 'monseigneur'?"

"Say 'my friend.'"

At this moment her hand touched that of the unknown.

"Madame Desroches, are you there?" asked Helene, drawing back.

"Madame Desroches," said the voice, "tell mademoiselle that she is as safe as in a temple before God."

"Ah! monseigneur, I am at your feet, pardon me."

"Rise, my child, and seat yourself there. Madame Desroches, close all the doors; and now," continued he, "give me your hand, I beg."

Helene's hand again met that of the stranger, and this time it was not withdrawn.

"He seems to tremble also," murmured she.

"Tell me are you afraid, dear child?"

"No," replied Helene; "but when your hand clasps mine, a strange thrill passes through me."

"Speak to me, Helene," said the unknown, with an expression of tenderness. "I know already that you are beautiful, but this is the first time I have heard your voice. Speak—I am listening."

"But have you seen me, then?" asked Helene.

"Do you remember that two years ago the abbess had your portrait taken?"

"Yes, I remember—an artist came expressly from Paris."

"It was I who sent him."

"And was the portrait for you?"

"It is here," said the unknown, taking from his pocket a miniature, which Helene could feel, though she could not see it.

"But what interest could you have in the portrait of a poor orphan?"

"Helene, I am your father's friend."

"My father! Is he alive?"

"Yes."

"Shall I ever see him?"

"Perhaps."

"Oh!" said Helene, pressing the stranger's hand, "I bless you for bringing me this news."

"Dear child!" said he.

"But if he be alive," said Helene, "why has he not sought out his child?"

"He had news of you every month; and though at a distance, watched over you."

"And yet," said Helene, reproachfully, "he has not seen me for sixteen years."

"Believe me, none but the most important reasons would have induced him to deprive himself of this pleasure."

"I believe you, monsieur; it is not for me to accuse my father."

"No; it is for you to pardon him if he accuses himself."

"To pardon him!" cried Helene.

"Yes; and this pardon, which he cannot ask for himself, I ask in his name."

"Monsieur," said Helene, "I do not understand you.'"

"Listen, then, and give me back your hand."

"Here it is."

"Your father was an officer in the king's service; at the battle of Nerwinden, where he charged at the head of the king's household troops, one of his followers, called M. de Chaverny, fell near him, pierced by a ball. Your father wished to assist him, but the wound was mortal, and the wounded man, who knew that it was so, said, 'Think not of me, but of my child.' Your father pressed his hand as a promise, and the man fell back and died, as though he only waited this assurance to close his eyes. You are listening, are you not, Helene?"

"Oh! need you ask such a question?" said the young girl.

"At the end of the campaign, your father's first care was for the little orphan. She was a charming child, of from ten to twelve years, who promised to be as beautiful as you are. The death of M. de Chaverny, her father, left her without support or fortune; your father placed her at the convent of the Faubourg Saint Antoine, and announced that at a proper age he should give her a dowry."

"I thank God," cried Helene, "for having made me the child of a man who so nobly kept his promise."

"Wait, Helene," said the unknown, "for now comes the time when your father will not receive your praises."

Helene was silent.

The unknown continued: "Your father, indeed, watched over the orphan till her eighteenth year. She was an adorable young girl, and his visits to the convent became longer and more frequent than they should have been: your father began to love his protegée. At first he was frightened at his own love, for he remembered his promise to her dying father. He begged the superior to look for a suitable husband for Mademoiselle de Chaverny, and was told that her nephew, a young Breton, having seen her, loved her, and wished to obtain her hand."

"Well, monsieur?" asked Helene, hearing that the unknown hesitated to proceed.

"Well; your father's surprise was great, Helene, when he learned from the superior that Mademoiselle de Chaverny had replied that she did not wish to marry, and that her greatest desire was to remain in the convent where she had been brought up, and that the happiest day of her life would be that on which she should pronounce her vows."

"She loved some one," said Helene.

"Yes, my child, you are right—alas! we cannot avoid our fate—Mademoiselle de Chaverny loved your father. For a long time she kept her secret, but one day, when your father begged her to renounce her strange wish to take the veil, the poor child confessed all. Strong against his love when he did not believe it returned, he succumbed when he found he had but to desire and to obtain. They were both so young—your father scarcely twenty-five, she not eighteen—they forgot the world, and only remembered that they could be happy."

"But since they loved," said Helene, "why did they not marry?"

"Union was impossible, on account of the distance which separated them. Do you not know that your father is of high station?"

"Alas! yes," said Helene, "I know it."

"During a year," continued he, "their happiness surpassed their hopes; but at the end of that time you came into the world, and then——"

"Well?" asked the young girl, timidly.

"Your birth cost your mother's life."

Helene sobbed.

"Yes," continued the unknown, in a voice full of emotion, "yes, Helene, weep for your mother; she was a noble woman, of whom, through his griefs, his pleasures, even his follies—your father retains a tender recollection; he transferred to you all his love for her."

"And yet," said Helene, "he consented to remove me from him, and has never again seen me."

"Helene, on this point pardon your father, for it was not his fault. You were born in 1703, at the most austere period of Louis XIV.'s reign; your father was already out of favor with the king, or rather with Madame de Maintenon; and for your sake, as much or more than for his, he sent you into Bretagne, confiding you to Mother Ursula, superior of the convent where you were brought up. At length, Louis XIV. being dead, and everything having changed through all France, it is decided to bring you nearer to him. During the journey, however, you must have seen that his care was over you, and when he knew that you were at Rambouillet, he could not wait till to-morrow—he is come to you here, Helene."

"Oh, mon Dieu!" cried Helene, "is this true?"

"And in seeing, or rather in listening to you, he thinks he hears your mother—the same accent in the voice. Helene, Helene, that you may be happier than she was is his heartfelt prayer!"

"Oh, heavens!" cried Helene, "this emotion, your trembling hand. Monsieur, you said my father is come to meet me."

"Yes."

"Here at Rambouillet?"

"Yes."

"You say he is happy to see me again?"

"Oh yes, very happy!"

"But this happiness was not enough, is it not so? He wished to speak to me, to tell me himself the story of my life—that I may thank him for his love—that I may fall at his feet, that I may ask his blessing. Oh!" cried Helene, kneeling, "oh, I am at your feet; bless me, father!"

"Helene, my child, my daughter!" cried the unknown, "not at my feet, but in my arms!"

"My father, my father!" was Helene's only reply.

"And yet," continued he, "I came with a different intention, prepared to deny all, to remain a stranger to you; but having you so near me, pressing your hand, hearing your voice, I had not the strength; but do not make me repent my weakness, and let secrecy—"

"I swear by my mother's grave," cried Helene.

"That is all I desire," cried the unknown. "Now listen, for I must leave you."

"What, already!"

"It must be so."

"Speak, then, my father. I am ready to obey you."

"To-morrow you leave for Paris; there is a house there destined for you. Madame Desroches will take you there, and at the very first moment that I can do so, I will come there to see you."

"Soon, I hope, for do not forget that I am alone in the world."

"As soon as possible;" and pressing his lips to Helene's forehead, the unknown imprinted on it one of those kisses as sweet to the heart of a father as a kiss of love to the heart of a lover.

Ten minutes later Madame Desroches entered with a light. Helene was on her knees praying; without rising, she signed to Madame Desroches to place the light on the chimney-piece, which that lady did, and then retired.

Helene, after praying for some time, rose, and looked around her as though for some evidence that the whole was not a dream; her own emotion, however, assured her that it was really a great event in her life which had taken place. Then the thought of Gaston rose to her mind; this father whom she had so dreaded to see—this father, who himself had loved so ardently and suffered so deeply, would not do violence to her love; besides, Gaston was a scion of an ancient house, and beyond all this, she loved him, so that she would die if she were separated from him, and her father would not wish her death.

The obstacles on Gaston's side could be but the right, and would doubtless be easily overcome, and Helene fell asleep to dream of a happy and smiling future.

Gaston, on his part, set at liberty with many apologies from those who pretended to have mistaken him for another person, went back to fetch his coat and cloak, which he was overjoyed to find where he had left them; he anxiously opened his pocket-book—it was as he had left it, and for greater safety he now burned the address of La Jonquiere. He gave his orders for the next day to Owen and retired.

Meanwhile, two carriages rolled away from the door of the Tigre-Royal; in the first were two gentlemen in traveling costume, preceded and followed by outriders.

In the second was a single traveler, wrapped in a large cloak; this carriage followed close behind the other as far as the Barriere de l'Etoile, where they separated, and while the first stopped at the Palais Royal, the other drew up at the Rue de Valois.

CHAPTER X.

IN WHICH DUBOIS PROVES THAT HIS POLICE WAS BETTER ORGANIZED AT AN EXPENSE OF 300,000 FRANCS THAN THE GENERAL POLICE FOR THREE MILLIONS.

Whatever might have been the fatigues of the preceding night, the Duc d'Orleans still gave his mornings to business. He generally began to work with Dubois before he was dressed; then came a short and select levée, followed again by audiences, which kept him till eleven or twelve o'clock; then the chiefs of the councils (La Valliere and Le Blanc) came to give an account of their espionage, then Torcy, to bring any important letters which he had abstracted. At half-past two the regent had his chocolate, which he always took while laughing and chatting. This lasted half an hour, then came the audience hour for ladies, after that he went to the Duchesse d'Orleans, then to the young king, whom he visited every day, and to whom he always displayed the greatest reverence and respect.

Once a week he received foreign ministers, and on Sundays heard mass in his private chapel.

At six, on council days, at five on others, all business was over; then the regent would go to the opera, or to Madame de Berry, with whom, however, he had quarreled now, on account of her marriage with Riom. Then came those famous suppers.

They were composed of from ten to fifteen persons, and the regent's presence among them sometimes added to their license and freedom, but never restrained it. At these suppers, kings, ministers, chancellors, ladies of the court, were all passed in review, discussed, abused; everything might be said, everything told, everything done; provided only that it were wittily said, told, or done. When all the guests had arrived, the doors were closed and barred, so that it was impossible to reach the regent until the following morning, however urgent might be the necessity.

Dubois was seldom of the number, his bad health forbade it; and this was the time chosen to pick him to pieces, at which the regent would laugh as heartily as any one. Dubois knew that he often furnished the amusement of these suppers, but he also knew that by the morning the regent invariably forgot what had been said the night before, and so he cared little about it.

Dubois, however, watched while the regent supped or slept, and seemed indefatigable; he appeared to have the gift of ubiquity.

When he returned from Rambouillet, he called Maitre Tapin, who had returned on horseback, and talked with him for an hour, after which he slept for four or five, then, rising, he presented himself at the door of his royal highness; the regent was still asleep.

Dubois approached the bed and contemplated him with a smile which at once resembled that of an ape and a demon.

At length he decided to wake him.

"Hola, monseigneur, wake up!" he cried.

The duke opened his eyes, and seeing Dubois, he turned his face to the wall, saying—

"Ah! is that you, abbe; go to the devil!"

"Monseigneur, I have just been there, but he was too busy to receive me, and sent me to you."

"Leave me alone; I am tired."

"I dare say, the night was stormy."

"What do you mean?" asked the duke, turning half round.

"I mean that the way you spent the night does not suit a man who makes appointments for seven in the morning."

"Did I appoint you for seven in the morning?"

"Yes, yesterday morning, before you went to St. Germains."

"It is true," said the regent.

"Monseigneur did not know that the night would be so fatiguing."

"Fatiguing! I left table at seven."

"And afterward?"

"Well! what afterward?"

"Are you satisfied, monseigneur, and was the young person worth the journey?"

"What journey?"

"The journey you took after you left the table at seven."

"One would think, to hear you, that from St. Germains here, was a long distance."

"No, monseigneur is right; it is but a few steps, but there is a method of prolonging the distance."

"What is that?"

"Going round by Rambouillet."

"You are dreaming, abbe."

"Possibly, monseigneur. I will tell you my dream; it will at least prove to your highness that even in my dreams I do not forget you."

"Some new nonsense."

"Not at all. I dreamed that monseigneur started the stag at Le Treillage, and that the animal, after some battling, worthy of a stag of high birth, was taken at Chambourcy."

"So far, your dream resembles the truth; continue, abbe."

"After which, monseigneur returned to St. Germains, sat down to table at half-past five, and ordered that the carriage without arms should be prepared and harnessed, with four horses, at half-past seven."

"Not bad, abbe, not bad; go on."

"At half-past seven, monseigneur dismissed every one except Lafare, with whom he entered the carriage. Am I right?"

"Go on; go on."

"The carriage went toward Rambouillet, and arrived there at a quarter to ten, but at the entrance of the town it stopped, Lafare went on in the carriage to the Tigre-Royal, monseigneur following as an outrider."

"Here your dream becomes confused, abbe."

"No, no, not at all."

"Continue, then."

"Well, while Lafare pretended to eat a bad supper, which was served by waiters who called him Excellency, monseigneur gave his horse to a page and went to a little pavilion."

"Demon, where were you hidden?"

"I, monseigneur, have not left the Palais Royal, where I slept like a dormouse, and the proof is, that I am telling you my dream."

"And what was there in the pavilion?"

"First, at the door, a horrible duenna, tall, thin, dry, and yellow."

"Dubois, I will recommend you to Desroches, and the first time she sees you, she will tear your eyes out."

"Then inside, mon Dieu! inside."

"You could not see that, even in a dream, abbe."

"Monseigneur, you may take away the 300,000 francs which you allow me for my secret police, if—by their aid—I did not see into the interior."

"Well, what did you see?"

"Ma foi, monseigneur, a charming little Bretonne, sixteen or seventeen years old, beautiful, coming direct from the Augustine convent at Clisson, accompanied to Rambouillet by one of the sisters, whose troublesome presence was soon dispensed with, was it not?"

"Dubois, I have often thought you were the devil, who has taken the form of an abbe to ruin me."

"To save you, monseigneur, to save you."

"To save me; I do not believe it."

"Well," said Dubois, "are you pleased with her?"

"Enchanted, Dubois; she is charming."

"Well, you have brought her from so far, that if she were not, you would be quite cheated."

The regent frowned, but, reflecting that probably Dubois did not know the rest, the frown changed to a smile.

"Dubois," said he, "certainly, you are a great man."

"Ah, monseigneur, no one but you doubts it, and yet you disgrace me—"

"Disgrace you!"

"Yes, you hide your loves from me."

"Come, do not be vexed, Dubois."

"There is reason, however, you must confess, monseigneur."

"Why?"

"Why did you not tell me you wanted a Bretonne. Could not I have sent for one?"

"Yes."

"Yes, of course I could."

"As good?"

"Yes, and better. You think you have found a treasure, perhaps?"

"Hola, hola!"

"Well, when you know what she is, and to what you expose yourself."

"Do not jest, abbe, I beg."

"Ah! monseigneur, you distress me."

"What do you mean?"

"That you are taken by a glance, a single night fascinates you, and there is no one to compare to the new comer. Is she then very pretty?"

"Charming."

"And discreet: virtue itself, I suppose."

"You are right."

"Well, I tell you, monseigneur, you are lost."

"I?"

"Yes; your Bretonne is a jade."

"Silence, abbe."

"Why silence?"

"I forbid you to say another word."

"Monseigneur, you, too, have had a dream—let me explain it."

"Monsieur Joseph, I will send you to the Bastille."

"As you please, monseigneur, but still you must know that this girl—"

"Is my daughter, abbe."

Dubois drew back stupefied.

"Your daughter; and who is her mother?"

"An honest woman, who had the honor of dying without knowing you."

"And the child?"

"The child has been concealed, that she might not be sullied by the looks of such creatures as you."

Dubois bowed, and retired, respectfully.

The regent looked triumphant.

"Ah!" said Dubois, who had not quite closed the door, "I thought this plot would bring me my archbishop's miter—if I am careful, it will bring me my cardinal's hat."

CHAPTER XI.

RAMBOUILLET AGAIN.

At the appointed hour Gaston presented himself at Helene's domicile, but Madame Desroches made some difficulty about admitting him; Helene, however, said firmly that she was quite at liberty to judge for herself what was right, and that she was quite determined to see M. de Livry, who had come to take leave of her. It will be remembered that this was the name which Gaston had assumed during the journey, and which he intended to retain, except when with those connected with his mission to Paris.

Madame Desroches went to her room somewhat out of humor, and even attempted to overhear the conversation, but Helene bolted the outer door.

"Ah, Gaston," said she, "I have been expecting you. I did not sleep last night."

"Nor I, Helene; but I must admire all this splendor."

Helene smiled.

"And your head-dress—how beautiful you are, like this."

"You do not appear much pleased."

Gaston made no reply, but continued his investigations.

"These rich hangings, these costly pictures, all prove that your protectors are opulent, Helene."

"I believe so," said Helene, smiling, "yet I am told that these hangings, and this gilding, which you admire, are old and unfashionable, and must be replaced by new."

"Ah, Helene, you will become a great lady," said Gaston, sighing; "already I am kept waiting for an audience."

"My dear Gaston, did you not wait for hours in your little boat on the lake?"

"You were then in the convent. I waited the abbess's pleasure."

"That title is sacred, is it not?"

"Yes."

"It gives security, imposes respect and obedience."

"Doubtless."

"Well, judge of my delight. Here I find the same protection, the same love, only more powerful, more lasting."

"What!" exclaimed Gaston, surprised.

"I find—"

"Speak, in Heaven's name."

"Gaston, I have found a father."

"A father—ah, my dear Helene, I share your joy; what happiness! a father to watch over my Helene, my wife!"

"To watch from afar."

"Is he separated from you?"

"Alas, it seems the world separates us."

"Is it a secret?"

"A secret even to me, or you may be sure you should know all. I have no secrets from you, Gaston."

"A misfortune of birth—a prescription in your family—some temporary obstacle?"——"I do not know."

"Decidedly, it is a secret; but," said he, smiling, "I permit you to be discreet with me, if your father ordered it. However, may I ask some more questions?"

"Oh, yes."

"Are you pleased? Is your father one you can be proud of?"

"I think so, his heart seems noble and good. His voice is sweet and melodious."

"His voice! but is he like you?"

"I do not know. I have not seen him."

"Not seen him?"

"No, it was dark."

"Your father did not wish to see his daughter; and you so beautiful; oh, what indifference!"

"No, Gaston, he is not indifferent; he knows me well; he has my portrait—that portrait which made you so jealous last spring."

"But I do not understand this."

"It was dark, I tell you."

"In that case one might light these girandoles," said Gaston.

"That is well, when one wishes to be seen; but when one has reasons for concealment—"

"What!" interrupted Gaston; "what reason can a father have for hiding from his own daughter?"

"Excellent reasons, I believe, and you should understand them better than I can."

"Oh, Helene!" said Gaston, "with what terrible ideas you fill my mind."

"You alarm me, Gaston!"

"Tell me—what did your father speak of!"

"Of his deep love for me."

Gaston started.

"He swore to me that in future I should be happy; that there should be no more uncertainty as to my fate, for that he would despise all those considerations which had induced him as yet to disown me as a daughter."

"Words, words; but what proof did he give you? Pardon me these questions, Helene. I dread misfortune. I wish that for a time your angel's innocence could give place to the sharpness and infernal sagacity of a fiend; you would then understand me. I should not need to subject you to this interrogatory, which now is so necessary."

"I do not understand your question, Gaston. I do not know how to reply to you."

"Did he show you much affection?"

"Yes."

"But in the darkness, when he wished to speak to you?"

"He took my hand, and his trembled the most."

Gaston clenched his hands with rage.

"He embraced you paternally, did he not?"

"He gave me a single kiss on the forehead, which I received on my knees."

"Helene!" he cried, "my fears were not groundless; you are betrayed—you are the victim of a snare. Helene, this man who conceals himself, who fears the light, who calls you his child, is not your father."

"Gaston, you distress me."

"Helene, angels might envy your innocence; but on earth all is abused, even angels are insulted, profaned, by men. This man, whom I will know, whom I will seize and force to have confidence in your love and honor, shall tell me— if he be not the vilest of beings—whether I am to call him father, or kill him as a wretch!"

"Gaston, your brain is wandering; what can lead you to suspect such treachery? And, since you arouse my suspicions, since you hold a light over those ignoble labyrinths of the human heart which I refused to contemplate, I will speak to you with the same freedom. Was I not in this man's power? Is not this house his? Are not the people by whom I am surrounded devoted to his orders? Gaston, if you love me, you will ask my pardon for what you have thought and said of my father."

Gaston was in despair.

"Do not destroy one of the purest and holiest joys I have ever tasted. Do not poison the happiness of a life which I have often wept to think was solitary and abandoned, without other affection than that of which Heaven forbids us to be lavish. Let my filial ties compensate for the remorse which I sometimes feel for loving you almost to idolatry."

"Helene, forgive me," cried Gaston. "Yes, you are right; I sully your pure joys by my contact, and it may be the noble affection of your father, but in Heaven's name, Helene, give some heed to the fears of my experience and my love. Criminal passions often speculate on innocent credulity. The argument you use is weak. To show at once a guilty love would be unlike a skillful corrupter; but to win you by a novel luxury pleasing to your age, to accustom you gradually to new impressions, to win you at last by persuasion, is a sweeter victory than that of violence. Helene, listen to my prudence of five-and-twenty years—I say my prudence, for it is my love that speaks, that love which you should see so humble, so devoted, so ready to accept a father whom I knew to be really your parent."

Helene made no answer.

"I implore you," continued Gaston, "not to take any determination now, but to watch everything around you. Suspect the perfumes which are given you, the wine which you are offered—everything, Helene. Watch over yourself, you are my happiness, my honor, my life."

"My friend, I will obey you; this will not keep me from loving my father."

"Adore him, Helene, if I am wrong."

"You are a noble friend, Gaston. We are agreed then?"

"At the slightest suspicion write to me."

"Write! You leave me then?"

"I must go to Paris on business. I shall be at the hotel Muids d'Amour, Rue des Bourdonnais. Write down this address, and do not show it to any one."

"Why so many precautions?"

Gaston hesitated.

"Because, if your devoted protector were known, his plans for aiding you might be frustrated in case of bad intentions."

"You are somewhat mysterious, Gaston. I have a father who conceals himself, and a lover—this word I can hardly speak—who is going to do the same."

"But my intentions, you know," said Gaston, attempting to force a laugh.

"Ah, Madame Desroches is coming back. She thinks our interview too long. I am as much under tutelage as at the convent."

Gaston imprinted a kiss on the hand Helene held out to him. As Madame Desroches approached, Helene made a formal curtsey, which Gaston returned by an equally formal bow.

Gaston left for Paris. Owen awaited him with impatience, and this time could not reproach his master with being slow, for in three hours they were in Paris.

CHAPTER XII.

CAPTAIN LA JONQUIERE.

There was, as the reader has learned, in the Rue des Bourdonnais, a hotel where one could lodge, eat, and drink.

In his nocturnal interview with Dubois, Tapin had received the famous name of La Jonquiere, and had transmitted it to L'Eveille, who had passed it to all the chiefs of police, who had begun to search for the suspected officer in all the equivocal houses in Paris. The conspiracy of Cellamare, which we have related in a history of the Chevalier d'Harmental, had taught them that everywhere conspirators were to be found.

It was, however, by luck or by cleverness, Maitre Tapin himself who, in the Rue des Bourdonnais and in the hotel Muids d'Amour, found La Jonquiere, who was then a nightmare to Dubois.

The landlord took Tapin to be an old attorney's clerk, and replied to his questions politely, that "the Captain la Jonquiere was in the hotel, but was asleep."

Tapin asked no more. La Jonquiere was asleep, therefore he was in bed, for it was only six in the morning; if he were in bed, then he must be stopping at the inn.

Tapin went back to the Palais Royal, and found Dubois, who had just left the regent. A number of false La Jonquieres had already been discovered by his emissaries. One was a smuggler, called Captain la Jonciere, whom L'Eveille had found and arrested. A second was La Jonquille, sergeant in the French guards, and many others.

"Well," said Dubois, when Tapin had made his report, "you have found the real Captain la Jonquiere, then?"

"Yes, monseigneur."

"Is he called La Jonquiere?"

"Yes, monseigneur."

"L-a, la; J-o-n, jon; q-u-i-e-r-e, quiere?" continued he, spelling the word.

"La Jonquiere," repeated Tapin.

"A captain."

70

"Yes, monseigneur."

"What is he doing?"

"Waiting and drinking."

"That must be he," said Dubois; "and does he pay?"

He evidently attached great importance to the question.

"Very well, monsieur."

"A la bonne heure, Tapin. You have some sense."

"Monseigneur," said Tapin, modestly, "you flatter me; it is quite clear, if he had not paid he could not have been a dangerous man."

Dubois gave him ten louis as a reward, gave him some further orders, and set out at once to go to the Rue des Bourdonnais.

Let us say a word regarding the interior of the hotel. It was partly hotel, partly public house; the dwelling rooms were on the first-floor, and the tavern rooms on the ground-floor.

The principal of these, the common room, had four oak tables, and a quantity of red and white curtains; some benches along the walls, some glasses on a sideboard, some handsomely framed pictures, all blackened and rendered nauseous by smoke, completed the tout ensemble of this room, in which sat a fat man, with a red face, thirty-five or forty years old, and a little pale girl of twelve or fourteen.

This was the landlord and his only daughter and heiress.

A servant was cooking a ragout in the kitchen.

As the clock struck one, a French guard entered, and stopping at the threshold, murmured, "Rue des Bourdonnais, Muids d'Amour, in the common room, to sit at the table on the left, and wait."

Then, in accordance with this, the worthy defender of his country, whistling a tune and twirling his mustache, seated himself at the place indicated.

Scarcely had he had time to seat himself and strike his fist on the table, which, in the language of all taverns, means "Some wine," than a second guard, dressed exactly like the first, appeared at the door, murmured some words, and, after a little hesitation, seated himself by the other.

The two soldiers looked at each other, and both exclaimed:

"Ah!" which in all languages means surprise.

"It is you, Grippart," said one.

"It is you, L'Eulevant," said the other.

"What are you doing in this tavern?"

"And you?"

"I do not know."

"Nor I."

"You come here, then?"

CAPTAIN LA JONQUIERE.—*Page* 463.

Link to larger image

"Under orders."

"That is my case."

"And you are waiting?"

"For a man who is coming."

"With a watchword?"

"And on this watchword?"

"I am to obey as though it were Tapin himself."

"Just so; and, in the mean time, I have a pistole for drink."

"I have a pistole also, but I was not told to drink."

"And it being doubtful?"

"In doubt, as the sage says, I do not abstain."

"In that case, let us drink."

And he raised his hand to call the landlord, but it was not necessary, for he was standing near, expecting orders.

"Some wine," cried the two guards.

"Orleans," added one; "I like that."

The landlord brought an inclosed bottle.

The two drinkers filled their glasses, emptied them, and then placed them on the table, each with a different grimace, but both intended to express the same opinion.

When the host was gone, one said to the other:

"You know more of this than you have told me?"

"I know it concerns a certain captain," answered the other.

"Yes; just so. But I suppose we shall have aid to arrest him?"

"Doubtless; two to one is not enough."

"You forget the man with the watchword."

"Ah! I think I hear something."

"Yes; some one coming downstairs."

"Chut!"

"Silence!"

And the soldiers, much more occupied by their commission than if they had really been soldiers, kept an eye turned toward the staircase while they drunk.

They were not deceived; the step on the staircase approached, and they saw, first, some legs, then a body, then a head descending. The legs were covered with fine silk stockings and white cashmere breeches, the body with a tight blue coat, and the head with a three-cornered hat, jauntily placed over one ear; his epaulets left no doubt that he held the rank of captain.

This man, who was, in fact, Captain la Jonquiere, was about five feet five,

73

rather fat, and had a sagacious air; one would almost have supposed that he suspected spies in the two soldiers, for he turned his back to them at once, and entered into conversation with his host in a somewhat assumed tone and manner.

"In truth," said he, "I should have dined here, and this delicious perfume of stewed kidneys would have tempted me, but some bons vivants are expecting me at the 'Galoubet de Paphos.' Perhaps a young man may come here this morning, but I could not wait any longer. Should he ask for a hundred pistoles, say that I shall be back in an hour, if he will wait."

"Very well, captain," said the host.

"Some wine," said the guard.

"Ah," said the captain, throwing an apparently careless glance at the drinkers, "here are some soldiers who have but little respect for an epaulet." Then, turning to the host—

"Serve these gentlemen; you see they are in a hurry."

"Ah," said one, rising, "as soon as monsieur will permit."

"Certainly I permit it," said La Jonquiere; and he stepped toward the door.

"But, captain," said the host, stopping him, "you have not told me the name of the gentleman you expect."

La Jonquiere hesitated. After a moment:

"Monsieur Gaston de Chanlay," he replied.

"Gaston de Chanlay," repeated the host. "I hope I shall remember the name. Gaston—Gascon. Ah, I shall remember Gascon. Chanlay; ah, I shall think of Chandelle."

"That is it," repeated La Jonquiere, gravely; "Gascon de Chandelle."

And he went out, but not without looking round the corners of the street and the angles of the houses.

He had not taken a hundred steps in the Rue St. Honoré before Dubois presented himself at the door. He had passed La Jonquiere, but, never having seen him, could not recognize him.

He presented himself boldly, dressed as a shopkeeper.

CHAPTER XIII.

MONSIEUR MOUTONNET, DRAPER AT ST. GERMAIN-EN-LAYE.

Dubois at once accosted the host.

"Monsieur," said he, timidly, "does Captain la Jonquiere lodge here? I wish to speak to him."

"You wish to speak to him?" said the host, examining the new-comer from head to foot.

"If possible," said Dubois.

"Are you sure that is the person you want?" asked the host, who did not think this was the man La Jonquiere expected.

"I think so," said Dubois modestly.

"A short, fat man?"

"Yes."

"Drinks his brandy neat?"

"That is the man."

"Always ready with his cane if he is not attended to directly!"

"Ah, that is Captain la Jonquiere!"

"You know him, then?"

"Not in the least," said Dubois.

"True, for you must have met him at the door."

"Diable! Is he out?" said Dubois, with a start of ill-humor badly repressed. "Thank you," and he called up an amiable smile.

"He has not been gone five minutes."

"But he is coming back?"

"In an hour."

"May I wait for him, monsieur?"

"Certainly, if you take something."

"Give me some brandy-cherries," said Dubois. "I never drink wine except with meals."

The two guards exchanged a contemptuous smile.

The host hastened to bring the cherries.

"Ah!" said Dubois; "only five! At St. Germain-en-Laye they give six."

"Possibly, monsieur; for at St. Germain-en-Laye they have no excise to pay."

"Yes, I forgot that," and he began to eat a cherry, which he could not, however, accomplish without a grimace.

"Where does the captain lodge?" asked Dubois.

"There is the door of his room; he preferred the ground-floor."

"Yes," murmured Dubois; "the windows look into the public road."

"And there is a door opening into the Rue des Deux-Boules."

"Oh, how convenient! And does not the noise annoy him?"

"There is another room above: sometimes he sleeps in one, sometimes in the other."

"Like Denis the tyrant," said Dubois, who could not refrain from Latin or historical quotations.

"What?" said mine host.

Dubois bit his lip. At this moment one of the soldiers called for wine, and the host darted off to wait upon him.

Dubois turned to the two guards.

"Thank you," said he.

"What is it, bourgeois?" asked they.

"France and the regent," replied Dubois.

"The watchword!" cried both, rising.

"Enter this room," said Dubois, showing La Jonquiere's room. "Open the door into the Rue des Deux-Boules, and hide behind a curtain, under a table, in a closet, wherever you can. If, when I come in, I can see so much as an ear, you will have no pay for six months."

The two men emptied their glasses, and entered the room, while Dubois, who saw they had forgotten to pay, put a piece of twelve sous on the table, then, opening the window, and calling to the driver of a hackney carriage standing before the door—"L'Eveille," said he, "bring the carriage to the little door in the Rue des Deux-Boules, and tell Tapin to come up when I knock on the windows with my fingers; he has his orders; be off."

The host reappeared.

"Hola!" cried, "where are my men?"

"A sergeant came and called them away."

"But they have not paid."

"Yes, they left a twelve-sou piece on the table."

"Diable! twelve sous; and my wine is eight sous the bottle."

"Ah!" said Dubois, "no doubt they thought that as they were soldiers you would make a reduction."

"At any rate," said the host, consoling himself, "it is not all lost; and in our trade one must expect this kind of thing."

"You have nothing of the sort to fear with Captain la Jonquiere?"

"Oh, no, he is the best of lodgers; he pays without a word, and ready money. True, he never likes anything."

"Oh, that may be his manner," said Dubois.

"Exactly."

"What you tell me of his prompt payment pleases me."

"Have you come to ask for money? He said he expected some one to whom he owed a hundred pistoles."

"No; on the contrary, I owe him fifty louis."

"Fifty louis! peste!" said the host, "what a pretty sum! Perhaps I was mistaken, and he said receive, not pay. Are you the Chevalier Gaston de Chanlay?"

"Does he expect the Chevalier Gaston de Chanlay?" said Dubois, with a joy he could not conceal.

"He told me so," said the host. "Is that you?"

"No; I am not noble. I am called Moutonnet."

"Nobility is nothing," said the host. "One may be called Moutonnet and be an honest man."

"Yes; Moutonnet, draper at St. Germain-en-Laye."

"And you have fifty louis for the captain?"

"Yes. In turning over some old accounts of my father's, I find he owed fifty louis to Captain la Jonquiere's father; and I have had no peace till, instead of the father, who is dead, I had found the son."

"Do you know there are not many debtors like you?"

"The Moutonnets are all the same, from father to son. When we are owed anything we are pitiless. Listen. There is an honest fellow who owed Moutonnet & Son one hundred and sixty francs; my grandfather put him in prison, and there he has been for the three generations, and he has just died there. I calculated that, during the thirty years he was there, he cost us twelve thousand francs; but we maintained the principle. But I beg your pardon for keeping you with all this nonsense; and here is a new customer for you."

"Ah!" said the host, "it is Captain la Jonquiere himself. Captain," continued he, "some one is waiting for you."

The captain entered suspiciously—he had seen some strange, and, he thought, sinister faces about.

Dubois saluted him politely.

La Jonquiere asked the host if the friend he had expected had arrived.

"No one but monsieur. However, you lose nothing by the exchange, since one was to fetch away money, and the other brings it."

La Jonquiere, surprised, turned to Dubois, who repeated the same story he had told to the host, and with such success that La Jonquiere, calling for wine, asked Dubois to follow him into his room.

Dubois approached the window, and quietly tapped on it with his fingers.

"But shall I not be in the way in your room?" asked Dubois.

"Not at all, not at all—the view is pleasant—as we drink we can look out and see the passers-by: and there are some pretty women in the Rue des Bourdonnais."

They entered the room. Dubois made a sign to Tapin, who appeared in the first room, followed by two men, then shut the door behind him.

Tapin's two followers went to the window of the common room, and drew the curtains, while Tapin placed himself behind the door of Jonquiere's room, so as to be hidden by it when it opened. The host now returned from La Jonquiere's room, to write down the receipt for the money which La Jonquiere had just paid him for the wine, when Tapin threw a handkerchief over his mouth, and carried him off like a feather to a second carriage standing at the door. One of the men seized the little girl who was cooking

78

eggs, the other carried off the servant, and soon they were all on the way to St. Lazare, drawn by two such good horses that it was evidently not a real hired car.

Tapin remained behind, and taking from a closet a calico apron and waistcoat, signed to a loiterer who was looking in at the window, and who quickly transformed himself into a publican.

At this moment a violent noise was heard in the captain's room, as of a table thrown down with bottles and glasses; then oaths, then the clinking of a sword, then silence.

Presently a carriage was heard rolling away up the Rue de Deux-Boules. Tapin looked joyous.

"Bravo," said he, "that is done."

"It was time, masters," said the pretended publican, "for here is a customer."

CHAPTER XIV.

TRUST TO SIGNS OF GRATITUDE.

Tapin at first thought that it was the Chevalier de Chanlay, but it was only a woman who wanted a pint of wine.

"What has happened to poor M. Bourguignon?" asked she. "He has just been taken away in a coach."

"Alas!" said Tapin, "we were far from expecting it. He was standing there talking, and was suddenly seized with apoplexy."

"Gracious heavens!"

"We are all mortal," said Tapin, throwing up his eyes.

"But why did they take the little girl?"

"To attend to her father—it is her duty."

"But the servant?"

"To cook for them."

"Ah, I could not understand it all, so I came to buy a pint of wine, though I did not want it, that I might find out."

"Well, now you know."

"Yes, but who are you?"

"I am Champagne, Bourguignon's cousin. I arrived by chance this morning; I brought him news of his family, and the sudden joy overcame him; ask Grabigeon," continued Tapin, showing his assistant, who was finishing an omelet commenced by the landlord's daughter.

"Oh, yes, everything passed exactly as M. Champagne says," replied Grabigeon, wiping away a tear with the handle of his spoon.

"Poor M. Bourguignon! then you think that we should pray for him?"

"There is never any harm in praying," said Tapin, sententiously.

"Ah, stop a minute, give me good measure."

Bourguignon would have groaned in spirit, could he have seen the wine that Tapin gave for her two sous.

"Well," said she, "I will go and tell the neighbors, who are very anxious, and I promise you my custom, M. Champagne; indeed, if M. Bourguignon were not your cousin, I would tell you what I think."

"Oh, tell me, never mind that."

"I perceive that he cheated me shamefully. What you have given me for two sous, he would hardly have given me for four; but if there is no justice here there is in heaven, and it is very providential that you are to continue his business."

"I believe so," said Tapin, in a half voice, "particularly for his customers."

And he dismissed the woman just as the door opened, and a young man entered, dressed in a blue cloak.

"Is this the hotel Le Muids d'Amour?" asked he.

"Yes, monsieur."

"Does Captain la Jonquiere lodge here?"

"Yes, monsieur."

"Is he within?"

"Yes, he has just returned."

"Tell him, if you please, that the Chevalier Gaston de Chanlay is here."

Tapin offered the chevalier a chair, and went into La Jonquiere's room.

Gaston shook the snow from his boots and cloak, and proceeded leisurely to examine the picture on the wall, never supposing that he had close to him three or four swords, which, at a sign from the polite host, would leave their sheaths to be plunged into his breast.

Tapin returned, saying, "Captain la Jonquiere waits for M. de Chanlay."

Gaston proceeded to the room where sat a man whom the host pointed out as Captain la Jouquiere, and—without being much of a physiognomist—he perceived at once that he was no bully.

Little, dry, gray-eyed, uneasy in his uniform, such appeared the formidable captain whom Gaston had been recommended to treat with so much consideration.

"This man is ugly, and looks like a sexton," thought Gaston; then, as the stranger advanced toward him—

"Have I the honor of speaking to Captain la Jonquiere?" asked Gaston.

"Himself," said Dubois; "and are you M. le Chevalier Gaston de

Chanlay?"——"I am, monsieur."

"Have you the sign of recognition?" asked the false La Jonquiere.

"Here is the half of the gold piece."

"And here the other," said Dubois.

They tried the two, which fitted exactly.

"And now," continued Gaston, "the papers;" and he drew from his pocket the strangely folded paper, on which was written the name of La Jonquiere.

Dubois took from his pocket a similar paper, bearing Gaston's name: they were precisely alike.

"Now," said Gaston, "the pocket-book."

They found that their new pocket-books were precisely similar, and both, though new, contained an almanac for the year 1700, nineteen years previous.

"And now, monsieur," said Gaston.

"Now we will talk of business: is not that your meaning, chevalier?"

"Exactly; are we safe?"

"As though in a desert."

They seated themselves by a table, on which were a bottle of sherry and two glasses.

Dubois filled one, and was about to fill the other, when Gaston stopped him.

"Peste!" thought Dubois, "he is slender and sober, bad signs; Cæsar mistrusted thin people who did not drink, and Brutus and Cassius were such."

"Captain," said Gaston, after a short silence, "when we undertake, as now, an affair in which we risk our heads, I think we should know each other, so that the past may vouch for the future. Montlouis, Talhouet, De Couëdic, and Pontcalec have told you my name and condition. I was brought up by a brother, who had reasons for personal hatred to the regent. This hatred I have imbibed; therefore, three years ago, when the league was formed among the nobility in Bretagne, I entered the conspiracy; now I have been chosen to come to Paris to receive the instructions of Baron de Valef, who has arrived from Spain, to transmit them to the Duc d'Olivares, his Catholic Majesty's agent in Paris, and to assure myself of his assent."

"And what is Captain la Jonquiere to do in all this?" asked Dubois, as though he were doubting the chevalier's identity.

"To present me to the Duc d'Olivares. I arrived two hours ago; since then I have seen M. de Valef, and now I come to you. Now you know my history."

Dubois listened, and, when Gaston had finished—"As to me, chevalier," said he, throwing himself back indolently in his chair, "I must own my history is somewhat longer and more adventurous; however, if you wish to hear it, I obey."

"I think it necessary, in our position, to know each other," said Gaston.

"Well," said Dubois, "as you know, I am called Captain la Jonquiere; my father was, like myself, a soldier of fortune; this is a trade at which one gains in general a good deal of glory and very little money; my glorious father died, leaving me, for sole inheritance, his rapier and his uniform; I girded on the rapier, which was rather too long, and I wore the uniform, which was rather too large. From that time," said Dubois, calling the chevalier's attention to the looseness of his coat, "from that time I contracted the habit of always having plenty of room to move easily."

Gaston nodded, as though to express his approbation of this habit.

"Thanks to my good looks I was received in the Royal Italian, which was then recruiting in France. I held a distinguished post; when—the day before the battle of Malplaquet—I had a slight quarrel with my sergeant about an order which he gave me with the end of his cane raised instead of lowered, as it should have been."

"Pardon me," said Gaston, "but I cannot see what difference that could make to the order he was giving."

"It made this difference, that in lowering his cane it struck against my hat, which fell to the ground; the result was a duel, in which I passed my saber through his body. Now, as I certainly should have been shot if I had waited to be arrested, I made off, and woke the next morning—devil take me if I know how it happened—in Marlborough's army."

"That is to say, you deserted," said Gaston, smiling.

"I had Coriolanus and the great Condé for examples," said Dubois, "and this appeared to me to be sufficient to excuse me in the eyes of posterity. I assisted then, I must tell you, as we are to hide nothing from one another, at the battle of Malplaquet; but instead of being on one side of the brook, I was on the other, and instead of having the village behind me, I faced it. I think this was a lucky exchange for your humble servant; the Royal Italian left eight hundred men on the field of battle, my company was cut to pieces, and my own comrade and bedfellow killed by a cannon-ball. The glory with which my late regiment covered itself so much delighted Marlborough, that he made me an ensign on the field of battle. With such a protector I ought to have done well, but his wife, Lady Marlborough, whom Heaven confound, having been awkward enough to spill a bowl of water over Queen Anne's dress, this great event changed the face of things in Europe. In the overthrow which resulted, I found myself without any other protector than my own merit, and the enemies I had gained thereby."

"And what did you do then?" asked Gaston, somewhat interested in the adventurous life of the pretended captain.

"What could I do? I was forced to enter the service of his Catholic majesty, who, to his honor be it said, graciously acceded to my demand for a commission. In three years I was a captain; but, out of our pay of thirty reals a day, they kept back twenty, telling us what an honor it was for us to lend money to the king of Spain. As the security did not appear good in my eyes, I asked leave of my colonel to quit the service and return to my beautiful country, accompanied by a recommendation, in order that the Malplaquet affair might not be too much brought on the tapis. The colonel referred me to the Prince do Cellamare, who, recognizing in me a natural disposition to obey, without discussion, any orders given in a proper manner and accompanied by a certain music, employed me actively in the famous conspiracy which bears his name, when, all at once, the whole affair blew up, as you know, by the double denunciation of La Fillon and a wretched writer called Buvat; but his highness, wisely thinking that what is deferred is not lost, recommended me to his successor, to whom, I hope, my services may be useful, and whom I thank most heartily for procuring me the acquaintance of so accomplished a cavalier as yourself. Count on me then, chevalier, as your most humble and obedient servant."

"I ask nothing of you, captain," replied Gaston, "but to present me to the duke, the only person to whom my instructions permit me to speak openly, and to whom I am to deliver the Baron de Valef's dispatches. I beg, therefore, that you will present me to his excellency."

"This very day, chevalier," said Dubois, who seemed to have decided on his course of action; "in an hour if you like, in ten minutes if necessary."

"As soon as possible."

"Listen," said Dubois; "I was a little too quick when I said you should see his excellency in an hour—in Paris one is never sure; perhaps he does not know of your coming, and I may not find him at home."

"I understand."

"Perhaps even I may be prevented from coming back to fetch you."

"How so?"

"Peste, chevalier; it is easy to see that this is your first visit to Paris."

"What do you mean?"

"I mean that in Paris there are three distinct bodies of police, who all unite to torment those honest people who only desire to substitute what is not for what is. First, the regent's police, which is not much to be feared; secondly, that of Messire Voyer d'Argenson—this has its days, when he is in a bad humor, or has been ill received at the convent of the Madeleine du Tresnel; thirdly, there is Dubois's police; ah! that is a different thing. Dubois is a—"

"A wretch," cried Gaston; "I am well aware of that."

Dubois smiled his sinister smile.

"Well, to escape these three police?" said Gaston.

"One must be prudent, chevalier."

"Instruct me, captain; for you seem to know more about it than I, who am a provincial."

"First, we must not lodge in the same hotel."

"Diable!" said Gaston, who remembered the address given to Helene; "I had a great wish to remain here."

"I will be the one to turn out then, chevalier. Take one of my rooms, this one, or the one above."

"I prefer this."

"You are right; on the ground-floor, a window looking into one street, a secret door to the other. You have a quick eye; we shall make something of you."

"Let us return to our business."

"Right; where was I?"

"You said you might not be able to come back and fetch me."

"Yes, but in that case take care not to follow any one without sufficient signs."

"By what signs shall I recognize any one as coming from you?"

"First, he must have a letter from me."

"I do not know your writing."

"True; I will give you a specimen."

And Dubois wrote the following lines:

"Monsieur le Chevaliér—Follow without fear the man who brings this note, he is deputed by me to lead you to the house where the Duc d'Olivares and Captain la Jonquiere await you."

"Stay," said he, giving him the note, "if any one comes in my name, he will give you a similar letter."

"Is that enough?"

"One cannot be too careful; besides the letter, he will show you the half-coin, and at the door of the house to which he leads you, ask for the third sign."

"Which will be."

"The paper."

"It is well," said Gaston, "with these precautions—the devil is in it if we are mistaken. Now, what am I to do?"

"Wait; you will not go out to-day."

"No."

"Well, remain quiet in this hotel, where you will want for nothing. I will recommend you to the host."

"Thanks."

"My dear M. Champagne," said Dubois to Tapin, opening the door, "the Chevalier de Chanlay takes my room; attend to him as you would to me."

Then, closing it—

"That fellow is worth his weight in gold, Tapin," said he in a low voice, "do not lose sight of him for a moment; you will answer for him with your head."

CHAPTER XV.

HIS EXCELLENCY THE DUC D'ORLEANS.

Dubois, on leaving the chevalier, contemplated the chance which had again placed in his hands the future of the regent and of France. In crossing the hall he recognized L'Eveille, and signed to him to follow. It was L'Eveille who had undertaken to get the real La Jonquiere out of the way. Dubois became thoughtful: the easiest part of the affair was done; it now remained to persuade the regent to put himself in a kind of affair which he held in the utmost horror—the maneuvering of intrigue.

Dubois began by asking where the regent was, and how occupied? The prince was in his studio, finishing an etching commenced by Hubert, the chemist, who, at an adjoining table, was occupied in embalming an ibis, by the Egyptian method, which he professed to have recovered.

A secretary was reading some letters to the regent.

All at once, to the regent's astonishment—for this was his sanctum—the door opened, and an usher announced Captain la Jonquiere.

The regent turned.

"La Jonquiere?" said he; "who is this?"

Hubert looked surprised that a stranger should be thus unceremoniously intruded on their privacy.

At this moment a long-pointed head appeared at the open door.

The regent did not, at first, recognize Dubois in his disguise: but shortly, the pointed nose, which had not its match in the kingdom, betrayed him.

A merry look took the place of the astonishment which the regent's features had at first displayed.

"Ah, it is you, abbe!" said his highness, laughing, "and what is the meaning of this disguise?"

"It means that I have changed my skin, and from a fox have turned into a lion; and now Monsieur the Chemist and Monsieur the Secretary, do me the favor to take your bird and letters elsewhere."

"Why so?" asked the regent.

"Because I have important business to speak of with you."

"Go to the devil with your important business; it is too late: come to-morrow."

"Monseigneur," said Dubois, "do not force me to remain till to-morrow in this villainous disguise."

"Do what you please, but I have decided that the rest of this day shall be given to pleasure."

"Well, I come to propose a disguise to you also."

"A disguise! what do you mean, Dubois?" asked the regent, who thought it was probably one of his ordinary masquerades.

"Ah, it makes your mouth water, Monsieur Alain."

"Speak; what do you want to do?"

"First send away your chemist and secretary."

"You still wish it?"——"Decidedly."

"Very well, then."

The regent signed to them to leave: they did so.

"And now," said he, "what is it?"

"I want to present to you, monseigneur, a young man, a very delightful fellow, just arrived from Bretagne, and strongly recommended to me."

"His name?"

"The Chevalier Gaston de Chanlay."

"De Chanlay!" said the regent, "the name is not unknown to me."

"Indeed."

"Yes, I think I have heard it formerly; but I do not remember where or how. What does your protégé come to Paris for?"

"Monseigneur, I shall leave him to tell you that himself."

"Tell it to me."

"Yes; that is to say, to the Duc d'Olivares, whom you are about to personate. Ah, my protégé is a discreet conspirator, and I have had some trouble to get at the truth of things. He was addressed to Paris, to a certain La Jonquiere, who was to present him to the Duc d'Olivares. Do you understand now?"

"Not at all."

"Well, I have been Captain la Jonquiere, but I cannot be both La Jonquiere and his excellency."

"So, you reserve that part—"

"For you, monseigneur."

"Thank you. So you think that, under a false name, I will get at the secrets—"

"Of your enemies, monseigneur," interrupted Dubois. "Pardieu! what a dreadful crime, and how it would distress you, to change name and dress; you have never before learned secrets by such means. But remember, monseigneur, our many disguises, and after being called M. Alain and Maitre Jean, you may well, I think, without anything derogatory to your dignity, be called Le Duc d'Olivares."

"I ask no better than a disguise for amusement, but—"

"But a disguise," continued Dubois, "to preserve the peace of France, to prevent traitors from overthrowing the kingdom, to prevent assassins from murdering you—this, I suppose, is unworthy of you. I understand; ah, if it were only in pursuit of some little ironmongress in the Pont Neuf, or the pretty widow of the Rue Saint Augustine, it might be worth your while."

"If I do what you wish," said the regent, "what will be the result?"

"Probably, that you will own that I am no visionary, and that you will allow others to watch over you, since you will not watch over yourself."

"But, once for all, if the thing turns out not worth the trouble, shall I be freed from your worrying?"

"I promise you, on my honor."

"Abbe, if you have no objection, I should prefer another oath."

"Oh, monseigneur, you are too hard; but you consent?"

"Again this folly."

"You shall see if it be folly."

"I believe you make plots to frighten me."

"Then they are well made; you shall see."

"Are you certain?"

"Absolutely."

"If I am not frightened, look to yourself."

"Monseigneur exacts too much."

"You are not sure, Dubois."

"I swear to you, monsieur, that you will be moved, and will be glad to speak with his excellency's tongue."

And Dubois went out before the regent had time to withdraw his consent.

Five minutes after, a courier entered the antechamber, and gave a letter to a page, who brought it to the regent.

"Madame Desroches," said he, looking at the writing, and, breaking the seal, read as follows:

"MONSEIGNEUR—The young lady you left in my charge does not appear to be in safety here."

"Bah," exclaimed the regent, and then read on—

"The residence in the town, which your highness feared for her, would be a hundred times better than isolation; and I do not feel strong enough to defend her as I would wish, and as I ought."

"Ouais," said the regent, "it seems something is the matter."

"A young man, who had written to Mademoiselle Helene shortly before your arrival yesterday, presented himself this morning at the pavilion; I wished to refuse him admittance, but mademoiselle so peremptorily ordered me to admit him, and to retire, that in her look and tone I recognized the blood which commands."

"Yes, yes," said the regent, "she is, indeed, my daughter; but who can this young man be? Some coxcomb she must have seen in the convent parlor." Then he read on:

"I believe, monseigneur, that this young man and mademoiselle have met before. I did not think it wrong to listen, for your highness's service, and in spite of the double door I once heard him say, 'To see you as formerly.' Will your royal highness secure me against this danger, and send me a written order which I can use to shelter myself from the anger of mademoiselle."

"Diable!" exclaimed the regent, "it cannot be a love affair already; brought up in the only convent in France where men never pass the parlor. No, it is some foolish fear of Madame Desroches; but let us see what else she writes."

"P. S.—I have just been to the hotel Tigre-Royal for information. The young man arrived yesterday evening at seven o'clock, just three-quarters of an hour before mademoiselle; he came by the Bretagne road, that is, the road she also came. He travels under the name of M. de Livry."

"Oh!" said the regent, "this looks like a concerted plan. Pardieu! Dubois would laugh if he knew this; how he would talk! It is to be hoped he knows nothing of it, in spite of his police. Hola! page."

The page who had brought the letter entered.

"Where is the messenger from Rambouillet?"

"He is waiting for an answer."

"Give him this, and tell him to start at once."

As to Dubois, while preparing the interview between Gaston and the false duke, he made the following calculation.

"I hold the regent both by himself and his daughter. This intrigue of his is either serious or not; if it be not, I distress her in exaggerating it. If it be serious, I have the merit of having discovered it; but I must not strike both blows at once. First, I must save the duke, then his daughter, and there will be two rewards.—Is that the best?—Yes—the duke first—if a young girl falls, no one suffers, if a man falls, a kingdom is lost, let us begin with the duke." And Dubois dispatched a courier to M. de Montaran at Nantes.

M. de Montaran was, as we have said, the ancient governor of Bretagne.

As to Gaston, his plan was fixed. Ashamed of being associated with a man like Jonquiere, he congratulated himself that he was now to communicate with the chief of the enterprise, and resolved, if he also appeared base and venial, to return and take counsel with his friends at Nantes. As to Helene, he doubted not; he knew her courage and her love, and that she would die rather than have to blush before her dearest friend. He saw with joy that the happiness of finding a father did not lead her to forget the past, but still he had his fears as to this mysterious paternity; even a king would own such a daughter, were there not some disgraceful obstacle.

Gaston dressed himself carefully; there is a coquetry in danger as well as in pleasure, and he embellished his youth with every advantage of costume.

The regent, by Dubois's advice, dressed in black velvet and half hid his face in an immense cravat of Mechlin lace.

The interview was to take place in a house belonging to the regent, in the Faubourg Saint Germain: he arrived there at five o'clock, as night was falling.

CHAPTER XVI.

MONSEIGNEUR, WE ARE BRETONS.

Gaston remained in the room on the ground-floor, and dressed himself carefully, as we have said, while Tapin continued his apprenticeship. By the evening he knew how to measure a pint as well as his predecessor, and even better; for he thought that in the compensation which would be given to Bourguignon, waste would be considered, and that therefore the less waste the better; so the morning's customer on her return got badly served, and went off disgusted.

When his toilet was finished, Gaston began to inspect La Jonquiere's library, and found it composed of three sets of books: theatrical books, obscene books, and arithmetical books.

While he was thus engaged a man entered, introduced by Tapin, who went out directly, and left him alone with Gaston. The man announced that Captain La Jonquiere, not being able to return, had sent him in his stead. Gaston demanding proof, the man showed a letter in the same terms and the same writing as the specimen Gaston had received, and then the half coin, after which Gaston made no difficulty as to following him, and both got into a carefully closed carriage. They crossed the Pont-Neuf, and, in the Rue du Bac, stopped at the courtyard of a pavilion; then the man drew from his pocket the paper bearing the chevalier's name as the third signal of recognition.

Gaston and his companion alighted, ascended the four steps of the doorway, and entered a large circular corridor surrounding the pavilion. Gaston looked round and saw that his guide had disappeared, and that he was alone.

His heart beat quickly. He was about to face, not the tool, but the master and originator of the whole plot, the representative of a king; he was to play a kingdom against a kingdom.

A bell sounded within.

Gaston almost trembled. He looked in a glass and saw that he was pale; a thousand new ideas assailed him; the door opened, and La Jonquiere appeared.

"Come, chevalier," said he, "we are expected."

Gaston advanced with a firm step.

They found a man seated in an armchair, his back turned to the door. A single light, placed on a table and covered with a shade, lighted only the lower part of his body; his head and shoulders were in shadow.

Gaston thought the face noble, and understood at once that this was a man of worth, and no La Jonquiere. The mouth was benevolent and the eyes large, bold, and firm, like those of a king or a bird of prey; deep thought was written on his brow, prudence and some degree of firmness in the lower part of the face; all this, however, in the half-darkness, and in spite of the Mechlin cravat.

"At least this is an eagle," thought he, "the other was but a raven."

Gaston bowed silently, and the unknown, rising, went and leaned against the chimney.

"Monsieur is the person of whom I spoke to your excellency," said La Jonquiere, "M. le Chevalier Gaston de Chanlay."

The unknown bowed silently.

"Mordieu!" whispered Dubois in his ear, "if you do not speak he will not say anything."

"This gentleman comes from Bretagne, I believe," said the duke, coldly.

"Yes, monsieur; but will your excellency pardon me. Captain la Jonquiere has told my name, but I have not been told yours. Excuse my rudeness, monseigneur; it is not I who speak, it is my province, which sends me."

"You are right, monsieur," said La Jonquiere, quickly, taking from a portfolio on the table a paper, at the bottom of which was a large signature with the seal of the king of Spain.

"Here is the name," said he.

"Duc d'Olivares," read Gaston.

Then turning to him, he bowed respectfully.

"And now, monsieur," said the duke, "you will not, I presume, hesitate to speak."

"I thought I had first to listen," said Gaston, still on the defensive.

"True: but, remember, it is a dialogue; each one speaks in turn."

"Monseigneur, you do me too much honor, and I will set the example of confidence."

"I listen, monsieur."

"Monseigneur, the states of Bretagne—"

"The malcontents of Bretagne," interrupted the regent smiling, in spite of a sign from Dubois.

"The malcontents are so numerous," replied Gaston, "that they may be considered the representatives of the province: however, I will employ the word your excellency points out; the malcontents of Bretagne have sent me to you, monseigneur, to learn the intentions of Spain in this affair."

"First let us learn those of Bretagne."

"Monseigneur, Spain may count on us; we pledge our word, and Breton loyalty is proverbial."

"But what do you promise?"

"To second the efforts of the French nobility."

"But are you not French?"

"Monseigneur, we are Bretons. Bretagne, reunited to France by a treaty, may look on herself as separated from the moment when France no longer respects the rights of that treaty."

"Yes, I know; the old story of Anne de Bretagne's contract. It is a long time since that contract was signed, monsieur."

The false La Jonquiere pushed the regent violently.

"What matter," said Gaston, "if each one of us has it by heart?"

CHAPTER XVII.

MONSIEUR ANDRE.

"You said that the Breton nobility were ready to second the French nobility: now, what do the French nobility want?"

"They desire, in case of his majesty's death, to place the king of Spain on the throne of France, as sole heir of Louis XIV."

"Very good, very good," said La Jonquiere, taking snuff with an air of extreme satisfaction.

"But," said the regent, "the king is not dead, although you speak almost as if he were."

"The Grand Dauphin, the Duc and Duchesse de Bourgogne and their children, disappeared in a deplorable manner." The regent turned pale with anger; Dubois coughed.

"Then they reckon on the king's death?"

"Generally, monseigneur."

"Then that explains how the king of Spain hopes, in spite of the renunciation of his rights, to mount the throne of France. But, among the people attached to the regency, he may meet with some opposition."

The false Spaniard involuntarily lingered on these words.

"Monseigneur," replied the chevalier, "this case also has been foreseen."

"Ah!" said Dubois, "this has been foreseen. Did not I tell you, monseigneur, that the Bretons were valuable to us. Continue, monsieur, continue."

In spite of this invitation, Gaston was silent.

"Well, monsieur," said the pretended duke, "I am listening."

"This secret is not mine, monseigneur."

"Then," said the duke, "I have not the confidence of your chiefs?"

"On the contrary, you alone have it."

"I understand, monsieur; but the captain is my friend, and I answer for him as for myself."

"My instructions are, monseigneur, to speak to you alone."

"But, I tell you, I answer for the captain."

"In that case," said Gaston, bowing, "I have said all I have to say."

"You hear, captain," said the regent; "have the kindness to leave us alone."

"Yes, monseigneur; I have but two words to say to you."

Gaston drew back.

"Monseigneur," whispered Dubois, "press him hard—get out the whole affair —you will never have such another chance. What do you think of our Breton?"

"A noble fellow; eyes full of intelligence and a fine head."

"So much the better for cutting it off."

"What do you say?"

"Nothing, monseigneur; I am exactly of your opinion. M. de Chanlay, your humble servant; some might be angry that you would not speak before them, but I am not proud, and, provided all things turn out as I expect, I do not care for the means."

Chanlay bowed.

"Monsieur," said the regent, when Dubois had closed the door, "we are alone, and I am listening. Speak—you understand my impatience."

"Yes, monseigneur. You are doubtless surprised that you have not yet received from Spain a certain dispatch which you were to send to Cardinal Olocroni?"

"True, monsieur," said the regent, dissembling with difficulty.

"I will explain the delay. The messenger who should have brought this dispatch fell ill, and has not left Madrid. The Baron de Valef, my friend, who was in Spain, offered himself; and, after three or four day's hesitation, at length—as he was a man already tried in Cellamare's conspiracy—they trusted him."

"In fact," said the regent, "the Baron de Valef narrowly escaped Dubois's emissaries; it needed some courage to renew such a work. I know that when the regent saw Madame de Maine and Cellamare arrested; Richelieu, Polignac, Malezieux, and Mademoiselle de Launay in the Bastille; and that wretched Lagrange-Chancel at the Sainte Marguerite, he thought all was finished."

"You see he was mistaken, monseigneur."

"But do not these Breton conspirators fear that in thus rising they may sacrifice the heads of the Paris conspirators whom the regent has in his power?"

"They hope to save them, or die with them."

"How save them?"

"Let us return to the dispatch, if you please, monseigneur; here it is."

The regent took the paper, but seeing the address to his excellency the Duc d'Olivares, laid it on the table unopened. Strange inconsistency! This man opened two hundred letters a day by his spies; it is true that then he dealt with a Thorey or a Dubois, and not with a Chevalier de Chanlay.

"Well, monseigneur," said Gaston.

"You know, doubtless, what this dispatch contains, monsieur?"

"Not word for word, perhaps; but I know what was arranged."

"Well, tell me. I shall be glad to know how far you are admitted into the secrets of the Spanish cabinet."

"When the regent is got rid of," said Gaston, without noticing the slight start which his interlocutor gave at these words, "the Duc de Maine will be provisionally recognized in his place. The Duc de Maine will at once break the treaty of the quadruple alliance signed by that wretch Dubois."

"I wish La Jonquiere had been here to hear you speak thus; it would have pleased him. Go on, monsieur."

"The pretender will start with a fleet for the English shore; Prussia, Sweden, and Russia will then be engaged with Holland; the empire will profit by this war to retake Naples and Sicily, to which it lays claim through the house of Suabia; the Grand Duchy of Tuscany will be assured to the second son of the king of Spain, the Catholic low countries will be re-united to France, Sardinia given to the Duke of Savoy, Commachio to the pope. France will be the soul of the great league of the south against the north, and, if Louis XV. dies, Philip V. will be crowned king of half the world."

"Yes, I know all that," said the regent, "and this is Cellamare's conspiracy renewed. But you used a phrase I did not understand."

"Which, monseigneur?"

"You said, when the regent is got rid of. How is he to be got rid of?"

"The old plan was, as you know, to carry him off to the prison of Saragossa, or the fortress of Toledo."

"Yes; and the plan failed through the duke's watchfulness."

"It was impracticable—a thousand obstacles opposed it. How was it possible to take such a prisoner across France?"

"It was difficult," said the duke; "I never understood the adoption of such a plan. I am glad to find it modified."

"Monseigneur, it would be possible to seduce guards, to escape from a prison or a fortress, to return to France, retake a lost power, and punish those who had executed this abduction. Philip V. and Alberoni have nothing to fear; his excellency the Duc d'Olivares regains the frontier in safety; and, while half the conspirators escape, the other half pay for all."——"However—"

"Monseigneur, we have the example of the last conspiracy before our eyes, and you yourself named those who are in the Bastille."

"What you say is most logical," replied the duke.

"While, on the contrary, in getting rid of the regent—" continued the chevalier.

"Yes; you prevent his return. It is possible to return from a prison, but not from a tomb—that is what you would say?"

"Yes, monseigneur," replied Gaston, with a somewhat tremulous voice.

"Now I understand your mission. You come to Paris to make away with the regent?"

"Yes, monseigneur."

"Explain yourself."

"We were five Breton gentlemen, forming a small party or league in the midst of the general association, and it was agreed that the majority should decide on our plans."

"I understand, and the majority decided that the regent should be assassinated."

"Yes, monseigneur, four were for assassination, and one against it."

"And that one?"

"If I lose your excellency's confidence I must own that I was that one."

"But, then, why are you to accomplish a design you disapprove?"

"Chance was to decide the one who should strike the blow."

"And the lot?"

"Fell on me, monseigneur."

"Why did you not refuse?"

"The ballot was without names, no one knew my vote. I should have been taken for a coward."

"And you came to Paris?"

"For the task imposed on me."

"Reckoning on me?"

"As on an enemy of the regent, for aid in accomplishing an enterprise which not only concerns the interests of Spain, but which will save our friends from the Bastille."

"Do they run as much danger as you believe?"

"Death hovers over them; the regent has proofs, and has said of M. de Richelieu that if he had four heads he has wherewith to condemn them all."

"He said that in a moment of passion."

"What, monseigneur, you defend the duke—you tremble when a man devotes himself to save, not only his accomplices, but two kingdoms—you hesitate to accept that devotion."

"If you fail!"

"Everything has its good and evil side; if the happiness of being the savior of a country is lost, the honor of being a martyr to its cause is gained."

"But remember, in facilitating your access to the regent, I become your accomplice."

"Does that frighten you, monseigneur?"

"Certainly, for you being arrested—"

"Well—I being arrested?"

"They may force from you, by means of tortures, the names of those—"

Gaston's reply was a smile of supreme disdain.

"You are a foreigner and a Spaniard, monseigneur," said he, "and do not know what a French gentleman is, therefore I pardon you."

"Then I may reckon on your silence?"

"Pontcalec, Du Couëdic, Talhouet, and Montlouis, doubted me for an instant, and have since apologized to me for doing so."

"Well, monsieur, I will think seriously of what you have said, but in your place—"

"In my place?"

"I would renounce this enterprise."

"I wish I had never entered into it, monseigneur, I own, for since I did so a great change has taken place in my life, but I am in it, and must accomplish it."

"Even if I refuse to second you?"

"The Breton committee have provided for that emergency."

"And decided—"

"To do without you."

"Then your resolution—"

"Is irrevocable."

"I have said all I had to say," replied the regent, "since you are determined to pursue your undertaking."

"Monseigneur," said Gaston, "you seem to wish to retire."

"Have you anything more to say to me?"

"Not to-day; to-morrow, or the day after."

"You have the captain as go-between—when he gives me notice I will receive you with pleasure."

"Monseigneur," said Gaston firmly, and with a noble air, "let me speak freely. We should have no go-between; you and I—so evidently separated by rank and station—are equal before the scaffold which threatens us. I have even a superiority over you, since I run the greater danger; however, you are now, monseigneur, a conspirator, like the Chevalier de Chanlay, with this difference: that you have the right—being the chief—to see his head fall before yours—let me, then, treat as an equal with your excellency, and see you when it is necessary."

The regent thought for a moment.

"Very well," said he, "this house is not my residence; you understand I do not receive many at my house: since the war, my position is precarious and delicate in France; Cellamare is in prison at Blois; I am only a sort of consul —good as a hostage—I cannot use too many precautions."

The regent lied with a painful effort.

"Write, then, poste restante to M. Andre, you must name the time at which you wish to see me, and I will be there."

"Through the post?" asked Gaston.

"Yes, it is only a delay of three hours; at each post a man will watch for your letter, and bring it to me when it arrives; three hours after you can come here."

"Your excellency forgets," said Gaston, laughing, "that I do not know where I am, in what street, at what number; I came by night. Stay, let us do better than that; you asked for time to reflect, take till to-morrow morning, and at eleven o'clock send for me. We must arrange a plan beforehand, that it may not fail, like those plans where a carriage or a shower of rain disconcerts everything."

"That is a good idea," said the regent; "to-morrow, then, at eleven o'clock, you shall be fetched, and we will then have no secrets from each other."

Gaston bowed and retired. In the antechamber he found the guide who brought him, but he noticed that in leaving they crossed a garden which they had not passed through on entering, and went out by a different door. At this door the carriage waited, and it quickly arrived at the Rue des Bourdonnais.

CHAPTER XVIII.

THE FAUBOURG SAINT ANTOINE.

No more illusion for the chevalier. In a day or two he might be called to his work.

The Spanish envoy had deeply impressed Gaston—there was about him an air of greatness which surprised him.

A strange circumstance passed across his mind; there was, between his forehead and eyes and those of Helene, one of those vague and distant likenesses which seem almost like the incoherence of a dream. Gaston, without knowing why, associated these two faces in his memory, and could not separate them. As he was about to lie down, worn out with fatigue, a horse's feet sounded in the street, the hotel door opened, and Gaston heard an animated conversation; but soon the door was closed, the noise ceased, and he slept as a man sleeps at five-and-twenty, even if he be a conspirator.

However, Gaston was not mistaken; a horse had arrived, and a conversation had taken place. A peasant from Rambouillet brought in haste a note from a young and pretty woman to the Chevalier de Chanlay, Hotel Muids d'Amour.

We can imagine who the young and pretty woman was.

Tapin took the letter, looked at it, then, taking off his apron, left the charge of the hotel to one of his servants, and went off to Dubois.

"Oh," exclaimed the latter, "let us see; a letter!"

He unsealed it skillfully by aid of steam, and, on reading it, seemed pleased.

"Good! excellent! Let them alone to go their own way; we hold the reins, and can stop them when we like." Then, turning to Tapin, he gave him the letter, which he had resealed. "Here," said he, "deliver the letter."

"When?" asked Tapin.

"At once."

Tapin stepped toward the door.

"No, stop," said Dubois; "to-morrow morning will be soon enough."

"Now," said Tapin, "may I make an observation?"

"Speak."

"As monseigneur's agent, I gain three crowns a day."

"Well, is not that enough, you scoundrel?"

"It was enough as agent. I do not complain, but it is not enough as wine-merchant. Oh, the horrid trade!"

"Drink and amuse yourself."

"Since I have sold wine I hate it."

"Because you see how it is made; but drink champagne, muscat, anything: Bourguignon pays. Apropos, he has had a real attack; so your lie was only an affair of chronology."

"Indeed."

"Yes, fear has caused it; you want to inherit his goods?"

"No, no; the trade is not amusing."

"Well, I will add three crowns a day to your pay while you are there, and I will give the shop to your eldest daughter. Bring me such letters often, and you shall be welcome."

Tapin returned to the hotel, but waited for the morning to deliver the letter.

At six o'clock, hearing Gaston moving, he entered, and gave him the note.

This was what it contained:

"My Friend—I think of your advice, and that perhaps you were right at last, I fear. A carriage has just arrived—Madame Desroches orders departure—I tried to resist—they shut me up in my room; fortunately, a peasant passed by to water his horse; I have given him two louis, and he promised to take you this note. I hear the last preparations—in two hours we leave for Paris.

"On my arrival, I will send you my address, if I have to jump out of the window and bring it.

"Be assured, the woman who loves you will remain worthy of herself and you."

"Ah, Helene!" cried Gaston; "I was not deceived. Eight o'clock, but she must have arrived. Why was not this letter brought to me at once?"

"You were asleep, monsieur. I waited your awaking."

There was no reply to be made. Gaston thought he would go and watch at the barrier, as Helene might not have arrived. He dressed quickly, and set out, after saying to Tapin:

"If Captain La Jonquiere comes here, say I shall be back at nine."

While Gaston waits uselessly for Helene, let us look back.

We saw the regent receive Madame Desroches' letter and send a reply. Indeed, it was necessary to remove Helene from the attempts of this M. de Livry.

But who could he be? Dubois alone could tell. So when Dubois appeared—

"Dubois," said the regent, "who is M. de Livry, of Nantes?" "Livry—

Livry," said he. "Stay!"

"Yes, Livry."

"Who knows such a name? Send for M. d'Hozier."

"Idiot!"

"But, monseigneur, I do not study genealogies. I am an unworthy plebeian."

"A truce to this folly."

"Diable! it seems monseigneur is in earnest about these Livrys. Are you going to give the order to one of them? because, in that case, I will try and find a noble origin."

"Go to the devil, and send me Nocé."

Dubois smiled, and went out.

Nocé quickly appeared. He was a man about forty, distinguished-looking, tall, handsome, cold and witty, one of the regent's most faithful and favorite friends.

"Monseigneur sent for me."

"Ah, Nocé, good-day."

"Can I serve your royal highness in anything?"

"Yes; lend me your house in the Faubourg St. Antoine, but empty, and carefully arranged. I will put my own people in it."

"Is it to be for—?"

"For a prude, Nocé."

"The houses in the faubourg have a bad name, monseigneur."

"The person for whom I require it does not know that; remember, absolute silence, Nocé, and give me the keys."

"A quarter of an hour, monseigneur, and you shall have them."

"Adieu, Nocé, your hand; no spying, no curiosity, I beg."

"Monseigneur, I am going to hunt, and shall only return at your pleasure."

"Thanks; adieu till to-morrow."

The regent sat down and wrote to Madame Desroches, sending a carriage with an order to bring Helene, after reading her the letter without showing it to her.

The letter was as follows:

"MY DAUGHTER—On reflection, I wish to have you near me. Therefore follow Madame Desroches without loss of time. On your arrival at Paris, you shall hear from me. Your affectionate father."

PHILIP V.—*Page 477.*

Link to larger image

Helene resisted, prayed, wept, but was forced to obey. She profited by a moment of solitude to write to Gaston, as we have seen. Then she left this dwelling which had become dear to her, for there she had found her father and received her lover.

As to Gaston, he waited vainly at the barrier, till, giving up all hope, he returned to the hotel. As he crossed the garden of the Tuileries, eight o'clock struck.

At that moment Dubois entered the regent's bedchamber with a portfolio under his arm, and a triumphant smile on his face.

CHAPTER XIX.

THE ARTIST AND THE POLITICIAN.

"Ah! it is you, Dubois," exclaimed the regent, as his minister entered.

"Yes, monseigneur," said Dubois, taking out some papers. "Well, what do you say to our Bretons now?"

"What papers are those?" asked the regent, who, in spite of the preceding day's conversation, or perhaps because of it, felt a secret sympathy with De Chanlay.

"Oh, nothing at all, first a little report of what passed yesterday evening between M. de Chanlay and his excellency the Duc d'Olivares."

"You listened, then?" said the regent.

"Pardieu, monseigneur, what did you expect that I should do?"

"And you heard?"

"All. What do you think of his Catholic majesty's pretensions?"

"I think that perhaps they use his name without his consent."

"And Cardinal Alberoni? Tudieu! monseigneur, how nicely they manage Europe: the pretender in England; Prussia, Sweden, and Russia tearing Holland to pieces; the empire recovering Sicily and Naples; the grand duchy of Tuscany for Philip the Fifth's son; Sardinia for the king of Savoy; Commanchio for the pope; France for Spain; really, this plan is somewhat grand, to emanate from the brain of a bell-ringer."

"All smoke! these prospects," said the duke; "mere dreams."

"And the Breton league, is that all smoke?"

"I am forced to own that that really exists."

"And the dagger of our conspirator; is that a dream?"

"No; it even appeared to me likely to be vigorously handled."

"Peste! monseigneur, you complained in the other plot that you found none but rose-water conspirators. Well, this time I hope you are better pleased. These fellows strike hard."

"Do you know," said the regent, thoughtfully, "that the Chevalier de Chanlay is of an energetic and vigorous nature."

"Ah, the next thing will be, you will conceive a great admiration for this fellow. I know, monseigneur, that you are capable of it."

"How is it that a prince always finds such natures among his enemies, and not among friends?"

"Because, monseigneur, hatred is a passion, and devotion often only a weakness; but if you will descend from the height of philosophy and deign to a simple act, namely, to give me two signatures—"

"What signatures?" asked the regent.

"First, there is a captain to be made a major."

"Captain la Jonquiere?"

"Oh, no; as to him, we'll hang him when we have done with him; but meanwhile, we must treat him with care."

"Who, then, is this captain?"

"A brave officer whom monseigneur eight days, or rather eight nights ago, met in a house in the Rue St. Honoré."

"What do you mean?"

"Ah, I see I must aid your memory a little, monseigneur, since you have such a bad one."

"Speak, one can never get at the truth with you."

"In two words, eight nights ago you went out disguised as a musketeer through the little door in the Rue Richelieu, accompanied by Nocé and Simiane."

"It is true; what passed in the Rue St. Honore?"

"Do you wish to know, monseigneur?"

"I do."

"I can refuse you nothing."

"Speak, then."

"You supped at the house—that house, monseigneur."

"Still with Nocé and Simiane?"

"No, monseigneur, tete-à-tete. Nocé and Simiane supped too, but separately. You supped, then, and were at table, when a brave officer, who probably mistook the door, knocked so obstinately at yours, that you became impatient, and handled the unfortunate who disturbed you somewhat roughly, but he, who, it seems, was not of an enduring nature, took out his sword, whereupon you, monseigneur, who never look twice before committing a folly, drew your rapier and tried your skill with the officer."

"And the result?" asked the regent.

"Was, that you got a scratch on the shoulder, in return for which you bestowed on your adversary a sword-thrust in the breast."

"But it was not dangerous?" asked the regent, anxiously.

"No; fortunately the blade glided along the ribs."

"So much the better."

"But that is not all."

"How?"

"It appears that you owed the officer a special grudge."

"I had never seen him."

"Princes strike from a distance."

"What do you mean?"

"This officer had been a captain for eight years, when, on your highness's coming into power, he was dismissed."

"Then I suppose he deserved it."

"Ah, monseigneur, you would make us out as infallible as the pope!"

"He must have committed some cowardly act."

"He is one of the bravest officers in the service."

"Some infamous act then?"

"He is the most honest fellow breathing."

"Then this is an injustice to be repaired."

"Exactly; and that is why I prepared this major's brevet."

"Give it to me, Dubois, you have some good in you sometimes."

A diabolical smile passed over Dubois's face as he drew from his portfolio a second paper.

The regent watched him uneasily.

"What is that paper?" asked he.

"Monseigneur, you have repaired an act of injustice, now do an act of justice."

"The order to arrest the Chevalier Gaston de Chanlay, and place him in the Bastille," cried the regent. "Ah! I see now why you bribed me with a good action; but stay, this requires reflection."

"Do you think I propose to you an abuse of power, monseigneur?" asked Dubois, laughing.

"No, but yet—"

"Monseigneur," continued Dubois, "when we have in our hands the government of a kingdom, the thing most necessary is, to govern."

"But it seems to me that I am the master."

"To reward, yes; but on condition of punishing—the balance of justice is destroyed, monseigneur, if an eternal and blind mercy weighs down one of the scales. To act as you always wish, and often do, is not good, but weak. What is the reward of virtue, if you do not punish vice?"

"Then," said the regent, the more impatiently that he felt he was defending a bad though generous cause, "if you wished me to be severe, you should not have brought about an interview between me and this young man; you should not have given me the opportunity of appreciating his worth, but have allowed me to suppose him a common conspirator."

"Yes; and now, because he presented himself to your highness under a romantic guise, your artistic imagination runs away with you. Diable! monseigneur, there is a time for everything; so chemistry with Hubert, engraving with Audran, music with Lafare, make love with the whole world —but politics with me."

"Mon Dieu!" said the regent, "is it worth while to defend a life, watched, tortured, calumniated as mine is?"

"But it is not your life you are defending, monseigneur; consider, among all these calumnies which pursue you, and against which Heaven knows you should be steeled by this time; your most bitter enemies have never accused you of cowardice—as to your life, at Steinkirk, at Nerwinden, and at Lerida, you proved at what rate you valued it. Pardieu! if you were merely a private gentleman, a minister, or a prince of the blood, and you were assassinated, a man's heart would cease to beat, and that would be all; but wrongly or rightly, you coveted a place among the powerful ones of the world; for that end you broke the will of Louis the Fourteenth, you drove the bastards from the throne whereon they had already placed their feet, you made yourself regent of France—that is to say, the keystone of the arch of the world. If you die, it is not a man who falls, it is the pillar which supports the European edifice which gives way; thus our four last years of watchfulness and struggles would be lost, and everything around would be shaken. Look at England; the Chevalier de Saint George will renew the mad enterprises of the pretender; look at Holland——Russia, Sweden, and Prussia would hunt her to the death; look at Austria—her two-headed eagle seizes Venice and Milan, as an indemnification for the loss of Spain; cast your eyes on France—no longer France, but Philip the Fifth's vassal; look, finally, at Louis the Fifteenth, the last descendant of the greatest monarch that ever gave light to the world, and the child whom by watchfulness and care we have saved from the fate of his father, his mother, and his uncles, to place him safe and sound on the throne of his ancestors; this child falls back again into the hands of those whom an adulterous law boldly calls to succeed him; thus, on all sides, murder, desolation, ruin, civil and foreign wars. And why? because it pleases Monsieur Philippe d'Orleans to think himself still major of the king's troops, or commandant of the army in Spain, and to forget that he ceased to be so from the moment he became regent of France."

"You *will* have it, then," said the duke.

"Stay, monseigneur," said Dubois, "it shall not be said that in an affair of this importance you gave way to my importunity. I have said what I had to say, now I leave you—do as you please. I leave you the paper; I am going to give some orders, and in a quarter of an hour I will return to fetch it."

And Dubois saluted the regent and went out.

Left alone, the regent became thoughtful—this whole affair, so somber and so tenacious of life, this remains of the former conspiracy, filled the duke's mind with gloomy thoughts; he had braved death in battle, had laughed at abductions meditated by the Spaniards and by Louis the Fourteenth's bastards; but this time a secret horror oppressed him; he felt an involuntary admiration for the young man whose poniard was raised against him; sometimes he hated him, at others he excused—he almost loved him. Dubois, cowering down over this conspiracy like an infernal ape over some dying prey, and piercing with his ravenous claws to its very heart, seemed to him to possess a sublime intelligence and power; he felt that he, ordinarily so courageous, should have defended his life feebly in this instance, and his eyes involuntarily sought the paper.

"Yes," murmured he, "Dubois is right, my life is no longer my own; yesterday, my mother also told me the same thing. Who knows what might happen if I were to fall? The same as happened at the death of my ancestor Henry the Fourth, perchance. After having reconquered his kingdom step by step, he was about—thanks to ten years of peace, economy, and prosperity—

to add Alsace, Lorraine, and perhaps Flanders, to France, while the Duke of Savoy, his son-in-law, descending the Alps, should cut out for himself a kingdom in the Milanais, and with the leavings of that kingdom enrich the kingdom of Venice and strengthen the dukes of Modena, Florence, and Mantua; everything was ready for the immense result, prepared during the whole life of a king who was at once a legislator and a soldier; then the 13th of May arrived; a carriage with the royal livery passed the Rue de la Feronniere, and the clock of Les Innocents struck three. In a moment all was destroyed; past prosperity, hopes of the future; it needed a whole century, a minister called Richelieu and a king called Louis the Fourteenth, to cicatrize the wound made in France by Ravaillac's knife. Yes, Dubois was right," cried the duke, "and I must abandon this young man to human justice; besides, it is not I who condemn him; the judges are there to decide; and," added he, with animation, "have I not still the power to pardon."

And quieted by the thought of this royal prerogative, which he exercised in the name of Louis XV., he signed the paper, and left the room to finish dressing.

Ten minutes after the door opened softly, Dubois carefully looked in, saw that the room was empty, approached the table near which the prince had been seated, looked rapidly at the order, smiled on seeing the signature, and folding it in four, placed it in his pocket, and left the room with an air of great satisfaction.

CHAPTER XX.

BLOOD REVEALS ITSELF.

When Gaston returned from the Barriere de la Conference, and left his room, he found La Jonquiere installed by the fireplace, and discussing a bottle of wine which he had just uncorked.

"Well, chevalier," said he, as Gaston entered, "how do you like my room? it is convenient, is it not? Sit down and taste this wine; it rivals the best Rosseau. Do you drink Rosseau? No, they do not drink wine in Bretagne; they drink cider or beer, I believe. I never could get anything worth drinking there, except brandy."

Gaston did not reply, for he was so occupied that he had not even heard what La Jonquiere said. He threw himself in an easy chair, with his hand in his pocket, holding Helene's first letter.

"Where is she?" he asked himself; "this immense, unbounded Paris may keep her from me forever. Oh! the difficulty is too great for a man without power or experience!"

"Apropos," said La Jonquiere, who had followed the young man's ideas easily, "there is a letter for you."

"From Bretagne?" asked the chevalier, trembling.

"No; from Paris. A beautiful writing—evidently a woman's."

"Where is it?" cried Gaston.

"Ask our host. When I came in he held it in his hands."

"Give it to me," cried Gaston, rushing into the common room.

"What does monsieur want?" asked Tapin, with his usual politeness.

"My letter."

"What letter?"

"The letter you received for me."

"Pardon, monsieur; I forgot it."

And he gave Gaston the letter.

"Poor imbecile!" said the false La Jonquiere, "and these idiots think of conspiring. It is like D'Harmental; they think they can attend to love and politics at the same time. Triple fools; if they were to go at once to La Fillon's for the former, the latter would not be so likely to bring them to the Place de Greve."

Gaston returned joyously, reading and re-reading Helene's letter. "Rue de Faubourg St. Antoine; a white house behind trees—poplars, I think. I could not see the number, but it is the thirty-first or thirty-second house on the left side, after passing a chateau with towers, resembling a prison."

"Oh," cried Gaston, "I can find that; it is the Bastille."

Dubois overheard these words.

"Parbleu; I will take care you shall find it, if I lead you there myself."

Gaston looked at his watch, and finding that it wanted two hours of the time appointed for his rendezvous in the Rue du Bac, took up his hat and was going out.

"What! are you going away?" asked Dubois.

"I am obliged to do so."

"And our appointment for eleven o'clock?"

"It is not yet nine."

"You do not want me?"

"No, thank you."

"If you are preparing an abduction, for instance, I am an adept, and might assist you."

"Thank you," said Gaston, reddening involuntarily, "but I am not."

Dubois whistled an air, to show that he took the answer for what it was worth.

"Shall I find you here on my return?" asked Gaston.

"I do not know; perhaps I also have to reassure some pretty creature who is interested in me; but, at any rate, at the appointed hour you will find your yesterday's guide with the same carriage and the same coachman."

Gaston took a hasty leave. At the corner of the cemetery of the Innocents he took a carriage, and was driven to the Rue St. Antoine. At the twentieth house he alighted, ordering the driver to follow him; then he proceeded to examine the left side of the street. He soon found himself facing a high wall, over which he saw the tops of some tall poplars; this house, he felt sure, was the one where Helene was.

But here his difficulties were but commencing. There was no opening in the wall, neither bell nor knocker at the door; those who came with couriers galloping before them to strike with their silver-headed canes could dispense with a knocker. Gaston was afraid to strike with a stone, for fear of being denied admittance, he therefore ordered the coachman to stop, and going up a narrow lane by one side of the house, he imitated the cry of the screech-owl— a signal preconcerted.

Helene started. She recognized the cry, and it seemed to her as though she were again in the Augustine convent at Clissons, with the chevalier's boat under her windows. She ran to the window; Gaston was there.

Helene and he exchanged a glance; then, re-entering the room, she rang a bell, which Madame Desroches had given her, so violently that two servants and Madame Desroches herself all entered at once.

"Go and open the door," said Helene, imperiously. "There is some one at the door whom I expect."

"Stop," said Madame Desroches to the valet, who was going to obey; "I will go myself."

"Useless, madame. I know who it is, and I have already told you that it is a person whom I expect."

"But mademoiselle ought not to receive this person," replied the duenna, trying to stand her ground.

"I am no longer at the convent, madame, and I am not yet in prison," replied Helene; "and I shall receive whom I please."

"But, at least, I may know who this is?"

"I see no objection. It is the same person whom I received at Rambouillet."

"M. de Livry?"

"Yes."

"I have positive orders not to allow this young man to see you."

"And *I* order you to admit him instantly."

"Mademoiselle, you disobey your father," said Madame Desroches, half angrily, half respectfully.

"My father does not see through your eyes, madame."

"Yet, who is master of your fate?"

"I alone," cried Helene, unwilling to allow any domination.

"Mademoiselle, I swear to you that your father—"

"Will approve, if he be my father."

These words, given with all the pride of an empress, cowed Madame Desroches, and she had recourse to silence.

"Well," said Helene, "I ordered that the door should be opened; does no one obey when I command?"

No one stirred; they waited for the orders of Madame Desroches.

Helene smiled scornfully, and made such an imperious gesture that Madame Desroches moved from the door, and made way for her; Helene then, slowly and with dignity, descended the staircase herself, followed by Madame Desroches, who was petrified to find such a will in a young girl just out of a convent.

"She is a queen," said the waiting-maid to Madame Desroches; "I know I should have gone to open the door, if she had not done so herself."

"Alas!" said the duenna, "they are all alike in that family."

"Do you know the family, then?" asked the servant, astonished.

Madame Desroches saw that she had said too much.

"Yes," said she; "I formerly knew the marquis, her father."

Meanwhile Helene had descended the staircase, crossed the court, and opened the door; on the step stood Gaston.

"Come, my friend," said Helene.

Gaston followed her, the door closed behind them, and they entered a room on the ground-floor.

"You called me, and I am here, Helene," said the young man; "what do you fear, what dangers threaten you?"

"Look around you," said Helene, "and judge."

The room in which they were was a charming boudoir, adjoining the dining-room, with which it communicated not only by folding doors, but also by an opening almost concealed by rare and peculiar flowers. The boudoir was hung with blue satin; over the doors were pictures by Claude Audran, representing the history of Venus in four tableaux, while the panels formed other episodes of the same history, all most graceful in outline and voluptuous in expression. This was the house which Nocé, in the innocence of his heart, had designated as fit for a prude.

"Gaston," said Helene, "I wonder whether I should really mistrust this man, who calls himself my father. My fears are more aroused here than at

Rambouillet."

After examining the boudoir, Gaston and Helene passed into the dining-room, and then into the garden, which was ornamented with marble statues of the same subjects as the pictures. As they returned, they passed Madame Desroches, who had not lost sight of them, and who, raising her hands in a despairing manner, exclaimed:

"Oh, mon Dieu! what would monseigneur think of this?"

These words kindled the smoldering fire in Gaston's breast.

"Monseigneur!" cried he; "you heard, Helene—monseigneur! We are then, as I feared, in the house of one of those great men who purchase pleasure at the expense of honor. Helene, do not allow yourself to be deceived. At Rambouillet I foresaw danger; here I see it."

"Mon Dieu," said Helene, "but if, by aid of his valets, this man should retain me here by force."

"Do not fear, Helene; am not I here?"

"Oh!" said Helene, "and must I renounce the sweet idea of finding a father, a preceptor, a friend."

"And at what a moment, when you are about to be left alone in the world," said Gaston, unconsciously betraying a part of his secret.

"What were you saying, Gaston? What is the meaning of these words?"

"Nothing—nothing," replied the young man; "some meaningless words which escaped me, and to which you must not attach any consequence."

"Gaston, you are hiding some dreadful secret from me, since you speak of abandoning me at the moment I lose a father."

"Helene, I will never abandon you except with life."

"Ah," cried the young girl, "your life is in danger, and it is thus that you fear to abandon me. Gaston, you betray yourself; you are no longer the Gaston of former days. You met me to-day with a constrained joy; losing me yesterday did not cause you intense sorrow: there are more important prospects in your mind than in your heart. There is something in you—pride, or ambition, more powerful than your love. You turn pale, Gaston; your silence breaks my heart."

"Nothing—nothing, Helene, I assure you. Is it surprising that I am troubled to find you here, alone and defenseless, and not know how to protect you; for doubtless this is a man of power. In Bretagne I should have had friends and two hundred peasants to defend me; here I have no one."

"Is that all, Gaston?"

"That is, it seems to me, more than enough."

"No, Gaston, for we will leave this house instantly."

Gaston turned pale; Helene lowered her eyes, and placing her hand in that of her lover—

"Before these people who watch us," said she; "before the eyes of this woman, we will go away together."

Gaston's eyes lighted up with joy; but somber thoughts quickly clouded them again. Helene watched this changing expression.

"Am I not your wife, Gaston?" said she; "is not my honor yours? Let us go."

"But where to place you?" said Gaston.

"Gaston," replied Helene, "I know nothing, I can do nothing; I am ignorant of Paris—of the world; I only know myself and you; well, you have opened my eyes; I distrust all except your fidelity and love."

Gaston was in despair. Six months previous, and he would have paid with his life the generous devotion of the courageous girl.

"Helene, reflect," said Gaston; "if we were mistaken, and this man be really your father!"

"Gaston, do you forget that you first taught me to distrust him?"

"Oh, yes, Helene, let us go," cried Gaston.

"Where are we to go?" asked Helene; "but you need not reply—if you know, it is sufficient."

"Helene," said Gaston, "I will not insult you by swearing to respect your honor; the offer which you have made to-day I have long hesitated to make—rich, happy, sure for the present of fortune and happiness, I would have placed all at your feet, trusting to God for the future; but at this moment I must tell you, that you were not mistaken; from day to day, from this day to the next, there is a chance of a terrible event. I must tell you now, Helene, what I can offer you. If I succeed, a high and powerful position; but if I fail, flight, exile, it may be poverty. Do you love me enough, Helene, or rather do you love your honor enough, to brave all this and follow me?"

"I am ready, Gaston; tell me to follow you, and I do so."

"Well, Helene, your confidence shall not be displaced, believe me; I will take you to a person who will protect you, if necessary, and who, in my absence, will replace the father you thought to find, but whom you have, on the contrary, lost a second time."

"Who is this person, Gaston? This is not distrust," added Helene, with a charming smile, "but curiosity."

"Some one who can refuse me nothing, Helene, whose days are dependent on mine, and who will think I demand small payment when I exact your peace and security."

"Still mysterious, Gaston: really, you frighten me."

"This secret is the last, Helene; from this moment my whole life will be open to you."

"I thank you, Gaston."

"And now I am at your orders, Helene."

"Let us go then."

Helene took the chevalier's arm, and crossed the drawing-room, where sat Madame Desroches, pale with anger, and scrawling a letter, whose destination we can guess.

"Mon Dieu! mademoiselle, where are you going? what are you doing?"

"I am going away from a house where my honor is threatened."

"What!" cried the old lady, springing to her feet, "you are going away with your lover."

"You are mistaken, madame," replied Helene, in an accent of dignity, "it is with my husband."

Madame Desroches, terrified, let her hands fall by her side, powerless.

"You shall not go, mademoiselle, even if I am forced to use violence."

"Try, madame," said Helene, in the queenly tone which seemed natural to her.

"Hola, Picard, Coutourier, Blanchet."

The servants appeared.

"The first who stops me I kill," said Gaston quietly, as he drew his sword.

"What a will," cried Madame Desroches; "ah, Mesdemoiselles de Chartres and de Valois, I recognize you there."

The two young people heard this exclamation, but did not understand it.

"We are going, madame," said Helene; "do not forget to repeat, word by word, what I told you."

And, hanging on Gaston's arm, flushed with pleasure and pride, brave as an ancient Amazon, the young girl ordered that the door should be opened for her; the Swiss did not dare to resist. Gaston took Helene by the hand, summoned the carriage in which he had come, and seeing that he was to be followed, he stepped toward the assailants, and said in a loud voice:

"Two steps further, and I tell this history aloud, and place myself and mademoiselle under the safeguard of the public honor."

Madame Desroches believed that Gaston knew the mystery, and would declare it: she therefore thought best to retire quickly, followed by the servants.

The intelligent driver started at a gallop.

CHAPTER XXI.

WHAT PASSED IN THE RUE DU BAC
WHILE WAITING FOR GASTON.

"What, monseigneur, you here!" cried Dubois, entering the room of the house in the Rue du Bac, and finding the regent seated in the same place as on the previous day.

"Yes; is there anything wonderful in that? Have I not an appointment at noon with the chevalier?"

"But I thought the order you signed would have put an end to these conferences."

"You were mistaken, Dubois; I wish to have another interview with this young man. I shall make one more effort to induce him to renounce his plans."

"And if he should do so?"

"Then all will be at an end—there will be no conspiracy—there will have been no conspirators. I cannot punish intentions."

"With any other I should not allow this; but with him I say, as you please."

"You think he will remain firm?"

"Oh! I am quite easy. But when he has decidedly refused, when you are quite convinced that he persists in his intention of assassinating you, then you will give him over to me, will you not?"

"Yes, but not here."

"Why not here?"'

"Better to arrest him at his hotel."

"There, at the Muids d'Amour, with Tapin and D'Argenson's people— impossible, monsieur. Bourguignon's affair is still in everybody's mouth in that quarter. I am not sure that they even quite believe in the attack of apoplexy, since Tapin now gives strict measure. It will be much better to arrest him as he leaves here, monseigneur; the house is quiet; four men could easily do it, and they are already here. I will move them, as you insist on seeing him; and, instead of arresting him as he enters, it must be done as he leaves. At the door a carriage shall be ready to take him to the Bastille; so that even the coachman who brings him here shall not know what has become of him. No one but Monsieur de Launay shall know; and I will answer for his discretion."

"Do as you please."

"That is my usual custom."

"Rascal that you are!"

"But I think monseigneur reaps the benefit of the rascality."

"Oh, I know you are always right."

"But the others?"

"What others?"

"The Bretons, Pontcalec, Du Couëdic, Talhouet, and Montlouis?"

"Oh, the unfortunates; you know their names."

"And how do you think I have passed my time at the hotel Muids d'Amour?"

"They will know of their accomplice's arrest."

"How?"

"Having no letter from Paris, they will fear that something is wrong."

"Bah! Is not Captain la Jonquiere there to reassure them?"

"True; but they must know the writing?"

"Not bad, monseigneur, you are improving; but you take useless precautions, as Racine says. At this moment, probably, they are arrested."

"And who dispatched the order?"

"I. Pardieu! I am not your minister for nothing. Besides, you signed it."

"I! Are you mad?"

"Assuredly, these men are not less guilty than the chevalier; and in authorizing me to arrest one, you authorized me to arrest all."

"And when did the bearer of this order leave?"

Dubois took out his watch.

"Just three hours ago. Thus, it was a poetical license when I said they were all arrested; they will not be till to-morrow morning."

"Bretagne will be aroused, Dubois."

"Bah! I have taken measures."

"The Breton tribunals will not condemn their compatriots."

"That case is foreseen."

"And, if they should be condemned, none will be found to execute them. It will be a second edition of the affair at Chalais. Remember, it was at Nantes that *that* took place, Dubois. I tell you, Bretons are unaccommodating."

"This is a point to settle with the commissioners, of whom this is a list. I will send three or four executioners from Paris—men accustomed to noble deeds —who have preserved the traditions of the Cardinal de Richelieu."

"Good God!" cried the regent; "bloodshed under my reign—I do not like it. As to Count Horn, he was a thief, and Duchaffour a wretch; but I am tender, Dubois."

"No, monseigneur, you are not tender; you are uncertain and weak; I told you so when you were my scholar—I tell you so again, now that you are my master. When you were christened, your godmothers, the fairies, gave you every gift of nature—strength, beauty, courage, and mind: only one—whom they did not invite because she was old, and they probably foresaw your aversion to old women—arrived the last, and gave you weakness—that spoiled all."

"And who told you this pretty tale? Perrault or St. Simon?"

"The princess palatine, your mother."

The regent laughed.

"And whom shall we choose for the commission?" asked he.

"Oh, monseigneur, people of mind and resolution, be sure; not provincials; not very sensitive to family scenes; men old in the dust of tribunals, whom the Breton men will not frighten with their fierce eyes, nor the Breton women seduce with their beautiful languid ones."

The regent made no reply.

"After all," continued Dubois, "these people may not be as guilty as we suppose. What they have plotted let us recapitulate. Bah! mere trifles. To bring back the Spaniards into France, what is that? To call Philip the Fifth king, the renouncer of his country; to break all the laws of the State—these good Bretons."

"Dubois, I know the national law as well as you."

"Then, monseigneur, if you speak truly, you have only to approve the nomination of the commissioners I have chosen."

"How many are there?"

"Twelve."

"Their names?"

Dubois gave in the list.

"Ah, you were right—a happy choice; but who is to preside over this amiable assembly?"

"Guess, monseigneur."

"Take care; you must have an honest man at the head of these ravagers."

"I have one."

"Who is it?"

"An ambassador."

"Cellamare, perhaps."

"Ma foi! I think if you would let him come out of Blois he would not refuse you even the heads of his accomplices."

"Let him stop at Blois. Who is to preside?"

"Chateau-Neuf."

"The ambassador from Holland, from the great king. Dubois, I do not generally compliment you, but this time you have done wonders."

"You understand, monseigneur: he knows that these people wish to make a republic; and he, who is brought up to know none but sultans, and who has a horror of Holland through the horror of Louis XIV. for republics, has accepted with a good grace. We shall have Argram for prosecutor. Cayet shall be our secretary. We go to work quickly and well, monseigneur, for time presses."

"But shall we at least have quiet afterward?"

"I believe so. We may sleep all day and all night; that is to say, when we have finished the war in Spain."

"Oh!" cried the regent, "why did I strive for the regency? I should laugh to see M. de Maine freeing himself with his Jesuits and his Spaniards! Madame de Maintenon and her politics, with Villeroy and Villars, would drive away the spleen; and Hubert says it is good to laugh once a day."

"Apropos of Madame de Maintenon," replied Dubois; "you know, monseigneur, that she is very ill, and that she cannot live a fortnight."

"Bah!"

"Since the imprisonment of Madame de Maine and the exile of her husband, she says that decidedly Louis XIV. is dead, and that she goes weeping to rejoin him."

"Which does not trouble you, eh?"

"Oh! I confess that I hate her cordially; it was she who made the king open his eyes so wide when I asked for the red hat at your marriage; and, corbleu! it was not an easy thing to arrange, monseigneur, as you know. If you had not been there to redress my wrongs, she would have spoiled my career. If I could but have crammed her M. de Maine into this Bretagne affair; but it was impossible—the poor man is half dead with fear, so that he says to every one he meets, 'Do you know there has been a conspiracy against the government of the king and against the person of the regent? it is a disgrace to France. Ah! if all men were only like me!'"

"No one would conspire—that is certain," said the regent.

"He has disowned his wife," added Dubois, laughing.

"And she has disowned her husband," said the regent, laughing also.

"I should not advise you to imprison them together—they would fight."

"Therefore I have placed one at Doulens, and the other at Dijon."

"From whence they bite by post."

"Let us put all that aside, Dubois."

"Ah, monseigneur! you have, I see, sworn the loss of the blood of Louis XIV.; you are a true executioner."

This audacious joke proved how sure Dubois felt of his ascendency over the prince.

The regent signed the order naming the tribunal, and Dubois went out to prepare for Gaston's arrest.

Gaston, on his return to the Muids d'Amour, found the same carriage and the same guide awaiting him that had before conducted him to the Rue du Bac. Gaston, who did not wish Helene to alight, asked if he could continue his route in the hired carriage in which he had just arrived; the man replied that he saw no objection, and mounted on the box by the driver, to whom he told the address.

During the drive, Gaston, instead of displaying the courage which Helene had expected, was sad, and yet gave no explanation of his sadness. As they entered the Rue du Bac, Helene, in despair at finding so little force of character in him on whom she leaned for protection, said: "Gaston, you frighten me."

"Helene, you shall see before long if I am acting for your good or not."

The carriage stopped.

"Helene, there is one in this house who will stand in the place of a father to you. Let me go first, and I announce you."

"Ah!" cried Helene, trembling, she knew not why; "and you are going to leave me here alone?"

"You have nothing to fear, Helene; besides, in a few minutes I will return and fetch you."

The young girl held out her hand, which Gaston pressed to his lips; the door opened; the carriage drove into the courtyard, where Gaston felt that Helene ran no danger; the man who had come to the hotel to fetch him opened the carriage door; Gaston again pressed Helene's hand, alighted, ascended the steps, and entered the corridor, when his guide left him as before.

Gaston, knowing that Helene waited his return, at once tapped at the door of the room.

"Enter," said the voice of the false Spaniard.

Gaston knew the voice, entered, and with a calm face approached the Duc d'Olivares.

"You are punctual, monsieur," said the latter; "we named noon, and it is now striking."

"I am pressed for time, monseigneur; my undertaking weighs on me; I fear to feel remorse. That astonishes and alarms you, does it not, monseigneur? But reassure yourself; the remorse of a man such as I am troubles no one but himself."

"In truth, monsieur," cried the regent, with a feeling of joy he could not quite conceal, "I think you are drawing back."

"Not so, monseigneur; since fate chose me to strike the prince, I have gone steadily forward, and shall do so till my mission is accomplished."

"Monsieur, I thought I detected some hesitation in your words; and words are of weight in certain mouths, and under certain circumstances."

"Monsieur, in Bretagne we speak as we feel, but we also do as we promise."

"Then you are resolved?"

"More than ever."

"Because, you see," replied the regent, "there is still time—the evil is not yet done."

"The evil, you call it, monseigneur," said Gaston; "what shall I call it then?"

"It is thus that I meant it," replied the regent; "the evil is for you, since you feel remorse."

"It is not generous, monseigneur, to dwell on a confidence which I should not have made to any person of less merit than yourself."

"And it is because I appreciate your worth, monsieur, that I tell you there is yet time to draw back; that I ask if you have reflected—if you repent having mixed yourself with all these—" the duke hesitated—"these audacious enterprises. Fear nothing from me—I will protect you, even if you desert us; I have seen you but once, but I think I judge of you as you deserve—men of worth are so rare that the regrets will be for us."

"Such kindness overwhelms me, monseigneur," said Gaston, who, in spite of his courage, felt some indecision. "My prince, I do not hesitate; but my reflections are those of a duelist, who goes to the ground determined to kill his enemy, yet deploring the necessity which forces him to rob a man of life. But here the interest is so great, so superior to the weaknesses of our nature, that I will be true to my friendship if not my sympathies, and will conduct myself so that you shall esteem in me even the momentary weakness which for a second held back my arm."

"Well," said the regent, "how shall you proceed?"

"I shall wait till I meet him face to face, and then I shall not use an arquebuse, as Paltrot did, nor a pistol, as Vitry did. I shall say, 'Monseigneur, you are the curse of France—I sacrifice you to her salvation;' and I shall stab him with my poniard."

"As Ravaillac did," said the duke, with a serenity which made Gaston shudder; "it is well."

Gaston did not reply.

"This plan appears to me the most secure, and I approve of it; but I must ask you one other question: suppose you should be taken and interrogated?"

"Your excellency knows what men do in such cases—they die, but do not answer; and since you have quoted Ravaillac, I think, if my memory serves me, that was what he did—and yet Ravaillac was not a gentleman."

Gaston's pride did not displease the regent, who had a young heart and a chivalric mind; besides, accustomed to worn-out and time-serving courtiers, Gaston's vigorous and simple nature was a novelty to him; and we know how the regent loved a novelty.

"I may then reckon," said he, "that you are immovable?"

Gaston looked surprised that the duke should repeat this question.

"Yes," said the regent; "I see you are decided."

"Absolutely, and wait your last instructions."

"How? *my* instructions?"

"Certainly; I have placed myself body and soul at your disposal."

The duke rose.

"Well," said he, "you must go out by that door, and cross the garden which surrounds the house. In a carriage which awaits you at the bottom you will find my secretary, who will give you a pass for an audience with the regent; besides that, you will have the warranty of my word."

"That is all I have to ask on that point, monseigneur."

"Have you anything else to say?"

"Yes; before I take leave of you, whom I may never see again in this world, I have a boon to ask."

"Speak, monsieur, I listen."

"Monsieur," said Gaston, "do not wonder if I hesitate a moment, for this is no personal favor and no ordinary service—Gaston de Chanlay needs but a dagger, and here it is; but in sacrificing his body he would not lose his soul; mine, monseigneur, belongs first to God and then to a young girl whom I love to idolatry—sad love, is it not, which has bloomed so near a tomb? To abandon this pure and tender girl would be to tempt God in a most rash manner, for I see that sometimes he tries us cruelly, and lets even his angels suffer. I love, then, an adorable woman, whom my affection has supported and protected against infamous schemes; when I am dead or banished, what will become of her? *Our* heads fall, monseigneur; they are those of simple gentlemen; but you are a powerful adversary, and supported by a powerful king; *you* can conquer evil fortune. I wish to place in your hands the treasure of my soul. You will bestow on her all the protection which, as an accomplice, as an associate, you owe to me."

"Monsieur, I promise you," replied the regent, deeply moved.

"That is not all, monseigneur; misfortune may overtake me, and find me not able to bestow my person upon her; I would yet leave her my name. If I die she has no fortune, for she is an orphan. On leaving Nantes I made a will wherein I left her everything I possessed. Monseigneur, if I die, let her be a widow—is it possible?"

"Who opposes it?"

"No one; but I may be arrested to-morrow, this evening, on putting my foot outside this house."

The regent started at this strange presentiment.

"Suppose I am taken to the Bastille; could you obtain for me permission to marry her before my execution?"

"I am sure of it."

"You will use every means to obtain this favor for me? Swear it to me, monseigneur, that I may bless your name, and that, even under torture, nothing may escape but a thanksgiving when I think of you."

"On my honor, monsieur, I promise you that this young girl shall be sacred to me; she shall inherit in my heart all the affection which I involuntarily feel for you."

"Monseigneur, one word more."

"Speak, monsieur; I listen with the deepest sympathy."

"This young girl knows nothing of my project; she does not know what has brought me to Paris, nor the catastrophe which threatens us, for I have not had the courage to tell her. You will tell it to her, monseigneur—prepare her for the event. I shall never see her again, but to become her husband. If I were to see her again at the moment of striking the blow which separates me from her, my hand might tremble, and this must not be."

"On my word of honor, monsieur," said the regent, softened beyond all expression, "I repeat, not only shall this young girl be sacred to me, but I will do all you wish for her—she shall reap the fruits of the respect and affection with which you have inspired me."

"Now," said Gaston, "I am strong."

"And where is this young girl?"

"Below, in the carriage which brought me. Let me retire, monseigneur, and only tell me where she will be placed."

"Here, monsieur; this house, which is not inhabited, and which is very suitable for a young girl, shall be hers."

"Monseigneur, your hand."

The regent held out his hand, but hearing a little dry cough, he understood that Dubois was becoming impatient, and he indicated to Gaston that the audience was over.

"Once more, monseigneur, watch over this young girl; she is beautiful, amiable and proud—one of those noble natures which we meet but seldom. Adieu, monseigneur, I go to find your secretary."

"And must I tell her that you are about to take a man's life?" asked the regent, making one more effort to restrain Gaston.

"Yes, monseigneur," said the chevalier; "but you will add that I do it to save France."

"Go then, monsieur," said the duke, opening a door which led into the garden, "and follow the directions I have given you."

"Wish me good fortune, monseigneur."

"The madman," thought the regent; "does he wish me to pray for success to his dagger's thrust? Ma foi, no!"

Gaston went out, the gravel, half-covered with snow, creaked under his feet— the regent watched him for some time from the window of the corridor—then, when he had lost sight of him—

"Well," said he, "each one must go his own way. Poor fellow!"

And he returned to the room, where he found Dubois, who had entered by another door, and was waiting for him.

Dubois's face wore an expression of malicious satisfaction which did not escape the regent, who watched him some time in silence, as if trying to discover what was passing through the brain of this second Mephistopheles.

Dubois was the first to speak.

"Well, monseigneur, you are rid of him at last, I hope."

"Yes," replied the duke; "but in a manner which greatly displeases me—I do not like playing a part in your comedies, as you know."

"Possibly; but you might, perhaps, do wisely in giving me a part in yours."

"How so?"

"They would be more successful, and the denouements would be better."

"I do not understand—explain yourself, and quickly, for I have some one waiting whom I must receive."

"Oh! certainly, monseigneur, receive them, and we will continue our conversation later—the denouement of this comedy has already taken place, and cannot be changed."

And with these words, Dubois bowed with the mock respect which he generally assumed whenever, in the eternal game they played against each other, he held the best cards.

Nothing made the regent so uneasy as this simulated respect; he held him back—

"What is there now?" asked he; "what have you discovered?"

"That you are a skillful dissimulator, peste!"

"That astonishes you?"

"No, it troubles me; a few steps further, and you will do wonders in this art—you will have no further need of me; you will have to send me away to educate your son, whom, it must be confessed, requires a master like myself."

"Speak quickly."

"Certainly, monseigneur; it is not now, however, a question of your son, but of your daughter."

"Of which daughter?"

"Ah! true; there are so many. First, the Abbess of Chelles, then Madame de Berry, then Mademoiselle de Valois; then the others, too young for the world, and therefore for me, to speak of; then, lastly, the charming Bretagne flower, the wild blossom which was to be kept away from Dubois's poisoning breath, for fear it should wither under it."

"Do you dare to say I was wrong?"

"Not so, monseigneur: you have done wonders; not wishing to have anything to do with the infamous Dubois, for which I commend you, you—the archbishop of Cambray being dead—have taken in his place the good, the worthy, the pure Nocé, and have borrowed his house."

"Ah!" said the regent, "you know that?"

"And what a house! Pure as its master—yes, monseigneur, you are full of prudence and wisdom. Let us conceal the corruptions of the world from this innocent child, let us remove from her everything that can destroy her primitive naïveté; this is why we choose this dwelling for her—a moral sanctuary, where the priestesses of virtue, and doubtless always under pretext of their ingenuousness, take the most ingenuous but least permitted of positions."

"Nocé told me that all was proper."

"Do you know the house, monseigneur?"

"Do I look at such things?"

"Ah! no; your sight is not good, I remember."

"Dubois!"

"For furniture your daughter will have strange couches, magic sofas; and as to books, ah! that is the climax. Nocé's books are good for the instruction and formation of youth; they would do well to go with the breviary of Bussy-Rabutin, of which I presented you a copy on your twelfth birthday."

"Yes; serpent that you are."

"In short, the most austere prudery prevails over the dwelling. I had chosen it for the education of the son; but monseigneur, who looks at things differently, chose it for the daughter."

"Ah, ca! Dubois," said the regent, "you weary me."

"I am just at the end, monseigneur. No doubt your daughter was well pleased with the residence; for, like all of your blood, she is very intelligent."

The regent shuddered, and guessed that some disagreeable news was hidden under the long preamble and mocking smile of Dubois.

"However, monseigneur, see what the spirit of contradiction will do; she was not content with the dwelling you chose for her, and she is moving."

"What do you mean?"

"I am wrong—she *has* moved."

"My daughter gone!" cried the regent.

"Exactly," said Dubois.

"How?"

"Through the door. Oh, she is not one of those young ladies who go through the windows, or by night—oh, she is of your blood, monseigneur; if I had ever doubted it, I should be convinced now."

"And Madame Desroches?"

"She is at the Palais Royal, I have just left her; she came to announce it to your highness."

"Could she not prevent it?"

"Mademoiselle commanded."

"She should have made the servants close the doors: they did not know that she was my daughter, and had no reason to obey her."

"Madame Desroches was afraid of mademoiselle's anger, but the servants were afraid of the sword."

"Of the sword! are you drunk, Dubois?"

"Oh, I am very likely to get drunk on chicory water! No, monseigneur; if I am drunk, it is with admiration of your highness's perspicacity when you try to conduct an affair all alone."

"But what sword do you mean?"

"The sword which Mademoiselle Helene disposes of, and which belongs to a charming young man—"

"Dubois!"

"Who loves her!"

"Dubois! you will drive me mad."

"And who followed her from Nantes to Rambouillet with infinite gallantry."

"Monsieur de Livry?"

"Ah! you know his name; then I am telling you nothing new, monseigneur."

"Dubois, I am overwhelmed."

"Not without sufficient cause, monseigneur; but see what is the result of your managing your own affairs, while you have at the same time to look after those of France."

"But where is she?"

"Ah! where indeed—how should I know?"

"Dubois, *you* have told me of her flight—I look to you to discover her retreat. Dubois, my dear Dubois, for God's sake find my daughter!"

"Ah! monseigneur, you are exactly like the father in Moliere, and I am like Scapin—'My good Scapin, my dear Scapin, find me my daughter.' Monseigneur, I am sorry for it, but Geroute could say no more; however, we will look for your daughter, and rescue her from the ravisher."

"Well, find her, Dubois, and ask for what you please when you have done so."

"Ah, that is something like speaking."

The regent had thrown himself back in an armchair, and leaned his head upon his hands. Dubois left him to his grief, congratulating himself that this affection would double his empire over the duke. All at once, while Dubois was watching him with a malicious smile, some one tapped at the door.

"Who is there?" asked Dubois.

"Monseigneur," said an usher's voice at the door, "there is in the carriage which brought the chevalier a young woman who wishes to know if he is coming down soon."

Dubois made a bound toward the door, but he was too late; the regent, to whom the usher's words had recalled the solemn promise he had made to Gaston, rose at once.

"Where are you going, monseigneur?" asked Dubois.

"To receive this young girl."

"That is my affair, not yours—you forget that you abandoned this conspiracy to me."

"I gave up the chevalier to you, but I promised him to be a father to this girl whom he loves. I have pledged my word, and I will keep it; since through me she loses her lover, I must at least console her."

"I undertake it," said Dubois, trying to hide his paleness and agitation under one of his own peculiar smiles.

"Hold your tongue and remain here," said the regent.

"Let me at least speak to her, monseigneur."

"I will speak to her myself—this is no affair of yours; I have taken it upon myself, have given my word as a gentleman. Silence, and remain here."

Dubois ground his teeth; but when the regent spoke in this tone, he knew he must obey: he leaned against the chimney-piece and waited.

Soon the rustling of a silk dress was heard.

"Yes, madame," said the usher, "this way."

"Here she is," said the duke, "remember one thing, Dubois: this young girl is in no way responsible for her lover's fault; consequently, understand me, she must be treated with the greatest respect;" then, turning to the door, "Enter," said he; the door was hastily opened, the young girl made a step toward the regent, who started back thunderstruck.

"My daughter!" murmured he, endeavoring to regain his self-command, while Helene, after looking round for Gaston, stopped and curtseyed.

Dubois's face would not be easy to depict.

"Pardon me, monseigneur," said Helene, "perhaps I am mistaken. I am seeking a friend who left me below, who was to come back to me; but, as he delayed so long, I came to seek for him. I was brought here, but perhaps the usher made a mistake."

"No, mademoiselle," said the duke, "M. de Chanlay has just left me, and I expected you."

As the regent spoke, the young girl became abstracted, and seemed as though taxing her memory; then, in answer to her own thoughts, she cried—

"Mon Dieu! how strange."

"What is the matter?" asked the regent.

"Yes: that it is."

"Explain!" said the duke, "I do not understand you."

"Ah! monsieur," said Helene, trembling, "it is strange how your voice resembles that of another person."

"Of your acquaintance?" asked the regent.

"Of a person in whose presence I have been but once, but whose accents live in my heart."

"And who was this person?" asked the regent, while Dubois shrugged his shoulders at this half recognition.

"He called himself my father," replied Helene.

"I congratulate myself upon this chance, mademoiselle," said the regent, "for this similarity in my voice to that of a person who is dear to you may give greater weight to my words. You know that Monsieur de Chanlay has chosen me for your protector?"

"He told me he would bring me to some one who would protect me from the danger—"

"What danger?" asked the regent.

Helene looked round her, and her glance rested uneasily on Dubois, and there was no mistaking her expression. Dubois's face inspired her with as much distrust as the regent's did with confidence.

"Monseigneur," said Dubois (who did not fail to notice this expression), in an undertone to the regent, "I think I am de trop here, and had better retire; you do not want me, do you?"

"No; but I shall presently; do not go away."——"I will be at your orders."

This conversation was too low for Helene to hear; besides, she had stepped back, and continued watching the doors, in the hope of seeing Gaston return.

It was a consolation to Dubois to know she would be disappointed.

When Dubois was gone, they breathed more freely.

"Seat yourself, mademoiselle," said the duke; "I have much to tell you."

"Monsieur, one thing before all. Is the Chevalier Gaston de Chanlay in any danger?"

"We will speak of him directly, but first of yourself; he brought you to me as a protector. Now, tell me against whom I am to protect you?"

"All that has happened to me for some days is so strange, that I do not know whom to fear or whom to trust. If Gaston were there—"

"Yes, I understand; if he authorized you to tell me, you would keep nothing back. But if I can prove to you that I know nearly all concerning you?"

"You, monsieur!"

"Yes, I; are you not called Helene de Chaverny? Were you not brought up in the Augustine convent between Nantes and Clisson? Did you not one day receive an order to leave the convent from a mysterious protector who watches over you? Did you not travel with one of the sisters, to whom you gave a hundred louis for her trouble? At Rambouillet, did not a person called Madame Desroches await you? Did she not announce to you a visit from your father? The same evening, did not some one arrive who loved you, and who thought you loved him?"

"Yes, yes, monsieur, it is all true," said Helene, astonished that a stranger should thus know the details of her history.

"Then the next day," continued the regent, "did not Monsieur de Chanlay, who followed you under the name of De Livry, pay you a visit, which was vainly opposed by Madame Desroches?"

"You are right, monsieur, and I see that Gaston has told you all."

"Then came the order to leave for Paris. You would have opposed it, but were forced to obey. You were taken to a house in the Faubourg St. Antoine; but there your captivity became insupportable."

"You are mistaken, monsieur; it was not the captivity, but the prison."

"I do not understand you."

"Did not Gaston tell you of his fears, which I laughed at at first, but shared afterward?"

"No, tell me what did you fear?"

"But if *he* did not tell you, how shall *I*?"

"Is there anything one cannot tell to a friend?"

"Did he not tell you that this man whom I at first believed to be my father —?"

Gaston rose hastily, and met D'Argenson with a law officer.—*Page* 514.

Link to larger image

"Believed!"

"Yes; I swear it, monsieur. Hearing his voice, feeling my hand pressed by his, I had at first no doubt, and it almost needed evidence to bring fear instead of the filial love with which he at first inspired me."

"I do not understand you, mademoiselle; how could you fear a man who—to judge by what you tell me—had so much affection for you?"

"You do not understand, monsieur; as you say, under a frivolous pretext, I was removed from Rambouillet to Paris, shut in a house in the Faubourg Saint Antoine, which spoke more clearly to my eyes than Gaston's fears had done.

Then I thought myself lost—and that this feigned tenderness of a father concealed the wiles of a seducer. I had no friend but Gaston—I wrote to him —he came."

"Then," said the regent, filled with joy, "when you left that house it was to escape those wiles, not to follow your lover?"

"Oh, monsieur, if I had believed in that father whom I had seen but once, and then surrounded by mysteries, I swear to you that nothing would have led me from the path of duty."

"Oh, dear child!" cried the duke, with an accent which made Helene start.

"Then Gaston spoke to me of a person who could refuse him nothing—who would watch over me and be a father to me. He brought me here, saying he would return to me. I waited in vain for more than an hour, and at length, fearing some accident had happened to him, I asked for you." The regent's brow became clouded.

"Thus," said he, "it was Gaston's influence that turned you from your duty— his fears aroused yours?"

"Yes; he suspected the mystery which encircled me, and feared that it concealed some fatal project."

"But he must have given you some proof to persuade you."

"What proof was needed in that abominable house? Would a father have placed his daughter in such a habitation?"

"Yes, yes," murmured the regent, "he was wrong; but confess that without the chevalier's suggestions, you, in the innocence of your soul, would have had no suspicion."

"No," said Helene, "but happily Gaston watched over me."

"Do you then believe that all Gaston said to you was true?" asked the regent.

"We easily side with those we love, monsieur."

"And you love the chevalier?"

"Yes; for the last two years, monsieur."

"But how could he see you in the convent?"

"By night, with the aid of a boat."

"And did he see you often?"

"Every week."

"Then you love him?"

"Yes, monsieur."

"But how could you dispose of your heart, knowing that you were not your own mistress?"

"For sixteen years I had heard nothing of my family; how could I suppose that all at once it would reveal itself, or rather, that an odious maneuver should take me from my quiet retreat to my ruin?"

"Then you still think that that man lied, when he called himself your father?"

"I scarcely know what to think, and my mind becomes bewildered in contemplating this strange reality, which seems so like a dream."

"But you should not consult your mind here, Helene," said the regent; "you should consult your heart. When you were with this man, did not your heart speak to you?"

"Oh!" said Helene, "while he was there I was convinced, for I have never felt emotion such as I felt then."

"Yes," replied the regent, bitterly; "but when he was gone, this emotion disappeared, driven away by stronger influence. It is very simple, this man was only your father; Gaston was your lover."

"Monsieur," said Helene, drawing back, "you speak strangely."

"Pardon me," replied the regent, in a sweet voice; "I see that I allowed myself to be carried away by my interest. But what surprises me more than all, mademoiselle," continued he, "is that, being beloved as you are by Gaston, you could not induce him to abandon his projects."

"His projects, monsieur! what do you mean?"

"What! you do not know the object of his visit to Paris?"

"I do not, monsieur. When I told him, with tears in my eyes, that I was forced to leave Clisson, he said he must also leave Nantes. When I told him that I was coming to Paris, he answered, with a cry of joy, that he was about to set out for the same place."

"Then," cried the regent, his heart freed from an enormous load, "you are not his accomplice?"

"His accomplice!" cried Helene, alarmed; "ah, mon Dieu! what does this mean?"

"Nothing," said the regent, "nothing."

"Oh, yes, monsieur; you have used a word which explains all. I wondered what made so great a change in Gaston. Why, for the last year, whenever I spoke of our future, his brow became dark. Why, with so sad a smile, he said to me, 'Helene, no one is sure of the morrow.' Why he fell into such reveries, as though some misfortune threatened him. That misfortune you have shown me, monsieur. Gaston saw none but malcontents there—Montlouis, Pontcalec. Ah! Gaston is conspiring—that is why he came to Paris."

"Then you knew nothing of this conspiracy?"

"Alas, monsieur! I am but a woman, and, doubtless, Gaston did not think me worthy to share such a secret."

"So much the better," cried the regent; "and now, my child, listen to the voice of a friend, of a man who might be your father. Let the chevalier go on the path he has chosen, since you have still the power to go no further."

"Who? I, monsieur!" cried Helene; "I abandon him at a moment when you yourself tell me that a danger threatens him that I had not known! Oh, no, no, monsieur! We two are alone in the world, we have but each other: Gaston has no parents, I have none either; or if I have, they have been separated from me for sixteen years, and are accustomed to my absence. We may, then, lose ourselves together without costing any one a tear—oh, I deceived you, monsieur, and whatever crime he has committed, or may commit, I am his accomplice."

"Ah!" murmured the regent, in a choking voice, "my last hope fails me; she loves him."

Helene turned, with astonishment, toward the stranger who took so lively an interest in her sorrow. The regent composed himself.

"But," continued he, "did you not almost renounce him? Did you not tell him, the day you separated, that you could not dispose of your heart and person?"

"Yes, I told him so," replied the young girl, with exaltation, "because at that time I believed him happy, because I did not know that his liberty, perhaps his life, were compromised; then, my heart would have suffered, but my conscience would have remained tranquil; it was a grief to bear, not a remorse to combat; but since I know him threatened—unhappy—I feel that his life is mine."

"But you exaggerate your love for him," replied the regent, determined to ascertain his daughter's feelings. "This love would yield to absence."

"It would yield to nothing, monsieur; in the isolation in which my parents left me, this love has become my only hope, my happiness, my life. Ah!

monsieur, if you have any influence with him—and you must have, since he confides to you the secrets which he keeps from me—in Heaven's name, induce him to renounce these projects, of which you speak; tell him what I dare not tell him myself, that I love him beyond all expression; tell him that his fate shall be mine; that if he be exiled, I exile myself; if he be imprisoned, I will be so too; and that if he dies, I die. Tell him *that*, monsieur; and add— add that you saw, by my tears and by my despair, that I spoke the truth."

"Unhappy child!" murmured the regent.

Indeed, Helene's situation was a pitiable one. By the paleness of her cheeks, it was evident that she suffered cruelly; while she spoke, her tears flowed ceaselessly, and it was easy to see that every word came from her heart, and that what she had said she would do.

"Well," said the regent, "I promise you that I will do all I can to save the chevalier."

Helene was about to throw herself at the duke's feet, so humbled was this proud spirit by the thought of Gaston's danger; but the regent received her in his arms. Helene trembled through her whole frame—there was something in the contact with this man which filled her with hope and joy. She remained leaning on his arm, and made no effort to raise herself.

"Mademoiselle," said the regent, watching her with an expression which would certainty have betrayed him if Helene had raised her eyes to his face, "Mademoiselle, the most pressing affair first—I have told you that Gaston is in danger, but not in immediate danger; let us then first think of yourself, whose position is both false and precarious. You are intrusted to my care, and I must, before all else, acquit myself worthily of this charge. Do you trust me, mademoiselle?"

"Oh, yes; Gaston brought me to you."

"Always Gaston," sighed the regent, in an undertone; then to Helene he said:

"You will reside in this house, which is unknown, and here you will be free. Your society will consist of excellent books, and my presence will not be wanting, if it be agreeable to you."

Helene made a movement as if to speak.

"Besides," continued the duke, "it will give you an opportunity to speak of the chevalier."

Helene blushed, and the regent continued:

"The church of the neighboring convent will be open to you, and should you have the slightest fear, such as you have already experienced, the convent itself might shelter you—the superior is a friend of mine."

"Ah, monsieur," said Helene, "you quite reassure me; I accept the house you offer me—and your great kindness to Gaston and myself will ever render your presence agreeable to me."

The regent bowed.

"Then, mademoiselle," said he, "consider yourself at home here; I think there is a sleeping-room adjoining this room—the arrangement of the ground-floor is commodious, and this evening I will send you two nuns from the convent, whom, doubtless, you would prefer to servants, to wait on you."

"Ah, yes, monsieur."

"Then," continued the regent, with hesitation, "then you have almost renounced your—father?"

"Ah, monsieur, do you not understand that it is for fear he should not be my father."

"However," replied the regent, "nothing proves it; that house alone is certainly an argument against him but he might not have known it."

"Oh," said Helene, "that is almost impossible."

"However, if he took any further steps, if he should discover your retreat and claim you, or at least ask to see you?"

"Monsieur, we would inform Gaston, and learn his opinion."

"It is well," said the regent, with a smile; and he held out his hand to Helene, and then moved toward the door.

"Monsieur," said Helene, in a scarcely audible voice.

"Do you wish for anything?" asked the duke, returning.

"Can I see him?"

The words seemed to die away on her lips as she pronounced them.

"Yes," said the duke, "but is it not better for your sake to do so as little as possible?" Helene lowered her eyes.

"Besides," said the duke, "he has gone on a journey, and may not be back for some days."

"And shall I see him on his return?"

"I swear it to you."

Ten minutes after, two nuns and a lay sister entered and installed themselves in the house.

When the regent quitted his daughter, he asked for Dubois, but he was told that, after waiting half an hour, Dubois had returned to the Palais Royal.

The duke, on entering the abbe's room, found him at work with his secretaries; a portfolio full of papers was on the table.

"I beg a thousand pardons," said Dubois, on seeing the duke, "but as you delayed, and your conference was likely to be prolonged greatly, I took the liberty of transgressing your orders, and returning here."

"You did rightly; but I want to speak to you."

"To me?"

"Yes, to you."

"To me alone?"

"Alone."

"In that case, will monseigneur go into my cabinet, or into your own room?"

"Let us go into your cabinet."

The abbe made a respectful bow and opened the door—the regent passed in first, and Dubois followed when he had replaced the portfolio under his arm. These papers had probably been got together in expectation of this visit.

When they were in the cabinet, the duke looked round him.

"The place is safe?" asked he.

"Pardieu, each door is double, and the walls are two feet thick."

The regent sat down and fell into a deep reverie.

"I am waiting, monseigneur," said Dubois, in a few minutes.

"Abbe," said the regent, in a quick decided tone, as of a man determined to be answered, "is the chevalier in the Bastille?"

"Monseigneur," replied Dubois, "he must have been there about half an hour."

"Then write to M. de Launay. I desire that he be set free at once."

Dubois did not seem surprised; he made no reply, but he placed the portfolio on the table, opened it, took out some papers, and began to look over them quietly.

"Did you hear me?" asked the regent, after a moment's silence.

"I did, monseigneur."

"Obey, then."

"Write yourself, monseigneur," said Dubois.

"And why?"

"Because nothing shall induce this hand to sign your highness's ruin," said Dubois.

"More words," said the regent, impatiently.

"Not words, but facts, monseigneur. Is M. de Chanlay a conspirator, or is he not?"

"Yes, certainly! but my daughter loves him."

"A fine reason for setting him at liberty."

"It may not be a reason to you, abbe, but to me it is, and a most sacred one. He shall leave the Bastille at once."

"Go and fetch him, then; I do not prevent you."

"And did you know this secret?"

"Which?"

"That M. de Livry and the chevalier were the same?"

"Yes, I knew it. What, then?"

"You wished to deceive me."

"I wished to save you from the sentimentality in which you are lost at this moment. The regent of France—already too much occupied by whims and pleasures—must make things worse by adding passion to the list. And what a passion! Paternal love, dangerous love—an ordinary love may be satisfied, and then dies away—but a father's tenderness is insatiable, and above all, intolerable. It will cause your highness to commit faults which I shall prevent, for the simple reason that I am happy enough not to be a father; a thing on which I congratulate myself daily, when I see the misfortunes and stupidity of those who are."

"And what matters a head more or less?" cried the regent. "This De Chanlay will not kill me, when he knows it was I who liberated him."

"No; neither will he die from a few days in the Bastille; and there he must stay."

"And I tell you he shall leave it to-day."

"He must, for his own honor," said Dubois, as though the regent had not spoken; "for if he were to leave the Bastille to-day, as you wish, he would appear to his accomplices, who are now in the prison at Nantes, and whom I suppose you do not wish to liberate also, as a traitor and spy who has been pardoned for the information he has given."

The regent reflected.

"You are all alike," pursued Dubois, "you kings and reigning princes; a reason stupid enough, like all reasons of honor, such as I have just given, closes your mouth; but you will never understand true and important reasons of state. What does it matter to me or to France that Mademoiselle Helene de Chaverny, natural daughter of the regent, should weep for her lover, Monsieur Gaston de Chanlay? Ten thousand wives, ten thousand mothers, ten thousand daughters, may weep in one year for their sons, their husbands, their fathers, killed in your highness's service by the Spaniard who threaten you, who takes your gentleness for weakness, and who becomes emboldened by impunity. We know the plot; let us do it justice. M. de Chanlay—chief or agent of this plot, coming to Paris to assassinate you—do not deny it, no doubt he told you so himself—is the lover of your daughter; so much the worse—it is a misfortune which falls upon you, but may have fallen upon you before, and will again. I knew it all. I knew that he was beloved; I knew that he was called De Chanlay, and not De Livry; yes, I dissimulated, but it was to punish him exemplarily with his accomplices, because, it must be understood that the regent's head is not one of those targets which any one may aim at through excitement or ennui, and go away unpunished if they fail."

"Dubois, Dubois, I shall never sacrifice my daughter's life to save my own, and I should kill her in executing the chevalier; therefore no prison, no dungeon; let us spare the shadow of torture to him whom we cannot treat with entire justice; let us pardon completely; no half pardon, any more than half justice."

"Ah, yes; pardon, pardon; there it is at last; are you not tired of that word, monseigneur; are you not weary of harping eternally on one string?"

"This time, at least, it is a different thing, for it is not generosity. I call Heaven to witness that I should like to punish this man, who is more beloved as a lover than I as a father; and who takes from me my last and only daughter; but, in spite of myself, I stop, I can go no farther; Chanlay shall be set free."

"Chanlay shall be set free; yes, monseigneur; mon Dieu! who opposes it? Only it must be later, some days hence. What harm shall we do him? Diable! he will not die of a week in the Bastille; you shall have your son-in-law; be at peace; but do act so that our poor little government shall not be too much ridiculed. Remember that at this moment the affairs of the others are being looked into, and somewhat roughly too. Well, these others have also mistresses, wives, mothers. Do you busy yourself with them? No, you are not so mad. Think, then, of the ridicule if it were known that your daughter loved the man who was to stab you; the bastards would laugh for a month; it is enough to revive La Maintenon, who is dying, and make her live a year longer. Have patience, monseigneur; let the chevalier eat chicken and drink wine with De Launay. Pardieu! Richelieu does very well there; he is loved by another of your daughters, which did not prevent you from putting him in the Bastille."

"But," said the regent, "when he is in the Bastille, what will you do with him?"

"Oh, he only serves this little apprenticeship to make him your son-in-law. But, seriously, monseigneur, do you think of raising him to that honor?"

"Oh, mon Dieu! at this moment I think of nothing, Dubois, but that I do not want to make my poor Helene unhappy; and yet I really think that giving him to her as a husband is somewhat derogatory, though the De Chanlays are a good family."

"Do you know them, monseigneur? Parbleu! it only wanted that."

"I heard the name long ago, but I cannot remember on what occasion; we shall see; but, meanwhile, whatever you may say, one thing I have decided— he must not appear as a traitor; and remember, I will not have him maltreated."

"In that case he is well off with M. de Launay. But you do not know the Bastille, monseigneur. If you had ever tried it, you would not want a country house. Under the late king it was a prison—oh, yes, I grant that, but under the gentle reign of Philippe d'Orleans, it is a house of pleasure. Besides, at this moment, there is an excellent company there. There are fetes, balls, vocal concerts; they drink champagne to the health of the Duc de Maine and the king of Spain. It is you who pay, but they wish aloud that you may die, and your race become extinct. Pardieu! Monsieur de Chanlay will find some acquaintances there, and be as comfortable as a fish in the water. Ah, pity him, monseigneur, for he is much to be pitied, poor fellow!"

"Yes, yes," cried the duke, delighted; "and after the revelations in Bretagne we shall see."

Dubois laughed.

"The revelations in Bretagne. Ah, pardieu! monseigneur, I shall be anxious to know what you will learn that the chevalier did not tell you. Do you not know enough yet, monseigneur? Peste! if it were me, I should know too much."

"But it is not you, abbe."

"Alas, unfortunately not, monseigneur, for if I were the Duc d'Orleans and regent, I would make myself cardinal. But do not let us speak of that, it will come in time, I hope; besides, I have found a way of managing the affair which troubles you."

"I distrust you, abbe. I warn you."

"Stay, monseigneur; you only love the chevalier because your daughter does?"

"Well?"

"But if the chevalier repaid her fidelity by ingratitude. Mon Dieu! the young woman is proud, monseigneur; she herself would give him up. That would be well played, I think."

"The chevalier cease to love Helene! impossible; she is an angel."

"Many angels have gone through that, monseigneur; besides, the Bastille does and undoes many things, and one soon becomes corrupted there, especially in the society he will find there."

"Well, we shall see, but not a step without my consent."

"Fear nothing, monseigneur. Will you now examine the papers from Nantes?"

"Yes, but first send me Madame Desroches."

"Certainly."

Dubois rang and gave the regent's orders.

Ten minutes after Madame Desroches entered timidly; but instead of the storm she had expected, she received a smile and a hundred louis.

"I do not understand it," thought she; "after all, the young girl cannot be his daughter."

CHAPTER XXII.

IN BRETAGNE.

Our readers must now permit us to look backward, for we have (in following the principal persons of our history) neglected some others in Bretagne, who deserve some notice; besides, if we do not represent them as taking an active part in this tale, history is ready with her inflexible voice to contradict us; we must, therefore, for the present, submit to the exigencies of history.

Bretagne had, from the first, taken an active part in the movement of the legitimated bastards; this province, which had given pledges of fidelity to monarchical principles, and pushed them to exaggeration, if not to madness, since it preferred the adulterous offspring of a king to the interests of a kingdom, and since its love became a crime by calling in aid of the pretensions of those whom it recognized as its princes, enemies against whom Louis XIV. for sixty years, and France for two centuries had waged a war of extermination.

We have seen the list of the principal names which constituted this revolt; the regent had wittily said that it contained the head and tail; but he was mistaken —it was the head and body. The head was the council of the legitimated princes, the king of Spain, and his imbecile agent, the prince of Cellamare; the body was formed by those brave and clever men who were now in the Bastille; but the tail was now agitating in Bretagne among a people unaccustomed to the ways of a court, and it was a tail armed with stings like those of a scorpion, and which was the most to be feared.

The Bretagne chiefs, then, renewed the Chevalier de Rohan, under Louis XIV.; we say the Chevalier de Rohan, because to every conspiracy must be given the name of a chief.

Along with the prince, who was a conceited and commonplace man, and even before him, were two men, stronger than he; one in thought and the other in execution. These two men were Letreaumont, a Norman gentleman, and Affinius Vanden-Enden, a Dutch philosopher; Letreaumont wanted money, he was the arm; Affinius wanted a republic, he was the soul. This republic, moreover, he wanted inclosed in Louis XIV.'s kingdom, still further to annoy the great king—who hated republicans even at a distance—who had persecuted and destroyed the Pensioner of Holland, John de Witt, more cruel in this than the Prince of Orange, who, in declaring himself De Witt's enemy, revenged personal injuries, while Louis XIV. had received nothing but friendship and devotion from this great man.

Now Affinius wanted a republic in Normandy, and got the Chevalier de Rohan named Protector; the Bretons wished to revenge themselves for certain injuries their province had received under the regency, and they decreed it a republic, with the power of choosing a protector, even were he a Spaniard; but Monsieur de Maine had a good chance.

This is what passed in Bretagne.

The Bretons lent an ear to the first overtures of the Spaniards; they had no more cause for discontent than other provinces, but to them it seemed a capital opportunity for war, and they had no other aim. Richelieu had ruled them severely; they thought to emancipate themselves under Dubois, and they began by objecting to the administrators sent by the regent; a revolution always commences by a riot.

Montesquieu was appointed viceroy to hold assemblies, to hear the people's complaints, and to collect their money. The people complained plentifully, but would not pay, because they did not like the steward; this appeared a bad reason to Montesquieu, who was a man of the old régime.

"You cannot offer these complaints to his majesty," said he, "without appearing to rebel: pay first, and complain afterward; the king will listen to your sorrows, but not to your antipathies to a man honored by his choice."

Monsieur de Montaran, of whom the Bretons complained, gave no offense; but, in being intendant of the province, any other would have been as much disliked, and they persisted in their refusal to pay.

"Monsieur le Marechal," said their deputies, "your language might suit a general treating with a conquered place, but cannot be accepted by free and privileged men. We are neither enemies nor soldiers—we are citizens and masters at home. In compensation of a service which we ask, namely—that Monsieur de Montaran, whom we dislike, should be removed, we will pay the tax demanded; but if the court takes to itself the highest prize, we will keep our money, and bear as we best can the treasurer who displeases us."

Monsieur de Montesquieu, with a contemptuous smile, turned on his heel— the deputies did the same, and both retired with their original dignity.

But the marshal was willing to wait; he behaved himself as an able diplomatist, and thought that private reunions would set all right; but the Breton nobles were proud—indignant at their treatment, they appeared no more at the marshal's reception; and he, from contempt, changed to angry and foolish resolves. This was what the Spaniards had expected. Montesquieu, corresponding with the authorities at Nantes, Quimper, Vannes, and Rennes, wrote that he had to deal with rebels and mutineers, but that ten thousand of his soldiers should teach the Bretons politeness.

The states were held again; from the nobility to the people in Bretagne is but a step; a spark lights the whole; the citizens declared to M. de Montesquieu that if he had ten thousand men, Bretagne had a hundred thousand, who would teach his soldiers, with stones, forks and muskets, that they had better mind their own business, and that only.

The marshal assured himself of the truth of this assertion, and was quiet, leaving things as they were for a while; the nobility then made a formal and moderate complaint; but Dubois and the council of the regency treated it as a hostile manifesto, and used it as an instrument.

Montaran, Montesquieu, Pontcalec and Talhouet were the men really fighting among themselves. Pontcalec, a man of mind and power, joined the malcontents and encouraged the growth of the struggle.

There was no drawing back; the court, however, only saw the revolt, and did not suspect the Spanish affair. The Bretons, who were secretly undermining the regency, cried aloud, "No impost, no Montaran," to draw away suspicion from their anti-patriotic plots—but the event turned out against them. The regent—a skillful politician—guessed the plot without perceiving it; he thought that this local veil hid some other phantom, and he tore off the veil. He withdrew Montaran, and then the conspirators were unmasked; all the others were content and quiet, they alone remained in arms.

Then Pontcalec and his friends formed the plot we are acquainted with, and used violent means to attain their ends.

Spain was watching; Alberoni, beaten by Dubois in the affair of Cellamare, waited his revenge, and all the treasures prepared for the plot of Paris were now sent to Bretagne; but it was late—he did not believe it, and his agents deceived him; he thought it was possible to recommence the war, but then France made war on Spain. He thought it possible to kill the regent; but he, and not Chanlay, should do what no one would then recommend to the most cruel enemy of France. Alberoni reckoned on the arrival of a Spanish vessel full of arms and money, and this ship did not arrive; he waited for news of Chanlay; it was La Jonquiere who wrote—and what a La Jonquiere!

One evening Pontcalec and his friends had met in a little room near the old castle; their countenances were sad and irresolute—Du Couëdic announced that he had received a note recommending them to take flight.

"I have a similar one to show you," said Montlouis; "it was slid under my glass at table, and my wife, who expected nothing, was frightened."

"I neither expect nor fear anything," said Talhouet; "the province is calm, the news from Paris is good; every day the regent liberates some one of those imprisoned for the Spanish affair."

"And I, gentlemen," said Pontcalec, "must tell you of a strange communication I have received to-day. Show me your note, Du Couëdic, and you yours, Montlouis; perhaps it is the same writing, and is a snare for us."

"I do not think so, for if they wish us to leave this, it is to escape some danger; we have nothing to fear for our reputation, for that is not at stake. The affairs of Bretagne are known to the world: your brother, Talhouet, and your cousin have fled to Spain: Solduc, Rohan, Sanbilly the counselor, have all disappeared, yet their flight was supposed to be natural, and from some simple cause of discontent. I confess, if the advice be repeated, I shall fly."

"We have nothing to fear, my friends," said Pontcalec, "our affairs were never more prosperous. See, the court has no suspicion, or we should have been molested already. La Jonquiere wrote yesterday; he announces that De Chanlay is starting for La Muette, where the regent lives as a private gentleman, without guards, without fear."——"Yet you are uneasy," said Du Couëdic.

"I confess it, but not for the reason you suppose."

"What is it, then?"

"A personal matter."

"Of your own!"

"Yes, and I could not confide it to more devoted friends, or any who know me better. If ever I were molested—if ever I had the alternative of remaining or of flying to escape a danger, I should remain; do you know why?"

"No, speak."

"I am afraid."

"You, Pontcalec?—afraid! What do you mean by these words, after those you have just uttered?"

"Mon Dieu! yes, my friend; the ocean is our safeguard; we could find safety on board one of those vessels which cruise on the Loire from Paimbœuf to Saint Nazaire; but what is safety to you is certain death to me."

"I do not understand you," said Talhouet.

"You alarm me," said Montlouis.

"Listen, then, my friends," said Pontcalec.

And he began, in the midst of the most scrupulous attention, the following recital, for they knew that if Pontcalec were afraid there must be a good cause.

CHAPTER XXIII.

THE SORCERESS OF SAVERNAY.

"I was ten years old, and I lived at Pontcalec, in the midst of woods, when one day my uncle Crysogon, my father, and I, resolved to have a rabbit hunt in a warren at five or six miles distance, found, seated on the heath, a woman reading. So few of our peasants could read that we were surprised. We stopped and looked at her—I see her now, as though it were yesterday, though it is nearly twenty years ago. She wore the dark costume of our Breton women, with the usual white head-dress, and she was seated on a large tuft of broom in blossom, which she had been cutting.

"My father was mounted on a beautiful bay horse, with a gold-colored mane, my uncle on a gray horse, young and ardent, and I rode one of those little white ponies, which to strength and activity unite the docility of a sheep.

"The woman looked up from her book at the group before her, and seeing me firm in my stirrups near my father, who seemed proud of me, she rose all at once, and approaching me, said—

"'What a pity!'

"'What do you mean?' asked my father.

"'It means that I do not like that white pony,' replied the woman.

"'And why not?'

"'Because he will bring misfortune to your child, Sirè de Pontcalec.'

"We Bretons are superstitious, you know; so that even my father, who, you know, Montlouis, was an enlightened as well as a brave man, stopped, in spite of my uncle Crysogon, who urged us to proceed, and trembling at the idea of danger to me, he added—

"'Yet the pony is gentle, my good woman, and Clement rides well for his age. I have often ridden the little animal in the park, and its paces are perfect.'

"'I do not know anything of that, Marquis de Guer,' replied the woman, 'but the little white horse will injure your son Clement, I tell you.'

"'And how can you know this?'

"'I see it,' replied she, in a strange voice.

"'When?' asked my father.

"'To-day.'

"My father turned pale, and I was afraid; but my uncle Crysogon, who had been in the Dutch wars, and had become somewhat hardened by combating the Huguenots, laughed till he nearly fell from his horse.

"'Parbleu!' said he, 'this good woman certainly is in league with the rabbits at Savernay. What do you say to it, Clement: would you like to go home and lose the sport?'

"'Uncle,' I replied, 'I would rather go on with you.'

"'You look pale and odd—are you afraid?'

"'I am not afraid,' said I.

"I lied, for I felt a certain shudder pass through me, which was very like fear.

"My father has since owned to me, that if it had not been for my uncle's words, which caused a certain false shame in him, he would have sent me home or given my horse to one of the servants; but what an example for a boy of my age, who declared himself to have no fear, and what a subject for ridicule to my uncle.

"I continued, then, to ride my pony; we reached the warren, and the chase commenced.

"While it lasted, the pleasures made us forget the prediction; but the chase over, and having started on our road home—

"'Well, Clement,' said my uncle, 'still on your pony; you are a brave boy.'

"My father and I both laughed; we were then crossing a plain as flat and even as this room—no obstacles in the way, nothing that could frighten a horse, yet at that moment my pony gave a bound which shook me from my seat, then he reared violently, and threw me off; my uncle laughed, but my father became as pale as death. I did not move, and my father leaped from his horse and came to me, and found that my leg was broken.

"To describe my father's grief and the cries of the grooms would be impossible; but my uncle's despair was indescribable—kneeling by my side, removing my clothes with a trembling hand, covering me with tears and caresses, his every word was a fervent prayer. My father was obliged to console him, but to all his consolations and caresses he answered not.

"They sent for the first surgeon at Nantes, who pronounced me in great danger. My uncle begged my mother's pardon all day long; and we remarked that, during my illness, he had quite changed his mode of life; instead of drinking and hunting with the officers—instead of going on fishing expeditions, of which he was so fond—he never left my pillow.

"The fever lasted six weeks, and the illness nearly four months; but I was saved, and retained no trace of the accident. When I went out for the first time, my uncle gave me his arm; but when the walk was over, he took leave of us with tears in his eyes.

"'Where are you going, Crysogon?' asked my father in astonishment.

"'I made a vow,' replied the good man, 'that if our child recovered, I would turn Carthusian, and I go to fulfill it.'

"This was a new grief. My father and my mother shed tears; I hung on my uncle's neck, and begged him not to leave us; but the viscount was a man who never broke a promise or a resolution. Our tears and prayers were vain.

"'My brother,' said he, 'I did not know that God sometimes deigns to reveal Himself to man in acts of mystery. I doubted, and deserve to be punished; besides, I do not wish to lose my salvation in the pleasures of this life.'

"At these words the viscount embraced me again, mounted his horse, and disappeared. He went to the Carthusian monastery at Morlaix. Two years afterward, fasts, macerations, and grief had made of this bon vivant, this joyous companion, this devoted friend, a premature skeleton. At the end of three years he died, leaving me all his wealth."

"Diable! what a frightful tale," said Du Couëdic; "but the old woman forgot to tell you that breaking your leg would double your fortune."

"Listen," said Pontcalec, more gravely than ever.

"Ah! it is not finished," said Talhouet.

"We are only at the commencement."

"Continue, we are listening."

"You have all heard of the strange death of the Baron de Caradec, have you not?"

"Our old college friend at Nantes," said Montlouis, "who was found murdered ten years ago in the forest of Chateaubriant?"

"Yes. Now listen; but remember that this is a secret which till this moment has been only known to me, and which even now must go no further than ourselves."

The three Bretons, who were deeply interested, gave the required promises.

"Well," said Pontcalec, "this college friendship of which Montlouis speaks had undergone some change between Caradec and myself, on account of a rivalry. We loved the same woman, and I was loved by her.

"One day I determined to hunt the stag in the forest of Chateaubriant; my dogs and huntsmen had been sent out the day before, and I was on my way to the rendezvous, when, on the road before me, I saw an enormous fagot walking along. This did not surprise me, for our peasants carry such enormous fagots, that they quite disappear under their load; but this fagot appeared from behind to move alone. Soon it stopped; an old woman, turning round, showed her face to me. As I approached, I could not take my eyes off her, for I recognized the sorceress of Savernay, who had predicted the misfortune caused by my white pony.

"My first impulse, I confess, was to take another road, and avoid the prophetess of evil; but she had already seen me, and she seemed to wait for me with a smile full of malice. I was ten years older than when her first threat had frightened me. I was ashamed to go back.

"'Good-day, Viscount de Pontcalec,' said she; 'how is the Marquis de Guer?'

"'Well, good woman; and I shall be quite easy about him, if you will assure me that nothing will happen to him during my absence.'

"'Ah! ah!' said she laughing; 'you have not forgotten the plains of Savernay. You have a good memory, viscount; but yet, if I gave you some advice, you would not follow it any more than the first time. Man is blind.'

"'And what is your advice?'

"'Not to go hunting to-day.'

"'Why not?'

"'And to return at once to Pontcalec.'

"'I cannot; I have a rendezvous with some friends at Chateaubriant.'

"'So much the worse, viscount, for blood will be spilled.'

"'Mine?'

"'Yours, and another's.'

"'Bah! are you mad?'

"'So said your uncle Crysogon. How is he?'

"'Do you not know that he died seven years ago at Morlaix?'

"'Poor fellow!' said the woman, 'like you, he would not believe: at length he beheld, but it was too late.'

"I shuddered involuntarily; but a false shame whispered that it would be cowardly to give way, and that doubtless the fulfillment of the pretended witch's former prediction had been but a chance.

"'Ah! I see that a former experience has not made you wiser, my fine fellow,' said she. 'Well, go to Chateaubriant then, since you must have it so, but at least send back that handsome hunting-knife.'

"'And with what will monsieur cut the stag's foot?' asked the servant who followed me.

"'With your knife,' said the old woman.

"'That stag is a royal animal,' replied the servant, 'and deserves a hunting-knife.'

"'Besides,' said I, 'you said my blood would flow. What means that?—I shall be attacked, and if so, I shall want it to defend myself.'

"'I do not know what it means,' replied the old woman; 'but I do know, that in your place, my brave gentleman, I would listen to a poor old woman, and that I would not go to Chateaubriant; or, if I did go, it would be without my hunting-knife.'

"'Do not listen to the old witch, monsieur,' said the servant, who was doubtless afraid to take the fatal weapon.

"If I had been alone, I should have returned; but before my servant I did not like to do so.

"'Thank you, my good, woman,' said I, 'but really I do not see what reason there is for not going to Chateaubriant. As to my knife, I shall keep it; if I be attacked, I must have a weapon to defend myself.'

"'Go, then, and defend yourself,' said the old woman, shaking her head; 'we cannot escape our destiny.'

"I heard no more. I urged my horse to a gallop; but, turning a corner, I saw that the old woman had resumed her route, and I lost sight of her.

"An hour after I was in the forest of Chateaubriant; and I met you, Montlouis and Talhouet, for you were both of the party."

"It is true," said Talhouet, "and I began to understand."

"And I," said Montlouis.

"But I know nothing of it," said Du Couëdic; "so pray continue, Pontcalec."

"Our dogs started the deer, and we set off in pursuit; but we were not the only hunters in the forest—at a distance we heard the sound of another pack, which gradually approached; soon the two crossed, and some of my dogs by mistake

157

went after the wrong deer. I ran after them to stop them, which separated me from you. You followed the rest of our pack; but some one had forestalled me. I heard the howls of my dogs under the lash of a whip; I redoubled my pace, and found the Baron de Caradec striking them. I told you there were causes of dislike between us, which only needed an opportunity to burst out. I asked him why he struck my dogs. His reply was haughtier than my question. We were alone—we were both twenty years of age—we were rivals—each was armed. We drew our knives—threw ourselves one upon the other, and Caradec fell from his horse, pierced through the body. To tell you what I felt when I saw him, bleeding and writhing in agony, would be impossible; I spurred my horse, and darted through the forest like a madman.

"I heard the voices of the hunters, and I arrived, one of the first, but I remember—do you remember it, Montlouis?—that you asked me why I was so pale."

"I do," said Montlouis.

"Then I remembered the advice of the sorceress, and reproached myself bitterly for neglecting it. This solitary and fatal duel seemed to me like an assassination. Nantes and its environs became insupportable to me, for every day I heard of the murder of Caradec. It is true that no one suspected me, but the secret voice of my conscience spoke so loud that twenty times I was on the point of denouncing myself.

"Then I left Nantes and went to Paris, but not until I had searched for the sorceress; not knowing either her name or her residence, I could not find her."

"It is strange," said Talhouet; "and have you ever seen her since?"

"Wait," said Pontcalec, "and listen, for now comes the terrible part. This winter—or rather last autumn—I say winter, because there was snow falling, though it was only in November—I was returning from Guer, and had ordered a halt at Pontcalec-des-Aulnes, after a day during which I had been shooting snipes in the marshes with two of my tenants. We arrived, benumbed with cold, at the rendezvous, and found a good fire and supper awaiting us.

"As I entered, and received the salutations and compliments of my people, I perceived in the chimney-corner an old woman wrapped in a large gray-and-black cloak, who appeared to be asleep.

"'Who is that?' I asked of the farmer, and trembling involuntarily.

"'An old beggar, whom I do not know, and she looks like a witch,' said he; 'but she was perishing with cold, hunger and fatigue. She came begging; I told her to come in, and gave her a piece of bread, which she eat while she warmed herself, and now she has gone to sleep.'

"The figure moved slightly in its corner.

"'What has happened to you, Monsieur le Marquis,' asked the farmer's wife, 'that you are so wet, and that your clothes are splashed with mud up to the shoulder?'

"'You nearly had to dine without me, my good Martine,' I replied, 'although this repast and this fire were prepared for me.'——"'Truly!' cried the good woman, alarmed.

"'Ah! monsieur had a narrow escape!' said the farmer.

"'How so, my good lord?'

"'You know your marshes are full of bogs; I ventured without sounding the ground, and all at once I felt that I was sinking in; so that, had it not been for my gun, which I held across, enabling your husband to come and pull me out, I should have been smothered, which is not only a cruel but a stupid death.'

"'Oh, monsieur,' said the wife, 'pray do not expose yourself in this way!'

"'Let him alone,' said the sepulchral voice of the figure crouched in the chimney-corner; 'he will not die thus; I foretell that.'

"And, lowering the hood of her gray cloak, she showed me the face of that woman who had twice crossed my path with sad prediction.

"I remained motionless and petrified.

"'You recognize me?' she asked, without moving.

"I made a sign of assent, but had not really the courage to reply. All gathered in a circle round us.

"'No, no,' continued she; 'be easy, Marquis de Guer; you will not die thus.'

"'How do you know?' I stammered out, with a conviction, however, that she did know.

"'I cannot tell you, for I do not know myself; but you know well that I do not make mistakes.'

"'And how shall I die?' asked I, making an effort over myself to ask this question and to listen to her reply.

"'You will die by the sea. Beware of the water, Marquis de Guer!' she replied.

"'How?' asked I. 'What do you mean?'

"'I have spoken, and cannot explain further, marquis; but again I say, *Beware of the water!*'

"All the peasants looked frightened; some muttered prayers, others crossed themselves; the old woman returned to her corner, buried herself again in her cloak, and did not speak another syllable.

CHAPTER XXIV.

THE ARREST.

"The details of this affair may some day escape my memory, but the impression it made will never be effaced. I had not the shadow of a doubt; and this prediction took the aspect of a reality, as far as I was concerned. Yes," continued Pontcalec, "even though you should laugh, like my Uncle Crysogon, you would never change my opinion, or take away from me the conviction that the prediction will be realized; therefore, I tell you, were it true that we are pursued by Dubois's exempts—were there a boat ready to take us to Belle Isle to escape them, so convinced am I that the sea will be fatal to me, and that no other death has any power over me, that I would give myself up to my pursuers, and say, 'Do your worst; I shall not die by your hands.'"

The three Bretons had listened in silence to this strange declaration, which gathered solemnity from the circumstances in which they stood.

"Then," said Du Couëdic, after a pause, "we understand your courage, my friend; believing yourself destined to one sort of death, you are indifferent to all other danger; but take care, if the anecdote were known, it would rob you of all merit; not in our eyes, for we know what you really are; but others would say that you entered this conspiracy because you can neither be beheaded, shot, nor killed by the dagger, but that it would have been very different if conspirators were drowned."

"And perhaps they would speak the truth," said Pontcalec, smiling.

"But, my dear marquis," said Montlouis, "we, who have not the same grounds for security, should, I think, pay some attention to the advice of our unknown friend, and leave Nantes, or even France, as soon as possible."

"But this may be wrong," said Pontcalec; "and I do not believe our projects are known at Nantes or elsewhere."

"And probably nothing will be known till Gaston has done his work," said Talhouet, "and then we shall have nothing to fear but enthusiasm, and that does not kill. As to you, Pontcalec, never approach a seaport, never go to sea, and you will live to the age of Methuselah!"

The conversation might have continued in this jocular strain; but at this moment several gentlemen, with whom they had appointed a meeting, came in by different secret ways, and in different costumes.

It was not that they had much to fear from the provincial police—that of Nantes, though Nantes was a large town, was not sufficiently well organized to alarm conspirators, who had in the locality the influence of name and social position—but the police of Paris—the regent's police, or that of Dubois—sent down spies, who were easily detected by their ignorance of the place, and the difference of their dress and speech.

Though this Breton association was numerous, we shall only occupy ourselves with its four chiefs, who were beyond all the others in name, fortune, courage, and intelligence.

They discussed a new edict of Montesquieu's, and the necessity of arming themselves in case of violence on the marshal's part: thus it was nothing less than the beginning of a civil war, for which the pretexts were the impiety of the regent's court and Dubois's sacrileges; pretexts which would arouse the anathemas of an essentially religious province, against a reign so little worthy to succeed that of Louis XIV.

Pontcalec explained their plan, not suspecting that at that moment Dubois's police had sent a detachment to each of their dwellings, and that an exempt was even then on the spot with orders to arrest them. Thus all who had taken part in the meeting, saw, from afar, the bayonets of soldiers at their houses: and thus, being forewarned, they might probably escape by a speedy flight; they might easily find retreats among their numerous friends: many of them might gain the coast, and escape to Holland, Spain, or England.

Pontcalec, Du Couëdic, Montlouis, and Talhouet, as usual, went out together; but, on arriving at the end of the street where Montlouis's house was situated, they perceived lights crossing the windows of the apartments, and a sentinel barring the door with his musket.

"Oh," said Montlouis, stopping his companions, "what is going on at my house?"

"Indeed, there is something," said Talhouet; "and just now I fancied I saw a sentinel at the Hotel de Rouen."

"Why did you not say so?" asked Du Couëdic, "it was surely worth mentioning."

"Oh, I was afraid of appearing an alarmist, and I thought it might be only a patrol."

"But this man belongs to the regiment of Picardy," said Montlouis, stepping back.

"It is strange," said Pontcalec; "let me go up the lane which leads to my house

—if that also be guarded, there will be no further doubt."

Keeping together, in case of an attack, they went on silently till they saw a detachment of twenty men grouped round Pontcalec's house.

"This passes a joke," said Du Couëdic, "and unless our houses have all caught fire at once, I do not understand these uniforms around them; as to me, I shall leave mine, most certainly."

"And I," said Talhouet, "shall be off to Saint-Nazaire, and from thence to Le Croisic; take my advice and come with me. I know a brig about to start for Newfoundland, and the captain is a servant of mine; if the air on shore becomes too bad, we will embark, set sail, and vogue la galères; come, Pontcalec, forget your old witch and come with us."

"No, no," said Pontcalec, "I will not rush on my fate; reflect, my friends; we are the chiefs, and we should set a strange example by flying before we even know if a real danger exists. There is no proof against us. La Jonquiere is incorruptible; Gaston is intrepid; our letters from him say that all will soon be over; perhaps, at this very moment, France may be delivered and the regent dead. What would be thought of us if, at such a time, we had taken flight? the example of our desertion would ruin everything here. Consider it well; I do not command you as a chief, but I counsel you as a friend; you are not obliged to obey, for I free you from your oath, but in your place I would not go. We have given an example of devotion; the worst that can happen to us is to give that of martyrdom; but this will not, I hope, be the case. If we are arrested, the Breton parliament will judge us. Of what is it composed?—of our friends and accomplices. We are safer in a prison of which they hold the key, than on a vessel at the mercy of the winds; besides, before the parliament has assembled, all Bretagne will be in arms; tried, we are absolved; absolved, we are triumphant!"

"He is right," said Talhouet; "my uncle, my brothers, all my family are compromised with me. I shall save myself with them, or die with him."

"My dear Talhouet," said Montlouis, "all this is very fine; but I have a worse opinion of this affair than you have. If we are in the hands of any one, it is Dubois, who is not a gentleman, and hates those who are. I do not like these people who belong to no class—who are neither nobles, soldiers, nor priests. I like better a true gentleman, a soldier, or a monk: at least they are all supported by the authority of their profession. However, I appeal, as we generally do, to the majority; but I confess, that if it be for flight, I shall fly most willingly."

"And I," said Du Couëdic; "Montesquieu may be better informed than we suppose; and if it be Dubois who holds us in his clutches, we shall have some difficulty in freeing ourselves."

"And I repeat, we must remain," said Pontcalec; "the duty of a general is to remain at the head of his soldiers; the duty of the chief of a conspiracy is to die at the head of the plot."

"My dear friend," said Montlouis, "your sorceress blinds you; to gain credence for her prediction, you are ready to drown yourself intentionally. I am less enthusiastic about this pythoness, I confess; and as I do not know what kind of death is in store for me, I am somewhat uneasy."

"You are mistaken, Montlouis," said Pontcalec, "it is duty above all which influences me, and besides, if I do not die for this, you will not, for I am your chief, and certainly before the judges I should reclaim the title which I have abjured to-day. If I do not die by Dubois, neither will you. We soldiers, and afraid to pay an official visit to parliament, for that is it, after all, and nothing else; benches covered with black robes—smiles of intelligence between the accused and the judge: it is a battle with the regent; let us accept it, and when parliament shall absolve us, we shall have done as well as if we had put to flight all the troops in Bretagne."

"Montlouis proposed to refer it to a majority," said Du Couëdic, "let us do so."

"I did not speak from fear," said Montlouis; "but I do not see the use of walking into the lion's mouth if we can muzzle him."

"That was unnecessary, Montlouis," said Pontcalec; "we all know you, and we accept your proposition. Let those who are for flight hold up their hands."

Montlouis and Du Couëdic raised their hands.

"We are two and two," said Montlouis; "we must, then, trust to inspiration."

"You forget," said Pontcalec, "that, as president, I have two votes."

"It is true."

"Let those, then, who are for remaining here hold up their hands."

Pontcalec and Talhouet raised their hands; thus the majority was fixed.

This deliberation in the open street might have seemed absurd, had it not involved in its results the question of life or death to four of the noblest gentlemen in Bretagne.

"Well," said Montlouis, "it appears, Du Couëdic, that we were wrong: and now, marquis, we obey your orders."

"See what I do," said Pontcalec, "and then do as you like."

And he walked straight up to his house, followed by his three friends.

Arriving at the door, he tapped a soldier on the shoulder.

"My friend," said he, "call your officer, I beg."

The soldier passed the order to the sergeant, who called the captain.

"What do you want?" asked the latter.——"I want to come into my house."

"Who are you?"

"I am the Marquis de Pontcalec."

"Silence!" said the officer, in a low voice, "and fly instantly—I am here to arrest you." Then aloud, "You cannot pass," said he, pushing back the marquis, and closing in his soldiers before him.

Pontcalec took the officer's hand, pressed it, and said:

"You are a brave fellow, but I must go in. I thank you, and may God reward you!"

The officer, surprised, opened his ranks, and Pontcalec, followed by his friends, crossed the court. On seeing him, his family uttered cries of terror.

"What is it?" asked the marquis, calmly; "and what is going on here?"

"I arrest you, Monsieur le Marquis," said an exempt of the provost of Paris.

"Pardieu! what a fine exploit!" said Montlouis; "and you seem a clever fellow —you, a provost's exempt, and absolutely those whom you are sent to arrest are obliged to come and take you by the collar."

The exempt saluted this gentleman, who joked so pleasantly at such a time, and asked his name.

"I am Monsieur de Montlouis. Look, my dear fellow, if you have not got an order against me, too—if you have, execute it."

"Monsieur," said the exempt, bowing lower as he became more astonished, "it is not I, but my comrade, Duchevon, who is charged to arrest you; shall I tell him?"——"Where is he?"

"At your house, waiting for you."

"I should be sorry to keep you waiting long," said Montlouis, "and I will go to him. Thanks, my friend."

The exempt was bewildered.

Montlouis pressed Pontcalec's hand and those of the others; then, whispering a few words to them, he set out for his house, and was arrested.

Talhouet and Du Couëdic did the same; so that by eleven at night the work was over.

The news of the arrest ran through the town, but every one said, "The parliament will absolve them."

The next day, however, their opinions changed, for there arrived from Nantes the commission, perfectly constituted, and wanting, as we have said, neither president, procureur du roi, secretary, nor even executioners. We use the plural, for there were three.

The bravest men are sometimes stupefied by great misfortune. This fell on the province with the power and rapidity of a thunderstroke; it made no cry, no movement; Bretagne expired.

The commission installed itself at once, and expected that, in consideration of its powers, people would bow before it rather than give offense; but the terror was so great, that each one thought of themselves alone, and merely deplored the fate of the others.

This, then, was the state of affairs in Bretagne three or four days after the arrest of Pontcalec and his three friends. Let us leave them awhile at Nantes, in Dubois's toils, and see what was passing in Paris.

CHAPTER XXV.

THE BASTILLE.

And now, with the reader's permission, we will enter the Bastille—that formidable building at which even the passing traveler trembled, and which, to the whole neighborhood, was an annoyance and cause of alarm; for often at night the cries of the unfortunate prisoners who were under torture might be heard piercing the thick walls, so much so, that the Duchesse de Lesdequieres once wrote to the governor, that, if he did not prevent his patients from making such a noise, she should complain to the king.

At this time, however, under the reign of Philippe d'Orleans, there were no cries to be heard; the society was select, and too well bred to disturb the repose of a lady.

In a room in the Du Coin tower, on the first floor, was a prisoner alone; the room was large, and resembled an immense tomb lighted by two windows, furnished with an unusual allowance of bars and irons. A painted couch, two rough wooden chairs, and a black table, were the whole furniture; the walls were covered with strange inscriptions, which the prisoner consulted from time to time when he was overcome by ennui.

ABBE BRIGAUD.—*Page* 517.

Link to larger image

He had, however, been but one day in the Bastille, and yet already he paced his vast chamber, examining the iron-barred doors, looking through the grated windows, listening, sighing, waiting. This day, which was Sunday, a pale sun silvered the clouds, and the prisoner watched, with a feeling of inexpressible melancholy, the walkers on the Boulevards. It was easy to see that every passer-by looked at the Bastille with a feeling of terror, and of self-gratulation at not being within its walls. A noise of bolts and creaking hinges drew the prisoner from this sad occupation, and he saw the man enter before whom he had been taken the day before. This man, about thirty years of age, with an agreeable appearance and polite bearing, was the governor, M. de Launay, father of that De Launay who died at his post in '89.

The prisoner, who recognized him, did not know how rare such visits were.

"Monsieur de Chanlay," said the governor, bowing, "I come to know if you have passed a good night, and are satisfied with the fare of the house and the conduct of the employés"—thus M. de Launay, in his politeness, called the turnkeys and jailers.

"Yes, monsieur; and these attentions paid to a prisoner have surprised me, I own."

"The bed is hard and old, but yet it is one of the best; luxury being forbidden by our rules. Your room, monsieur, is the best in the Bastille; it has been occupied by the Duc d'Angoulême, by the Marquis de Bassompierre, and by the Marshals de Luxembourg and Biron; it is here that I lodge the princes when his majesty does me the honor to send them to me."

"It is an excellent lodging," said Gaston, smiling, "though ill furnished; can I have some books, some paper, and pens?"

"Books, monsieur, are strictly forbidden; but if you very much wish to read, as many things are allowed to a prisoner who is ennuyé, come and see me, then you can put in your pocket one of those volumes which my wife or I leave about; you will hide it from all eyes; on a second visit you will take the second volume, and to this abstraction we will close our eyes."

"And paper, pens, ink?" said Gaston, "I wish most particularly to write."

"No one writes here, monsieur; or, at least, only to the king, the regent, the minister, or to me; but they draw, and I can let you have drawing-paper and pencils."

"Monsieur, how can I thank you sufficiently for your kindness?"

"By granting me the request I came to make, for my visit is an interested one. I came to ask if you would do me the honor to dine with me to-day?"

"With you, monsieur! truly, you surprise me; however, I cannot tell you how sensible I am of your courtesy, and should retain for it an everlasting gratitude if I had any prospect but death before my eyes."

"Death! monsieur, you are gloomy; you should not think of these things— forget them and accept—"

"I do, monsieur."

"A la bonne heure," said the governor, bowing to Gaston, "I will take back your answer;" and he went out, leaving the prisoner plunged in a new train of ideas.

The politeness which at first charmed the chevalier, on reflection began to arouse some suspicion. Might it not be intended to inspire him with confidence, and lead him on to betray himself and his companions; he remembered the tragic chronicle of the Bastille, the snares laid for prisoners, and that famous dungeon chamber so much spoken of, which none who had entered ever left alive. Gaston felt himself alone and abandoned. He also felt that the crime he had meditated deserved death; did not all these flattering and strange advances conceal some snare? In fact, the Bastille had done its ordinary work; the prison acted on the prisoner, who became cold, suspicious, and uneasy.

"They take me for a provincial," he thought, "and they hope that—prudent in my interrogatories—I shall be imprudent in my conduct; they do not, they cannot, know my accomplices; and they hope that in giving me the means of communicating with them, of writing to them, or of inadvertently speaking of them, they will get something out of me. Dubois and D'Argenson are at the bottom of this."

Then Gaston thought of his friends who were waiting for him without news from him, who would not know what had become of him, or, worse still, on some false news, might act and ruin themselves.

Then came the thought of his poor Helene, isolated, as he himself was, whom he had not even presented to the Duc d'Olivares, her sole protector for the future, and who might himself be arrested or have taken flight. Then, what would become of Helene, without support, and pursued by that unknown person, who had sought her even in the heart of Bretagne?

In a paroxysm of despair at this thought, Gaston threw himself on his bed, cursing the doors and bars which imprisoned him, and striking the stones with his hands.

At this moment there was a noise at the door. Gaston rose hastily, and met D'Argenson with a law officer, and behind them an imposing escort of soldiers. He understood that he was to be interrogated.

D'Argenson, with his great wig, large black eyes, and dark shaggy eyebrows, made little impression on the chevalier; he knew that in joining the conspiracy he sacrificed his happiness, and that in entering the Bastille he had sacrificed his life. In this mood, it was difficult to frighten him. D'Argenson asked a hundred questions which Gaston refused to answer, replying only by complaints of being unjustly arrested, and demanding proof. M. d'Argenson became angry, and Gaston laughed in his face; then D'Argenson spoke of the Breton conspiracy; Gaston assumed astonishment, and listened to the list of his accomplices with the greatest sangfroid. When the magistrate had finished, he thanked him for giving him intelligence of events which were quite new to him. D'Argenson again lost patience, and gave his ordinary angry cough. Then he passed from interrogatory to accusation.

"You wanted to kill the regent," said he, all at once, to the chevalier.

"How do you know that?" asked Gaston, calmly.

"Never mind how, since I know it."

"Then I will answer you as Agamemnon did Achilles. Why ask, since you know it?"

"Monsieur, I am not jesting," said D'Argenson.

"Nor I," said Gaston; "I only quote Racine."

"Take care, monsieur, you may find this system of defense do you no good."

"Do you think it would be better to confess what you ask me?"

"It is useless to deny a fact which I am aware of."

"Then permit me to repeat my question: what is the use of asking me about a project of which apparently you are so much better informed than I am?"

"I want the details."

"Ask your police, which reads even people's most secret thoughts."

"Hum, hum," said D'Argenson, in a tone which, in spite of Gaston's courage, made some impression on him, "what would you say if I asked news of your friend La Jonquiere?"

"I should say," replied Gaston, turning pale, "that I hope the same mistake has not been made about him as about me."

"Ah!" said D'Argenson, "that name touches you, I think—you know M. la Jonquiere?"

"I know him as a friend, recommended to me to show me Paris."

"Yes—Paris and its environs; the Palais Royal, the Rue du Bac, or La Muette: he was to show you all these, was he not?"

"They know all," thought Gaston.

"Well, monsieur," said D'Argenson, "can you find another verse from Racine which will serve as an answer to my question?"

"Perhaps I might, if I knew what you meant; certainly I wished to see the Palais Royal, for it is a curious place, and I have heard it much spoken of. As to the Rue du Bac, I know little of it; then there only remains La Muette, of which I know nothing."

"I do not say that you have been there; I say that La Jonquiere was to take you there—do you dare to deny it."

"Ma foi, monsieur, I neither deny nor avow; I refer you to him; he will answer you if he think fit."

"It is useless, monsieur; he has been asked, and has replied."

Gaston felt a shudder pass through him. He might be betrayed, but he would divulge nothing. He kept silence.

D'Argenson waited a moment, then, seeing that Gaston remained silent—

"Would you like to meet La Jonquiere?" asked he.

"You can do with me as you please, monsieur," said Gaston; "I am in your hands."

But at the same time he resolved, if he were to face La Jonquiere, he would crush him beneath his contempt.

"It is well. As you say, I am the master, and I choose just now to apply the ordinary and extraordinary question: Do you know what they are, monsieur?" said D'Argenson, leaning on each syllable.

A cold sweat bathed Gaston's temples, not that he feared to die, but torture was worse than death. A victim of the torture was always disfigured or crippled, and the best of these alternatives was a cruel one for a young man of five and twenty.

D'Argenson saw, as in a mirror, what was passing in Gaston's mind.

"Hola!" said the interrogator.

Two men entered.

"Here is a gentleman who seems to have no dislike to the question ordinary or extraordinary. Take him to the room."

"It is the dark hour, the hour I expected," murmured Gaston. "Oh, my God! give me courage."

Doubtless his prayer was heard, for, making a sign that he was ready, he followed the guards with a firm step.

D'Argenson came behind him.

They descended the stone staircase and passed the first dungeon in the tower. There they crossed two courts. As they crossed the second court, some prisoners, looking through their windows and seeing a gentleman well dressed, called out:

"Hola! monsieur, you are set free then?"

A woman's voice added:

"Monsieur, if you are asked about us when you are free from here, say that we said nothing."

A young man's voice said:

172

"You are happy, monsieur—you will see her you love."

"You are mistaken, monsieur," said the chevalier. "I am about to suffer the question."

A terrible silence succeeded. Then the sad procession went over the drawbridge, Gaston was placed in a closed and locked chair and taken to the arsenal, which was separated from the Bastille by a narrow passage.

D'Argenson had taken the lead, and awaited the prisoner, who found himself in a low room covered with damp. On the wall hung chains, collars, and other strange instruments; chafing dishes stood on the ground, and crosses of Saint Andre were in the corner.

"You see this," said D'Argenson, showing the chevalier two rings fastened into flagstones at six feet apart, and separated by a wooden bench about three feet high; "in these rings are placed the head and feet of the patient; then this tressel is placed under him, so that his stomach is two feet higher than his mouth; then we pour pots of water holding two pints each into his mouth. The number is fixed at eight for the ordinary, ten for the extraordinary question. If the patient refuses to swallow, we pinch his nose so that he cannot breathe; then he opens his mouth, then he swallows. This question," continued he, emphasizing every detail, "is very disagreeable, and yet I do not think I should prefer the boot. Both kill sometimes; the boot disfigures the patient, and it is true that the water destroys his health for the future; but it is rare, for the prisoner always speaks at the ordinary question if he be guilty, and generally at the extraordinary, if he be not."

Gaston, pale and silent, listened and watched.

"Do you prefer the wedges, chevalier? Here, bring the wedges."

A man brought six wedges and showed them, still stained with blood and flattened at the edges by the blows which had been struck upon them.

"Do you know the way in which these are used? The knees and ankles of the patient are pressed between two wooden slabs as tightly as possible, then one of these men forces a wedge between the knees, which is followed by a larger one. There are eight for the ordinary torture, and two larger for the extraordinary. These wedges, I warn you, chevalier, break bones like glass, and wound the flesh insupportably."

"Enough, enough," said Gaston, "unless you wish to double the torture by describing it; but, if it be only to guide my choice, I leave it to you, as you must know them better than I, and I shall be grateful if you will choose the one which will kill me most quickly."

D'Argenson could not conceal the admiration with which Gaston's strength of will inspired him.

"Come," said he, "speak, and you shall not be tortured."

"I have nothing to say, monsieur, so I cannot."

"Do not play the Spartan, I advise you. One may cry, but between the cries one always speaks under torture."

"Try," said Gaston.

Gaston's resolute air, in spite of the struggle of nature—a struggle which was evidenced by his paleness, and by a slight nervous tremor which shook him— gave D'Argenson the measure of his courage. He was accustomed to this kind of thing, and was rarely mistaken. He saw that he should get nothing out of him, yet he persisted.

"Come, monsieur," said he, "it is still time. Do not force us to do you any violence."

"Monsieur," said Gaston, "I swear before God who hears me, that if you put me to the torture, instead of speaking, I will hold my breath, and stifle myself, if the thing be possible. Judge, then, if I am likely to yield to threats, where I am determined not to yield to pain."

D'Argenson signed to the tormentors, who approached Gaston; but, as they did so, he seemed to gain new strength. With a calm smile, he helped them to remove his coat and to unfasten his cuffs.

"It is to be the water, then?" asked the man.

"The water first," said D'Argenson.

They passed the cords through the rings, brought the tressels, filled the vases —Gaston did not flinch.

D'Argenson reflected.

After about ten minutes' thought, which seemed an age to the chevalier—

"Let him go," said D'Argenson, with a grunt of discontent, "and take him back to the Bastille."

CHAPTER XXVI.

HOW LIFE PASSED IN THE BASTILLE
WHILE WAITING FOR DEATH.

Gaston was inclined to thank the lieutenant of police, but he refrained. It might appear as though he had been afraid. He took his hat and coat, and returned to the Bastille as he had come.

"They did not like to put a man of high birth to the torture," thought he; "they will try me and condemn me to death."

But death seemed easy when divested of the preliminary agonies which the lieutenant of police had so minutely described.

On re-entering his room, Gaston saw, almost with joy, all that had seemed so horrible to him an hour before. The prison seemed gay, the view charming, the saddest inscriptions on the walls were madrigals compared to the menacing appearance of the room he had just quitted.

The major of the Bastille came to fetch him about an hour afterward, accompanied by a turnkey.

"I understand," thought Gaston; "the governor's invitation is a pretext, in such a case, to take from the prisoner the anguish of expectation. I shall, doubtless, cross some dungeon, into which I shall fall and die. God's will be done." And, with a firm step, he followed the major, expecting every moment to be precipitated into some secret dungeon, and murmuring Helene's name, that he might die with it on his lips.

But, no accident following this poetical and loving invocation, the prisoner quietly arrived at the governor's door.

M. de Launay came to meet him.

"Will you give me your word of honor, chevalier," said he, "not to attempt to escape while you are in my house? It is understood, of course," he added, smiling, "that this parole is withdrawn as soon as you are taken back to your own room, and it is only a precaution to insure me a continuance of your society."

"I give you my word so far," said Gaston.

"'Tis well, monsieur, enter; you are expected."

And he led Gaston to a well-furnished room, where a numerous company was already assembled.

"I have the honor to present to you M. le Chevalier Gaston de Chanlay," said the governor. Then naming, in turn, each of the persons assembled—

"M. le Duc de Richelieu."

"M. le Comte de Laval."

"M. le Chevalier Dumesnil."

"M. de Malezieux."

"Ah," said Gaston, smiling, "all the Cellamare conspiracy."

"Except M. and Madame de Maine, and the Prince of Cellamare," said the Abbe Brigaud, bowing.

"Ah, monsieur," said Gaston, in a reproachful tone, "you forget the brave D'Harmental and the learned Mademoiselle de Launay."

"D'Harmental is kept in bed by his wounds," said Brigaud.

"As to Mademoiselle de Launay," said the Chevalier Dumesnil, reddening with pleasure, "here she comes; she does us the honor of dining with us."

"Present me, monsieur," said Gaston; "among prisoners we must not make ceremonies; I reckon, therefore, on you.'"

And Dumesnil, taking Gaston by the hand, presented him to Mademoiselle de Launay.

Gaston could not repress a certain expression of astonishment at all he saw.

"Ah, chevalier," said the governor, "I see that, like three-quarters of the inhabitants of Paris, you thought I devoured my prisoners."

"No, monsieur," said Gaston, "but I certainly thought for a moment that I should not have had the honor of dining with you to-day."——"How so?"

"Is it the habit to give your prisoners an appetite for their dinners by the walk I have had to-day?"

"Ah, yes," cried Mademoiselle de Launay, "was it not you who were being led to the torture just now?"

"Myself, mademoiselle; and be assured that only such a hindrance would have kept me from so charming a society."

"Ah, these things are not in my jurisdiction," said the governor; "thank Heaven, I am a soldier, and not a judge. Do not confound arms and the toga, as Cicero says. My business is to keep you here, and to make your stay as agreeable as possible, so that I may have the pleasure of seeing you again. M. d'Argenson's business is to have you tortured, hanged, beheaded, put on the wheel, quartered, if possible; each to his task. Mademoiselle de Launay," added he, "dinner is ready, will you take my arm? Your pardon, Chevalier Dumesnil; you think me a tyrant, I am sure, but as host I am privileged. Gentlemen, seat yourselves."

"What a horrible thing a prison is," said Richelieu, delicately turning up his cuffs, "slavery, irons, bolts, chains."

"Shall I pass you this potage à l'écrevisses?" said the governor.

"Yes, monsieur," said the duke, "your cook does it beautifully, and I am really annoyed that mine did not conspire with me; he might have profited by his stay in the Bastille."

"There is champagne," said De Launay, "I have it direct from Ai."

"You must give me the address," said Richelieu, "for if the regent leaves me my head, I shall drink no other wine than this. I have got accustomed to it during my sojourns here, and I am a creature of habit."

"Indeed," said the governor, "you may all take example by Richelieu; he is most faithful to me; and, in fact, unless we are overcrowded, I always keep his room ready for him."

"That tyrant of a regent may force us all to keep a room here," said Brigaud.

"Monsieur de Launay," said Laval, in an angry tone, "permit me to ask if it was by your orders that I was awoke at two o'clock this morning, and the meaning of this persecution?"

"It is not my fault, monsieur; you must blame these gentlemen and ladies, who will not keep quiet, in spite of all I tell them."

"We!" cried all the guests.

"Certainly," replied the governor, "you all break through rules; I am always having reports of communications, correspondences, notes, etc."

Richelieu laughed, Dumesnil and Mademoiselle de Launay blushed.

"But we will speak of that at dessert. You do not drink, M. de Chanlay?"

"No, I am listening."

"Say that you are dreaming; you cannot deceive me thus."

"And of what?" asked Malezieux.

"Ah, it is easy to see that you are getting old, my poetical friend; of what should M. de Chanlay dream but of his love."

"Is it not better, M. de Chanlay," cried Richelieu, "to have your head separated from your body, than your body from your soul?"

"Apropos," interrupted Laval, "is there any news from the court; how is the king?"

"No politics, gentlemen, if you please," said the governor. "Let us discuss poetry, arts, war, and even the Bastille, if you like, but let us avoid politics."

"Ah, yes," said Richelieu, "let us talk of the Bastille. What have you done with Pompadour?"

"I am sorry to say he forced me to place him in the dungeon."

"What had he done?" asked Gaston.

"He had beaten his jailer."

"How long has it been forbidden for a gentleman to beat his servant?" asked Richelieu.

"The jailers are servants of the king, M. le Duc," said De Launay, smiling.

"Say rather of the regent."

"A subtle distinction."

"A just one."

"Shall I pass you the Chambertin, M. de Laval?"

"If you will drink with me to the health of the king."

"Certainly—if afterward you will drink with me to the health of the regent."

"Monsieur," said Laval, "I am no longer thirsty."

"I believe it—you have just drunk some wine from his highness's cellar."

"From the regent's?"

"He sent it me yesterday, knowing that I was to have the pleasure of your company."

"In that case," said Brigaud, throwing the contents of his glass upon the floor, "no more poison."

"Oh!" said Malezieux, "I did not know you were such a fanatic for the good cause."

"You were wrong to spill it, abbe," said Richelieu, "I know that wine, and you will hardly find such out of the Palais Royal—if it were against your principles to drink it, you should have passed it to your neighbor, or put it back in the bottle. 'Vinum in amphoram,' said my schoolmaster."

"M. le Duc," said Brigaud, "you do not know Latin as well as Spanish."

"I know French still less, and I want to learn it."

"Oh! that would be long and tedious; better get admitted into the Academy, it would be far easier."

"And do you speak Spanish?" asked Richelieu of De Chanlay.

"Report says, monsieur, that I am here for the abuse of that tongue."

"Monsieur," said the governor, "if you return to politics I must leave the table."

"Then," said Richelieu, "tell Mademoiselle de Launay to talk mathematics; that will not frighten any one."

Mademoiselle de Launay started; she had been carrying on a conversation with Dumesnil, which had been greatly exciting the jealousy of Maison-Rouge, who was in love with her.

When dinner was over, the governor conducted each guest back to his own room, and when it came to Gaston's turn he asked M. de Launay if he could have some razors, instruments which appeared necessary in a place where such elegant company was assembled.

"Monsieur le Chevalier," said the governor, "I am distressed to refuse you a thing of which I see the necessity; but it is against the rules for any one to shave themselves unless they have special permission from the lieutenant of police—no doubt you will obtain the permission if you apply for it."

"But are those gentlemen whom I met here privileged, for they were well dressed and shaved?"

"No, they all had to ask permission; the Duc de Richelieu remained for a month with a beard like a patriarch."

"I find it difficult to reconcile such severity in detail with the liberty I have just seen."

"Monsieur, I also have my privileges, which do not extend to giving you books, razors, or pens, but which allow me to invite to my table such prisoners as I choose to favor—always supposing that it is a favor. True, it is stipulated that I shall give an account of anything which is spoken against the government, but by preventing my guests from touching on politics, I avoid the necessity of betraying them."

"Is it not feared, monsieur," said Gaston, "that this intimacy between you and your prisoners should lead to indulgences on your part, which might be contrary to the intentions of the government?"

"I know my duty, monsieur, and keep within its strict limits; I receive my orders from the court, and my guests—who know that I have nothing to do with them—bear me no ill will for them. I hope you will do the same."

"The precaution was not unnecessary," said Gaston, "for doubtless I shall not long be left in the enjoyment of the pleasure I have had to-day."

"You have doubtless some protector at court?"

"None," said Gaston.

"Then you must trust to chance, monsieur."

"I have never found it propitious."

"The more reason that it should weary of persecuting you."

"I am a Breton, and Bretons trust only in God."

"Take that as my meaning when I said chance."

Gaston retired, charmed with the manners and attentions of M. de Launay.

CHAPTER XXVII.

HOW THE NIGHT PASSED IN THE BASTILLE WHILE WAITING FOR THE DAY.

Gaston had already, on the preceding night, asked for a light, and been told that it was against the rules—this night he did not renew the request, but went quietly to bed; his morning's visit to the torture-room had given him a lesson in philosophy.

Thus, rather from youthful carelessness than from force of will or courage, he slept quietly and soundly.

He did not know how long he had slept when he was awoke by the sound of a small bell, which seemed to be in his room, although he could see neither bell nor ringer; it is true that the room was very dark, even by day, and doubly so at that hour. The bell, however, continued to sound distinctly, but with caution, as though it were afraid of being heard. Gaston thought the sound seemed to come from the chimney.

He rose, and approaching it gently, became convinced that he was right.

Presently he heard blows struck—under the floor on which he stepped—at regular intervals, with some blunt instrument.

It was evident that these were signals among the prisoners.

Gaston went to the window to raise the curtain of green serge which intercepted the rays of the moon, and in doing so he perceived an object hanging at the end of a string and swinging before the bars.

"Good," said he; "it appears that I shall have occupation, but each one in turn; regularity above all things; let us see what the bell wants, that was the first."

Gaston returned to the chimney, extended his hand, and soon felt a string, at the end of which a bell was hanging, he pulled, but it resisted.

"Good," said a voice, which came down the chimney, "you are there?"

"Yes," said Gaston; "what do you want?"

"Parbleu, I want to talk."

"Very well," said the chevalier, "let us talk."

"Are you not M. de Chanlay, with whom I had the pleasure of dining to-day?"

"Exactly so, monsieur."

"In that case I am at your service."

"And I at yours."

"Then have the goodness to tell me the state of the Bretagne affairs."

"You see they are in the Bastille."

"Good," said a voice, whose joyous tone Gaston could hear with ease.

"Pardon me," said Gaston, "but what interest have you in these affairs?"

"Why, when affairs are bad in Bretagne, they treat us well, and when they prosper we are treated badly; thus the other day, apropos of some affair, I do not know what, which they pretended was connected with ours, we were all put in the dungeon."

"Ah, diable!" said Gaston to himself, "if you do not know, I do." Then he added, aloud, "Well then, monsieur, be content, they are very bad, and that is perhaps the reason why we had the pleasure of dining togetherto-day."

"Eh, monsieur, are you compromised?"

"I fear so."

"Receive my excuses."

"I beg you, on the contrary, to accept mine, but I have a neighbor below who is becoming impatient, and who is striking hard enough to break the boards of my floor; permit me to reply to him."

"Do so, monsieur; if my topographical calculations are correct, it must be the Marquis de Pompadour."

"It will be difficult to ascertain."

"Not so difficult as you suppose."

"How so?"

"Does he not strike in a peculiar manner?"

"Yes; has it a meaning?"

"Certainly; it is our method of talking without direct communication."

"Have the kindness to give me the key to the vocabulary."

"It is not difficult; every letter has a rank in the alphabet."

"Decidedly."

"There are twenty-four letters."

"I have never counted them, but no doubt you are right."

"Well, one blow for a, two for b, three for c, and so on."

"I understand, but this method of communication must be somewhat lengthy, and I see a string at my window which is getting impatient—I will strike a blow or two to show my neighbor that I have heard him, and then attend to the string."

"Go, monsieur, I beg, for if I am not mistaken that string is of importance to me; but first strike three blows on the floor—in Bastille language that means patience; the prisoner will then wait for a new signal."

Gaston struck three blows with the leg of his chair, and the noise ceased.

He then went to the window.

It was not easy to reach the bars, but he at length succeeded in doing so and raising the string, which was gently pulled by some hand as a sign of acknowledgment.

Gaston drew the packet—which would scarcely pass the bars—toward him; it contained a pot of sweetmeats and a book. He saw that there was something written on the paper which covered the pot, but it was too dark to read it.

The string vibrated gently, to show that an answer was expected, and Gaston, remembering his neighbor's lesson, took a broom, which he saw in the corner, and struck three blows on the ceiling.

This, it will be remembered, meant patience.

The prisoner withdrew the string, freed from its burden.

Gaston returned to the chimney.

"Eh! monsieur," said he.

"All right, what is it?"

"I have just received, by means of a string, a pot of sweets and a book."

"Is not there something written on one of them?"

"About the book I do not know, but there is on the pot; unfortunately it is too dark to read."

"Wait," said the voice, "I will send a light."

"I thought lights were forbidden."

"Yes, but I have procured one."

"Well, then send it, for I am as impatient as you to know what is written to me." And Gaston, feeling cold, began to dress himself.

All at once he saw a light in his chimney; the bell came down again transformed into a lantern.

This transformation was effected in the most simple manner, the bell turned upside down, so as to form a vessel, into which some oil had been poured, and in the oil burned a little wick.

Gaston found this so ingenious that for a moment he forgot both the pot and the book. "Monsieur," said he to his neighbor, "may I, without indiscretion, ask you how you procured the different objects with which you fabricated this lamp?"

"Nothing more simple, monsieur; I asked for a bell, which was given me, then I saved some oil from my breakfasts and dinners, till I had a bottle full; I made wicks by unraveling one of my handkerchiefs; I picked up a pebble when I was walking in the yard; I made some tinder with burned linen; I stole some matches when I dined at the governor's: then I struck a light with a knife, which I possess; and with the aid of which I made the hole through which we correspond."

"Receive my compliments, monsieur, you are a man of great invention."

"Thank you, monsieur; will you now see what book has been sent you, and what is written on the paper of the pot of sweetmeats."

"Monsieur, the book is a Virgil."

"That is it—she promised it to me," cried the voice, in an accent of happiness which surprised the chevalier, who could not understand that a Virgil should be so impatiently expected.

"Now," said the prisoner with the bell, "pass on, I beg, to the pot of sweetmeats."

"Willingly," said Gaston, and he read:

"Monsieur le Chevalier—I hear from the lieutenant of the prison that you occupy the room on the first floor, which has a window immediately below mine. Prisoners should aid and help each other; eat the sweetmeats, and pass the Virgil up to the Chevalier Dumesnil, whose chimney looks into the court."

"That is what is expected," said the prisoner with the bell; "I was told at dinner to-day that I should receive this message."

"Then you are the Chevalier Dumesnil?"

"Yes, monsieur, and your humble servant."

"I am yours," replied Gaston, "I have to thank you for a pot of sweetmeats, and I shall not forget my obligation."

"In that case, monsieur," replied the prisoner, "have the kindness to detach the bell, and fasten on the Virgil instead."

"But if you have not the light, you cannot read."

"Oh, I will make another lantern."

Gaston, who trusted to his neighbor's ingenuity, after the proofs he had had of it, made no further difficulties; he took the bell, which he placed in the neck of an empty bottle, and fastened on the Virgil, conscientiously replacing a letter which fell from between the leaves.

"Thank you, monsieur," said Dumesnil; "and now, if you will reply to your neighbor below?"

"You give me liberty?"

"Yes, monsieur; though presently I shall make an appeal to your good nature."

"At your orders, monsieur; you say, then, that for the letters——?"

"One blow for A.; twenty-four for Z."

"Thank you."

The chevalier struck a blow with the handle of the broom, to give notice to his neighbor that he was ready to enter into conversation with him; it was instantly answered by another blow.

At the end of half an hour the prisoners had succeeded in saying this—

"Good-evening, monsieur; what is your name?"

"Thank you, monsieur; I am the Chevalier Gaston de Chanlay."

"And I, the Marquis de Pompadour."

At this moment Gaston, looking toward the windows, saw the string shaking convulsively.

He struck three blows, to ask for patience, and returned to the chimney.

"Monsieur," said he to Dumesnil, "I beg you to remember that the string at the window seems prodigiously ennuyé."

"Beg her to have patience; I will attend to her presently."

Gaston renewed the signal for patience on the ceiling, and then returned to the chimney, and the Virgil soon returned.

"Monsieur," said Dumesnil, "have the goodness to fasten the Virgil to the string; that is what she wants."

Gaston had the curiosity to see if Dumesnil had replied to Mademoiselle de Launay. He opened the Virgil; there was no letter, but some words were underlined in pencil, and Gaston read: "Meos amores," and "Carceris oblivia longa." He understood this method of correspondence, which consisted in underlining words which, placed together, made sense.

"Ah," said Gaston, fastening the book to the string, "it seems that I have become the postman."

Then he sighed deeply, remembering that he had no means of corresponding with Helene, and that she was entirely ignorant what had become of him. This gave him sympathy for the attachment of Mademoiselle de Launay and the Chevalier Dumesnil. He returned to the chimney.

"Monsieur," said he, "your letter is dispatched."

"A thousand thanks, chevalier. Now a word more, and I will leave you to sleep in peace."

"Oh, say whatever you wish, monsieur."

"Have you spoken with the prisoner below?"

"Yes."

"Who is he?"

"The Marquis de Pompadour."

"I thought so. What did he say?"

"'Good-evening,' and asked who I was; he had no time to ask more; the method of communication is not as expeditious as it is ingenious."

"You must make a hole, and then you can talk as we do."

"What with?"

"I will lend you my knife."

"Thank you."

"It will serve to amuse you, at least."

"Give it me."

"Here it is."

And the knife fell at Gaston's feet.

"Now, shall I send back the bell?"

"Yes; for my jailers might miss it to-morrow morning, and you do not want light for your conversation with Pompadour."

"No; certainly not."

And the bell was drawn up.

"Now," said the chevalier, "you must have something to drink with your sweets, and I will send you a bottle of champagne."

"Thank you," said Gaston, "do not deprive yourself of it; I do not care much for it."

"Then when you have made the hole, you shall pass it to Pompadour, who is of a very different opinion. Stay, here it is."

"Thank you, chevalier."

"Good-night."

"Good-night."

And the string ascended.

Gaston looked for the string at the window, and saw that it had disappeared.

"Ah," sighed he, "the Bastille would be a palace for me, if my poor Helene were in Mademoiselle de Launay's place."

Then he resumed a conversation with Pompadour, which lasted till three in the morning, and in which he told him that he was going to pierce a hole, that they might have more direct communication.

CHAPTER XXVIII.

A COMPANION IN THE BASTILLE.

Thus occupied, Gaston was more uneasy than ennuyé; besides, he found another source of amusement. Mademoiselle de Launay, who obtained whatever she liked from the lieutenant, Maison-Rouge, provided her request were only accompanied by a sweet smile, obtained paper and pens; she had sent some to Dumesnil, who had shared them with Gaston, with whom he still communicated, and with Richelieu, with whom also he managed to correspond. Then Gaston formed the idea of making some verses to Helene.

On his part, the Chevalier Dumesnil made some for Mademoiselle de Launay, who made them in return for him, so that the Bastille was a true Parnassus. There was only Richelieu who dishonored the society by writing prose.

Time passed, as it will pass, even in the Bastille.

Gaston was asked if he would like to attend mass, and as he was deeply religious, he had assented most gladly. The next day they came to fetch him.

The mass was celebrated in a little church, having, instead of chapels, separate closets, with bulls-eye windows into the choir, so that they could only see the officiating priest at the moment of elevation, and he could not see the prisoners at all.

Gaston saw M. de Laval and the Duc de Richelieu, who had apparently come to mass for the purpose of talking, for they knelt side by side, and kept up an incessant whispering. Monsieur de Laval appeared to have some important news to communicate, and kept looking at Gaston as though he were interested in it. As neither spoke to him, however, except in the way of mere salutation, he asked no questions.

When the mass was over, the prisoners were taken back. As they crossed a dark corridor, Gaston passed a man who seemed to be an employé of the house. This man sought Gaston's hand, and slipped a paper into it, which he put quietly into his waistcoat pocket.

When he was alone in his own room he eagerly took it out. It was written on sugar paper, with the point of a sharpened coal, and contained this line —"Feign illness from ennui."

It seemed to Gaston that the writing was not unknown to him, but it was so roughly traced that it was difficult to recognize. He waited for the evening impatiently, that he might consult with the Chevalier Dumesnil.

At night Gaston told him what had passed, asking him, as he had a longer acquaintance with the Bastille, what he thought of the advice of his unknown correspondent.

"Ma foi, though I do not understand the advice, I should follow it, for it cannot hurt you; the worse that can happen is, that they may give you less to eat."

"But," said Gaston, "suppose they discover the illness to be feigned."

"Oh! as to that," replied Dumesnil, "the doctor is entirely ignorant, and will give you whatever you may ask for; perhaps they will let you walk in the garden, and that would be a great amusement."

Gaston consulted Mademoiselle de Launay, whose advice, by logic or sympathy, was the same as that of the chevalier; but she added,

"If they diet you, let me know, and I will send you chicken, sweets, and Bordeaux."

Pompadour did not reply; the hole was not yet pierced.

Gaston then played the sick man, did not eat what they sent him, relying on his neighbor's liberality. At the end of the second day M. de Launay appeared —he had been told that Gaston was eating nothing, and he found the prisoner in bed.

"Monsieur," he said, "I fear you are suffering, and have come to see you."

"You are too good, monsieur," said Gaston; "it is true that I am suffering."

"What is the matter?"

"Ma foi, monsieur, I do not know that there is any amour propre here; I am ennuyé in this place."

"What, in four or five days?"

"From the first hour."

"What kind of ennui do you feel?"

"Are there several?"

"Certainly—one pines for his family."

"I have none."

"For his mistress."

Gaston sighed.

"For one's country."

"Yes," said Gaston, "it is that," seeing that he must say something.

The governor appeared to reflect.

"Monsieur," said he, "since I have been governor of the Bastille, my only agreeable moments have been those in which I have been of service to the gentlemen confided to my care by the king. I am ready to do anything for you if you will promise to be reasonable."

"I promise you, monsieur."

"I can put you in communication with one of your compatriots, or at least with a man who seems to know Bretagne perfectly."

"Is he a prisoner?"

"Like yourself."

A vague sentiment passed through Gaston's mind that it must be this man who had slipped the note into his hand. "I should be very grateful if you would do this," said he.

"Well, to-morrow you shall see him; but as I am recommended to be strict with him, you can only remain with him an hour, and as he may not quit his chamber, you must go to him."

"As you please, monsieur," said Gaston.

"Then it is decided; at five o'clock expect me or the major; but it is on one condition."

"What is it?"

"That in consideration of this distraction you will eat a little to-day."

"I will try."

Gaston eat a little chicken and drank a little wine to keep his promise.

In the evening he told Dumesnil what had passed.

"Ma foi," said he, "you are lucky; the Count de Laval had the same idea, and all he got was to be put into a room in the tower Du Tresor, where he said he was dreadfully dull, and had no amusement but speaking to the prison apothecary."

"Diable!" said Gaston, "why did you not tell me that before?"

"I had forgotten it."

This tardy recollection troubled Gaston somewhat; placed as he was between

Pompadour, Dumesnil, and Mademoiselle de Launay, his position was tolerable; if he were to be removed, he would be really attacked by the malady he had feigned.

At the appointed time the major of the Bastille came, and led Gaston across several courts, and they stopped at the tower Du Tresor. Every tower had its separate name.

In the room number one was a prisoner asleep on a folding bed, with his back turned to the light; the remains of his dinner were by him on a worn-out wooden table, and his costume, torn in many places, indicated a man of low station.

"Ouais," said Gaston, "did they think that I was so fond of Bretagne, that any fellows who happened to have been born at Nismes or at Penmarch may be raised to the rank of my Pylades? No, this fellow is too ragged, and seems to eat too much; but as one must not be too capricious in prison, let us make use of the hour—I will recount my adventure to Mademoiselle de Launay, and she will put it into verse for the Chevalier Dumesnil."

Gaston was now alone with the prisoner, who yawned and turned in his bed.

"Ugh! how cold it is in this cursed Bastille," said he, rubbing his nose.

"That voice, that gesture—it is he!" said Gaston, and he approached the bed.

"What," cried the prisoner, sitting up in bed, and looking at Gaston, "you here, M. de Chanlay?"

"Captain la Jonquiere," cried Gaston.

"Myself—that is to say, I am the person you name; but my name is changed."

"To what?"——"First Tresor."

"What?"

"First Tresor. It is a custom in the Bastille for the prisoner to take the name of his room—that saves the turnkey the trouble of remembering names; however, if the Bastille be full, and two or three prisoners in the same room, they take two numbers; for example: I am first Tresor, if you were put here you would be first Tresor number two; another would be first Tresor number three—the jailers have a kind of Latin literature for this."

"Yes, I understand," said Gaston, watching La Jonquiere intently; "then you are a prisoner?"

"Parbleu, you see for yourself; I presume we are neither of us here for pleasure."

"Then we are discovered."

"I am afraid so."

"Thanks to you."

"How to me?" cried La Jonquiere, feigning surprise. "No jokes, I beg."

"You have made revelations, traitor!"

"I! come, come, young man, you are mad; you ought not to be in the Bastille, but in the Petites Maisons."

"Do not deny it, M. d'Argenson told me!"

"D'Argenson; pardieu, the authority is good; and do you know what he told me?"

"No."

"That you had denounced me."

"Monsieur!"

"Well; what then? Are we to cut each other's throats because the police has followed out its trade and lied?"

"But how could he discover?"

"I ask the same of you. But one thing is certain; if I had told anything, I should not be here. You have not seen much of me, but you ought to know that I should not be fool enough to give information gratis; revelations are bought and sold, monsieur, and I know that Dubois pays high for them."

"Perhaps you are right," said Gaston; "but at least let us bless the chance which brings us together."

"Certainly."

"You do not appear enchanted, nevertheless."

"I am only moderately so, I confess."

"Captain!"

"Ah, monsieur, how bad-tempered you are."

"I?"

"Yes; you are always getting angry. I like my solitude; that does not speak."

"Monsieur!"

"Again. Now listen. Do you believe, as you say, that chance has brought us together?"

"What should it be?"

"Some combination of our jailers—of D'Argenson's, or perhaps Dubois's."

"Did you not write to me?"

"I?"

"Telling me to feign illness from ennui."

"And how should I have written?—on what?—by whom?"

Gaston reflected; and this time it was La Jonquiere who watched him.

"Then," said the captain presently, "I think, on the contrary, that it is to you we owe the pleasure of meeting in the Bastille."

"To me, monsieur?"

"Yes, chevalier; you are too confiding. I give you that information in case you leave here; but more particularly in case you remain here."

"Thank you."

"Have you noticed if you were followed?"

"No."

"A conspirator should never look before, but always behind him."

Gaston confessed that he had not taken this precaution.

"And the duke," asked La Jonquiere, "is he arrested?"

"I know not; I was going to ask you."

"Peste! that is disagreeable. You took a young woman to him?"

"You know that."

"Ah! my dear fellow, everything becomes known. Did not she give the information? Ah! woman, woman!"

"This was a brave girl, monsieur; I would answer for her discretion, courage, and devotion."

"Yes, I understand. We love her—so she is honey and gold. What an idea of a conspiracy you must have to take a woman to the chief of the plot!"

"But I told her nothing; and she could know no secrets of mine but such as she may have surprised."

"She has a keen eye."

"And if she knew my projects, I am convinced she would never have spoken."

"Oh, monsieur, without counting her natural disposition to that exercise, can we not always make a woman speak? Some one might have said, without any preparation 'Your love for M. de Chanlay will lose your head'—I will wager that she will speak."

"There is no danger—she loves me too much."

"That is the very reason, pardieu! that she would chatter like a magpie, and that we are both caged up. However, let us drop this. What do you do here?"

"Amuse myself."

"Amuse yourself—how?"

"With making verses, eating sweets, and making holes in the floor."

"Holes in the king's boards?" said La Jonquiere. "Oh, oh! that is good to know. Does not M. de Launay scold?"

"He does not know it; besides, I am not singular—everybody makes a hole in something; one his floor, the other his chimney, the next his wall. Do you not make holes in something?"

La Jonquiere looked to see if Gaston were not laughing at him.

"But now, monsieur," said La Jonquiere, "let us speak seriously. Are you condemned to death?"

"I?"

"Yes, you."

"You say that coolly."

"It is a habit in the Bastille. There are twenty here condemned to death, and not a bit the worse for it."

"I have been interrogated."

"Ah! you see."

"But I do not believe I am condemned."

"That will come."

"My dear captain, do you know that, although you do not look so, you are marvelously merry?"

"You think so?"

"Yes."

"Does it astonish you?"

"I did not know you were so brave."

"Then you would regret life?"

"I confess it; I only want one thing to make me happy, and that is to live."

"And you became a conspirator with a chance of happiness before you? I do not understand you; I thought people conspired from despair, as they marry when they have no other resource."

"When I joined the conspiracy I did not love."

"And afterward?"

"I would not draw back."

"Bravo! that is what I call character. Have you been tortured?"

"No; but I had a narrow escape."

"Then you will be."

"Why so?"

"Because I have been; and it would be unfair to treat us differently. Look at the state of my clothes."

"Which did they give you?" asked Gaston, shuddering at the recollection of what had passed between D'Argenson and himself.

"The water. They made me drink a barrel and a half; my stomach was like a bladder; I did not think I could have held so much."

"And did you suffer much?" asked Gaston, with interest.

"Yes; but my temperament is robust—the next day I thought no more of it. It is true that since then I have drunk a great deal of wine. If you have to choose, select the water—it cleans. All the mixtures doctors give us are only a means of making us swallow water. Fangon says the best doctor he ever heard of was Doctor Sangrado; he only existed in Le Sage's brain, or he would have done miracles."

"You know Fangon?" asked Gaston, surprised.

"By reputation; besides, I have read his works. But do you intend to persist in saying nothing?"

"Doubtless."

"You are right. I should tell you, if you regret life so much as you say, to whisper a few words to M. d'Argenson, but he is a talker who would reveal your confession."

"I will not speak, be assured; these are points on which I do not need strengthening."

"I believe it; pardieu! you seem to me like Sardanapalus in your tower. Here I have only M. de Laval, who takes medicine three times a day—it is an amusement he has invented. Well, tastes differ; and perhaps he wants to get accustomed to the water."

"But did you not say I should certainly be condemned?"

"Do you wish to know the whole truth?"

"Yes."

"Well, D'Argenson told me that you were."

Gaston turned pale, in spite of his courage. La Jonquiere remarked it.

"However," said he, "I believe you might save yourself by certain revelations."

"Why, do you think I should do what you refused?"

"Our characters and our positions are different—I am no longer young—I am not in love—I do not leave a mistress in tears." Gaston sighed.

"You see there is a great difference between us; when did you ever hear me sigh like that?"

"Ah! if I die, his excellency will take care of Helene."

"And if he be arrested?"

"You are right."

"Then—"

"God will protect her."

"Decidedly you are young," said La Jonquiere.

"Explain."

"Suppose his excellency be not arrested?"

"Well."

"What age is he?"

"Forty-five or six, I suppose."

"And if he fell in love with Helene; is not that her name?"

"The duke fall in love with her! he to whose protection I confided her! it would be infamous!"

"The world is full of infamy; that is how it gets on."

"Oh, I will not dwell on such a thought."

"I do not tell you to dwell on it; I only suggested it for you to make what use you liked of."

"Hush," said Gaston, "some one is coming."

"Have you asked for anything?"

"No."

"Then the time allowed for your visit is out," and La Jonquiere threw himself quickly on his bed.

The bolts creaked, the door opened, and the governor appeared.

"Well, monsieur," said he to Gaston; "does your companion suit you?"

"Yes, particularly as I know Captain la Jonquiere."

"That makes my task more delicate; but, however, I made you an offer, and I will not draw back. I will permit one visit daily, at any hour you please: shall it be morning or evening?"

Gaston looked at La Jonquiere.

"Say five in the evening," said La Jonquiere, quickly.

"In the evening at five o'clock, if you please."

"The same as to-day, then?"

"Yes."

"It shall be as you desire, monsieur."

Gaston and La Jonquiere exchanged a glance, and the chevalier was taken back to his chamber.

CHAPTER XXIX.

THE SENTENCE.

It was half-past six, and quite dark; the chevalier's first act on being left in his room was to run to the chimney.

"Chevalier," said he.

Dumesnil replied.

"I have paid my visit."

"Well?"

"I have found an acquaintance, if not a friend."

"A new prisoner."

"Of the same date as myself."

"His name?"

"Captain la Jonquiere."

"What?"

"Do you know him?"

"Yes!"

"Then do me a favor: what is he?"

"Oh, an enemy of the regent's."

"Are you sure?"

"Quite; he was in our conspiracy, and only withdrew because we preferred abduction to assassination."

"Then he was—?"

"For assassination."

"That is it," murmured Gaston; "he is a man to be trusted."

"If it be the same I mean, he lives in the Rue Bourdonnais, at the Muids d'Amour."

"The same."

"Then he is a safe man."

"That is well," said Gaston, "for he holds the lives of four brave gentlemen in his hands."

"Of whom you are one."

"No, I put myself aside, for it seems all is over with me."

"How all is over?"

"Yes, I am condemned."

"To what?"

"To death."

There was a moment's silence.

"Impossible!" cried the Chevalier Dumesnil, at length.

"Why impossible?"

"Because, if I be not mistaken, your affair is attached to ours."

"It follows on it."

"Well?"

"Well."

"Our affairs prospering, yours cannot go wrong."

"And who says you are prospering?"

"Listen, for with you I will have no secrets."

"I am listening."

"Mademoiselle de Launay wrote me this yesterday. She was walking with Maison-Rouge, who, as you know, loves her, and at whom we both laugh, but who is useful to us. On pretext of illness, she asked, as you did, for a doctor; he told her that the prison doctor was at her orders. I must tell you that we have known this doctor intimately; his name is Herment.

"However, she did not hope to get much out of him, for he is a timid man; but when he entered the garden, where she was walking, and gave her a consultation in the open air, he said to her, 'Hope!' In the mouth of any one else this would have been nothing—in his it was a vast deal; since *we* are told to hope, *you* have nothing to fear, as our affairs are intimately connected."

"However," said Gaston, "La Jonquiere seemed sure of what he said."

At this moment Pompadour knocked.

Gaston went to the hole, which, with the aid of his knife, he soon made practicable.

"Ask the Chevalier Dumesnil if he does not know anything more from Mademoiselle de Launay."

"About what?"

"One of us; I overheard some words between the governor and the major at my door—they were, 'condemned to death.'" Gaston shuddered.

"Be easy, marquis; I believe they spoke of me."

"Diable! that would not make me easy at all; firstly, because we have quickly become friends, and I should be grieved if anything were to happen to you; and, secondly, because what happened to you might well happen to us, our affairs being so similar."

"And you believe that Mademoiselle de Launay could remove your doubts."

"Yes, her windows look on the arsenal."

"Well."

"She would have seen if there were anything new going on there to-day."

"Ah! she is striking now!"

At that moment Mademoiselle de Launay struck two blows, which meant attention.

Gaston replied by one, which meant that he was listening.

Then he went to the window.

A minute after the string appeared with a letter.

Gaston took the letter, and went to the hole to Pompadour.

"Well?" said the marquis.

"A letter," replied Gaston.

"What does she say?"

"I cannot see, but I will send it to Dumesnil, who will read it."

"Make haste."

"Pardon," said Gaston, "I am as anxious as you;" and he ran to the chimney.

"The string," he cried.

"You have a letter."

"Yes; have you a light?"

"Yes."

"Lower the string."

Gaston tied on the letter, which was drawn up.

"It is for you and not for me," said Dumesnil.

"Never mind, read it, and tell me what it is; I have no light, and it would lose time to send me one."

MADEMOISELLE DE LAUNAY.—*Page* 538.

Link to larger image

"You permit me?"

"Certainly."

A moment's silence.

"Well," said Gaston.

"Diable!"

"Bad news, is it not?"

"Judge for yourself."

And Dumesnil read:

"MY DEAR NEIGHBOR—Some judge extraordinary has arrived at the arsenal this evening. I recognized D'Argenson's livery. We shall know more soon, when I see the doctor. A thousand remembrances to Dumesnil."

"That is what La Jonquiere told me; it is I that am condemned."

"Bah, chevalier," said Dumesnil; "you are too easily alarmed."

"Not at all. I know well what to think, and then—hark!"

"What!"

"Silence; some one is coming." And Gaston went away from the chimney.

The door opened, and the major and lieutenant, with four soldiers, came for Gaston, who followed them.

"I am lost," murmured he. "Poor Helene."

And he raised his head with the intrepidity of a brave man, who, knowing death was near, went boldly to meet it.

"Monsieur," said D'Argenson, "your crime has been examined by the tribunal of which I am the president. In the preceding sittings you were permitted to defend yourself; if you were not granted advocates, it was not with the intention of inquiring your defense, but, on the contrary, because it was useless to give you the extreme indulgence of a tribunal charged to be severe."

"I do not understand you."

"Then I will be more explicit. Discussion would have made one thing evident, even in the eyes of your defenders—that you are a conspirator and an assassin. How could you suppose that with these points established indulgence would be shown you. But here you are before us, every facility will be given for your justification. If you ask a delay, you shall have it. If you wish researches, they shall be made. If you speak, you have the reply, and it will not be refused you."

"I understand, and thank the tribunal for this kindness," replied Gaston. "The excuse it gives me for the absence of a defender seems sufficient. I have not to defend myself."

"Then you do not wish for witnesses, delays, or documents?"

"I wish my sentence—that is all."

"Do not be obstinate, chevalier; make some confessions."

"I have none to make, for in all my interrogatories you have not made one precise accusation."

"And you wish—?"

"Certainly—I should like to know of what I am accused."

"I will tell you. You came to Paris, appointed by the republican committee of Nantes, to assassinate the regent. You were referred to one La Jonquiere, your accomplice, now condemned with you."

Gaston felt that he turned pale at these true accusations. "This might be true, monsieur," said he, "but you could not know it. A man who wishes to commit such a deed does not confess it till it be accomplished."

"No; but his accomplices confess for him."

"That is to say, that La Jonquiere denounces me."

"I do not refer to La Jonquiere, but the others."

"The others!" cried Gaston; "are there, then, others arrested beside La Jonquiere and myself?"

"Yes. Messieurs de Pontcalec, de Talhouet, du Couëdic, and de Montlouis."

"I do not understand," said Gaston, with a vague feeling of terror—not for himself, but for his friends.

"What! do you not understand that Messieurs de Pontcalec, de Talhouet, du Couëdic, and de Montlouis are now being tried at Nantes?"

"Arrested!" cried Gaston, "impossible!"

"Yes," said D'Argenson, "you thought that the province would revolt rather than allow its defenders—as you rebels call yourselves—to be arrested. Well, the province has said nothing. The province has gone on singing, laughing, and dancing, and is already asking where they will be beheaded, in order to hire windows."

"I do not believe you, monsieur," said Gaston, coldly.

"Give me that portfolio," said D'Argenson to a man standing behind him. "Here, monsieur," continued he, "are the writs of arrest. Do you doubt their authenticity?"

"That does not say that they have accused me."

"They told all we wanted to know, and your culpability is the result."

"In that case, if they have told all you want to know, you have no need of my confession."

"Is that your final answer?"

"Yes."

"Officer, read the sentence."

The officer read—

"As the result of the investigation commenced on the 19th of February, that M. Gaston de Chanlay came from Nantes to Paris with the intention of committing the crime of murder on the person of his Royal Highness Monseigneur the Regent of France, which was to have been followed by a revolt against the authority of the king, the extraordinary commission instituted to inquire into this crime has adjudged the Chevalier Gaston de Chanlay worthy of the punishment for high treason, the person of the regent being as inviolable as that of the king. In consequence—We ordain that the Chevalier Gaston de Chanlay be degraded from all his titles and dignities; that he and his posterity be declared ignoble in perpetuity; that his goods be confiscated, his woods cut down to the height of six feet from the ground, and he himself beheaded on the Greve, or wheresoever it shall please the provost to appoint, saving his majesty's pardon."

Gaston was pale, but still as marble.

"And when am I to be executed?" asked he.

"As soon as it may please his majesty."

Gaston felt a cloud pass before his eyes, and his ideas became confused; but this soon vanished, and the serenity of his bearing returned, the blood rushed back to his cheeks, and a contemptuous smile settled on his lips.

"It is well, monsieur," said he; "at whatever moment his majesty's order may arrive, it will find me prepared; but I wish to know whether I may not see some persons who are very dear to me before I die, and I wish to ask a favor of the king."

D'Argenson's eyes glistened with malignant joy. "Monsieur," said he, "I told you that you would be treated with indulgence. You might therefore have spoken sooner, and perhaps his highness's kindness might not have waited for a prayer."

"You mistake me, monsieur," said Gaston, with dignity; "neither his majesty's honor nor mine will suffer from the favor which I shall ask."

"What would you ask?" said D'Argenson; "speak, and I will tell you at once if there be a chance of your request being granted."

"I ask, first, that my titles and dignities—which are not very great—should not be canceled, as I have no posterity. I am alone in the world; my name only survives me; but as that name is only noble, and not illustrious, it would not survive long."

"This is quite a royal favor, monsieur. His majesty alone can and will reply. Is that all you wish to ask?"

"No; I have another request to make, but I do not know to whom I should apply."

"First to me, monsieur, in my character of lieutenant of police. I shall see if I can grant it, or if I must refer it to his majesty."

"Well, then, monsieur, I desire to see Mademoiselle Helene de Chaverny, ward of his excellency the Duc d'Olivares, and also the duke himself."

D'Argenson, at this request, made a singular gesture, which Gaston interpreted as one of hesitation.

"Monsieur," said Gaston, "I would see them in any place, and for as short a time as may be thought advisable."

"You shall see them," said D'Argenson.

"Ah! monsieur," said Gaston, stepping forward as though to take his hand, "you lay me under the greatest obligation."

"On one condition, however, monsieur."

"What is it? there is no condition compatible with my honor that I will not accept in exchange for so great a favor."

"You must tell no one of your condemnation, and this on your word as a gentleman."

"I accede to that all the more willingly," said Gaston, "as one of the persons named would certainly die if she knew of it."

"Then all is well; have you anything further to say?"

"Nothing, monsieur, except to beg that you will record my denials."

"They are already firmly attached—officer, hand the papers to Monsieur de Chanlay, that he may read and sign them."

Gaston sat down by a table, and, while D'Argenson and the judges chatted around him, he carefully perused the papers and the report of his own answers to the interrogatory—then, finding all correct, he signed.

"Monsieur," said he, "here are the documents. Shall I have the pleasure of seeing you again?"

"I do not think so," said D'Argenson, with that brutality which was the terror of those who were subjected to him.

"Then to our meeting in another world, monsieur."

The major led Gaston to his own room.

CHAPTER XXX.

THE FAMILY FEUD.

When Gaston returned to his room, he was obliged to answer the questions of Dumesnil and Pompadour, who were waiting to hear news from him; but, in compliance with his promise made to D'Argenson, he did not mention his sentence, but simply announced a severer interrogatory than before—but as he wished to write some letters, he asked Dumesnil for a light. Dumesnil sent him a candle—things were progressing, it may be remarked; Maison-Rouge could refuse nothing to Mademoiselle de Launay, and she shared all with Dumesnil, who, in his turn, again shared with his neighbors, Gaston and Richelieu.

Gaston doubted whether, in spite of D'Argenson's promise, he would be allowed to see Helene, but he knew that at least he should see a priest before he died; there could be no doubt that the priest would forward two letters for him.

As he began to write, Mademoiselle de Launay made a signal that she had something to send him; it was a letter. Gaston read:

"Our friend—for you are our friend, and now we have no secrets from you— tell Dumesnil of the famous hope I conceived after the word that Herment said to me."

Gaston's heart beat. Might not he also find in this letter some ground for hope? Had they not said that his fate could not be separated from the others? It is true that those who had said so did not know of his conspiracy. He read on:

"An hour ago the doctor came, accompanied by Maison-Rouge; from the latter's manner I drew the most favorable augury; however, when I asked to speak in private, or, at least, to whisper to the doctor, he made some difficulties, which I removed with a smile. 'At least,' said he, 'no one must know that I am out of hearing. I should lose my place if it were known how weak I am.' This tone of love and interest combined seemed to me so grotesque that I laughingly promised him what he asked; you see how I keep my promise. He went to a distance, and Herment approached. Then commenced a dialogue, wherein the gestures meant one thing while the voice declared another. 'You have good friends,' said Herment; 'friends in good places, who are greatly interested for you.' I naturally thought of Madame de

Maine. 'Ah, monsieur,' I cried, 'have you anything for me?' 'Hush,' said Herment. Judge how my heart beat."

Gaston felt his own beating vigorously.

"'And what have you to give me?' 'Oh, nothing myself: but you will have the object agreed upon.' 'But what is the object? Speak!' 'The beds in the Bastille are known to be bad, and particularly badly covered, and I am commissioned to offer you—' 'What?' 'A coverlet.' I burst out laughing; the devotion of my friends was shown in preventing my catching cold. 'My dear Monsieur Herment,' said I, 'in my present position it would be better if my friends were to occupy themselves less about my feet and more about my head.' 'It is a female friend,' said he. 'Who is it?' 'Mademoiselle de Charolais,' said Herment, lowering his voice, so that I could scarcely hear him. Then he withdrew. I, my dear chevalier, am now waiting for Mademoiselle de Charolais's coverlet. Tell this to Dumesnil; it will make him laugh."

Gaston sighed. The gayety of those around him weighed heavily on his heart. It was a new torture which they had invented, in forbidding him to confide his fate to any one; it seemed to him that he should have found consolation in the tears of his two neighbors. He had not the courage to read the letter to Dumesnil, so he passed it on to him, and a moment after heard shouts of laughter.

At this moment Gaston was saying adieu to Helene.

After passing a part of the night in writing, he slept; at five-and-twenty one must sleep, even if it be just before death.

In the morning Gaston's breakfast was brought at the usual hour, but he remarked that it was more *recherché* than usual; he smiled at this attention, and as he was finishing, the governor entered.

Gaston with a rapid glance interrogated his expression, which was calm and courteous as ever. Was he also ignorant of the sentence, or was he wearing a mask?

"Monsieur," said he, "will you take the trouble to descend to the council-chamber?"

Gaston rose. He seemed to hear a buzzing in his ears, for to a man condemned to death every injunction which he does not understand is a torture.

"May I know the reason, monsieur?" asked Gaston, in so calm a tone that it was impossible to detect his real emotion.

"To receive a visit," replied the governor. "Yesterday, after the interrogatory, did you not ask the lieutenant of police to be allowed to see some one?"

Gaston started.

"And is it that person?" asked he.

"Yes, monsieur."

Gaston had asked for two persons; the governor only announced one; which one was it? He had not the courage to ask, and silently followed the governor.

De Launay led Gaston to the council-chamber; on entering, he cast an eager glance around, but the room was empty.

"Remain here, monsieur; the person whom you expect is coming," said the governor, who bowed and went out.

Gaston ran to the window, which was barred, and looked out—there was a sentinel before it.

The door opened, and Gaston, turning round, faced the Duc d'Olivares.

"Ah, monsieur," cried he, "how good of you to come at the request of a poor prisoner."

"It was a duty," replied the duke, "besides, I had to thank you."

"Me!" said Gaston, astonished; "what have I done to merit your excellency's thanks?"

"You have been interrogated, taken to the torture-chamber, given to understand that you might save yourself by naming your accomplices, and yet you kept silence."

"I made an engagement and kept it: that does not deserve any thanks, monseigneur."

"And now, monsieur, tell me if I can serve you in anything."

"First, tell me about yourself; have you been molested, monseigneur?"

"Not at all: and if all the Bretons are as discreet as you, I doubt not that my name will never be mentioned in these unfortunate debates."

"Oh, I will answer for them as for myself, monseigneur; but can you answer for La Jonquiere?"

"La Jonquiere!" repeated the duke.

"Yes. Do you not know that he is arrested?"

"Yes; I heard something of it."

"Well, I ask you, monseigneur, what you think of him?"

"I can tell you nothing, except that he has *my* confidence."

"If so, he must be worthy of it, monseigneur. That is all I wished to know."

"Then come to the request you had to make."

"Have you seen the young girl I brought to your house?"

"Mademoiselle Helene de Chaverny? Yes."

"Well, monsieur, I had not time to tell you then, but I tell you now, that I have loved her for a year. The dream of that year has been to consecrate my life to her happiness. I say the dream, monseigneur; for, on awaking, I saw that all hope of happiness was denied me; and yet, to give this young girl a name, a position, a fortune, at the moment of my arrest, she was about to become my wife."

"Without the knowledge of her parents or the consent of her family?" cried the duke.

"She had neither, monseigneur; and was probably about to be sold to some nobleman when she left the person who had been set to watch her."

"But who informed you that Mademoiselle Helene de Chaverny was to be the victim of a shameful bargain?"

"What she herself told me of a pretended father, who concealed himself; of diamonds which had been offered to her. Then, do you know where I found her, monseigneur? In one of those houses destined to the pleasures of our roués. She! an angel of innocence and purity. In short, monseigneur, this young girl fled with me, in spite of the cries of her duenna, in broad daylight, and in the face of the servants who surrounded her. She stayed two hours alone with me; and, though she is as pure as on the day when she received her mother's first kiss, she is not the less compromised. I wish this projected marriage to take place."

"In your situation, monsieur?"

"A still greater reason."

"But perhaps you may deceive yourself as to the punishment reserved for you!"

"It is probably the same which, under similar circumstances, was inflicted on the Count de Chalais, the Marquis de Cinq-Mars, and the Chevalier Louis de Rohan."

"Then you are prepared even for death, monsieur?"

"I prepared for it from the day I joined the conspiracy: the conspirator's only excuse is, that, while robbing others of their lives, he risks his own."

"And what will this young girl gain by the marriage?"

"Monseigneur, though not rich, I have some fortune; she is poor; I have a name, and she has none. I would leave her my name and fortune; and with that intention I have already petitioned the king that my goods may not be confiscated, nor my name declared infamous. Were it known for what reason I ask this, it would doubtless be granted; if I die without making her my wife, she will be supposed to be my mistress, and will be dishonored, lost, and there will be no future for her. If, on the contrary, by your protection, or that of your friends (and that protection I earnestly implore), we are united, no one can reproach her—the blood which flows for a political offense does not disgrace a family—no shame will fall on my widow; and if she cannot be happy, she will at least be independent and respected. This is the favor which I have to ask, monseigneur; is it in your power to obtain it for me?"

The duke went to the door and struck three blows: Maison-Rouge appeared.

"Ask M. de Launay, from me," said the duke, "whether the young girl who is at the door in my carriage may come in? Her visit, as he knows, is authorized. You will have the kindness to conduct her here."

"What! monseigneur; Helene is here—at the door?"

"Were you not promised that she should come?"

"Yes; but seeing you alone, I lost all hope."

"I wished to see you first, thinking that you might have many things to say which you would not wish her to hear; for I know all."

"You know all! What do you mean?"

"I know that you were taken to the arsenal yesterday!"

"Monseigneur!"

"I know that you found D'Argenson there, and that he read your sentence."

"Mon Dieu!"

"I know that you are condemned to death, and that you were bound not to speak of it to any one."

"Oh, monseigneur, silence! One word of this would kill Helene."

"Be easy, monsieur; but let us see; is there no way of avoiding this execution?"

"Days would be necessary to prepare and execute a plan of escape, and I scarcely have hours."

"I do not speak of escape; I ask if you have no excuse to give for your crime?"

"My crime!" cried Gaston, astonished to hear his accomplice use such a word.

"Yes," replied the duke: "you know that men stigmatize murder with this name under all circumstances; but posterity often judges differently, and sometimes calls it a grand deed."

"I have no excuse to give, monseigneur, except that I believe the death of the regent to be necessary to the salvation of France."

"Yes," replied the duke, smiling; "but you will see that that is scarcely the excuse to offer to Philippe d'Orleans. I wanted something personal. Political enemy of the regent's as I am, I know that he is not considered a bad man. Men say that he is merciful, and that there have been no executions during his reign."

"You forget Count Horn."

"He was an assassin."

"And what am I?"

"There is this difference: Count Horn murdered in order to rob."

"I neither can nor will ask anything of the regent," said Gaston.

"Not you, personally, I know; but your friends. If they had a plausible pretense to offer, perhaps the prince himself might pardon you."

"I have none, monseigneur."

"It is impossible, monsieur—permit me to say so. A resolution such as you have taken must proceed from a sentiment of some kind—either of hatred or vengeance. And stay; I remember you told La Jonquiere, who repeated it to me, that there was a family feud: tell me the cause."

"It is useless, monseigneur, to tire you with that; it would not interest you."

"Never mind, tell it me."

"Well, the regent killed my brother."

"The regent killed your brother! how so? it is—impossible, Monsieur de Gaston," said the Duc d'Olivares.

"Yes, killed; if from the effect we go to the cause."

"Explain yourself; how could the regent do this?"

"My brother, who, being fifteen years of age when my father died, three months before my birth, stood to me in the place of that father, and of mother, who died when I was still in the cradle—my brother loved a young girl who was brought up in a convent by the orders of the prince."

"Do you know in what convent?"

"No: I only know that it was at Paris."

The duke murmured some words which Gaston could not hear.

"My brother, a relation of the abbess, had seen this young girl and asked her hand in marriage. The prince's consent to this union had been asked, and he made a pretense of granting it, when this young girl, seduced by her so-called protector, suddenly disappeared. For three months my brother hoped to find her, but all his searches were vain; he found no trace of her, and in despair he sought death in the battle of Ramillies."

"And what was the name of this girl!"

"No one ever knew, monseigneur; to speak her name was to dishonor it."

"It was doubtless she," murmured the duke, "it was Helene's mother; and your brother was called—?" added he aloud.

"Olivier de Chanlay, monseigneur."

"Olivier de Chanlay!" repeated the duke, in a low voice. "I knew the name of De Chanlay was not strange to me." Then, aloud, "Continue, monsieur; I listen to you."

"You do not know what a family hatred is in a province like ours. I had lavished upon my brother all the love which would have fallen to the share of my father and mother, and now I suddenly found myself alone in the world. I grew up in isolation of heart, and in the hope of revenge; I grew up among people who were constantly repeating, 'It was the Duc d'Orleans who killed your brother.' Then the duke became regent, the Breton league was therefore organized. I was one of the first to join it. You know the rest. You see that there is nothing in all this which has any interest for your excellency."

"You mistake, monsieur; unfortunately, the regent has to reproach himself with many such faults."

"You see, therefore," said Gaston, "that my destiny must be accomplished, and that I can ask nothing of this man."

"You are right, monsieur; whatever is done must be done without you."

At this moment the door opened and Maison-Rouge appeared.

"Well, monsieur?" asked the duke.

"The governor has an order from the lieutenant of police to admit Mademoiselle Helene de Chaverny; shall I bring her here?"

"Monseigneur," said Gaston, looking at the duke with an air of entreaty.

"Yes, monsieur," said he, "I understand—grief and love do not need witnesses —I will come back to fetch Mademoiselle Helene."

"The permission is for half an hour," said Maison-Rouge.

"Then at the end of that time I will return," said the duke, and bowing to Gaston, he went out.

An instant after the door opened again, and Helene appeared, trembling, and questioning Maison-Rouge, but he retired without replying.

Helene looked round and saw Gaston, and for a few minutes all their sorrows were forgotten in a close and passionate embrace. "And now—" cried Helene, her face bathed in tears.

"Well! and now?" asked Gaston.

"Alas! to see you here—in prison," murmured Helene, with an air of terror, "here, where I dare not speak freely, where we may be watched—overheard."

"Do not complain, Helene, for this is an exception in our favor; a prisoner is never allowed to press one who is dear to him to his heart; the visitor generally stands against that wall, the prisoner against this, a soldier is placed between, and the conversation must be fixed beforehand."

"To whom do we owe this favor?"

"Doubtless to the regent; for yesterday, when I asked permission of Monsieur d'Argenson, he said that it was beyond his power to grant, and that he must refer it to the regent."

"But now that I see you again, Gaston, tell me all that has passed in this age of tears and suffering. Ah! tell me; but my presentiments did not deceive me; you were conspiring—do not deny it—I know it."

"Yes; Helene, you know that we Bretons are constant both in our loves and our hatreds. A league was organized in Bretagne, in which all our nobles took part—could I act differently from my brothers? I ask you, Helene, could I, or ought I to have done so? Would you not have despised me, if, when you had seen all Bretagne under arms, I alone had been inactive—a whip in my hand while others held the sword?"

"Oh! yes; you are right; but why did you not remain in Bretagne with the others?"

"The others are arrested also, Helene."

"Then you have been denounced—betrayed."

"Probably—but sit down, Helene; now that we are alone, let me look at you, and tell you that you are beautiful, that I love you. How have you been in my absence—has the duke—"

"Oh! if you only knew how good he is to me; every evening he comes to see me, and his care and attention—"

"And," said Gaston, who thought of the suggestion of the false La Jonquiere, "nothing suspicious in those attentions?"

"What do you mean, Gaston?"

"That the duke is still young, and that, as I told you just now, you are beautiful."

"Oh, Heaven! no! Gaston; this time there is not a shadow of doubt; and when he was there near me—as near as you are now—there were moments when it seemed as if I had found my father."

"Poor child!"

"Yes, by a strange chance, for which I cannot account, there is a resemblance between the duke's voice and that of the man who came to see me at Rambouillet—it struck me at once."

"You think so?" said Gaston, in an abstracted tone.

"What are you thinking of, Gaston?" asked Helene; "you seem scarcely to hear what I am saying to you."

"Helene, every word you speak goes to the inmost depth of my heart."

"You are uneasy, I understand. To conspire is to stake your life; but be easy, Gaston—I have told the duke that if you die I shall die too."

Gaston started.

"You are an angel," said he.

"Oh, my God!" cried poor Helene, "how horrible to know that the man I love runs a danger—all the more terrible for being uncertain; to feel that I am powerless to aid him, and that I can only shed tears when I would give my life to save him."

Gaston's face lit up with a flush of joy; it was the first time that he had ever heard such words from the lips of his beloved; and under the influence of an idea which had been occupying him for some minutes—

215

"Yes, dearest," said he, taking her hand, "you can do much for me."

"What can I do?"

"You can become my wife."

Helene started.

"I your wife, Gaston?" cried she.

"Yes, Helene; this plan, formed in our liberty, may be executed in captivity. Helene, my wife before God and man, in this world and the next, for time and for eternity. You can do this for me, Helene, and am I not right in saying that you can do much?"

"Gaston," said she, looking at him fixedly, "you are hiding something from me."

It was Gaston's turn to start now.

"I!" said he, "what should I conceal from you?"

"You told me you saw M. d'Argenson yesterday?"

"Well, what then?"

"Well, Gaston," said Helene, turning pale, "you are condemned."

Gaston took a sudden resolution.

"Yes," said he, "I am condemned to exile; and, egotist as I am, I would bind you to me by indissoluble ties before I leave France."

"Is that the truth, Gaston?"

"Yes; have you the courage to be my wife, Helene? to be exiled with me?"

"Can you ask it, Gaston?" said she, her eyes lighted with enthusiasm, "exile— I thank thee, my God—I, who would have accepted an eternal prison with you, and have thought myself blessed—I may accompany, follow you? Oh, this condemnation is, indeed, a joy after what we feared! Gaston, Gaston, at length we shall be happy."

"Yes, Helene," said Gaston, with an effort.

"Picture my happiness," cried Helene; "to me France is the country where you are; your love is the only country I desire. I know I shall have to teach you to forget Bretagne, your friends, and your dreams of the future; but I will love you, so that it will be easy for you to forget them."

Gaston could do nothing but cover her hands with kisses.

"Is the place of your exile fixed?" said she; "tell me, when do you go? shall we go together?"

"My Helene," replied Gaston, "it is impossible; we must be separated for a time. I shall be taken to the frontier of France—I do not as yet know, which—and set free. Once out of the kingdom, you shall rejoin me."

"Oh, better than that, Gaston—better than that. By means of the duke I will discover the place of your exile, and instead of joining you there, I will be there to meet you. As you step from the carriage which brings you, you shall find me waiting to soften the pain of your adieux to France; and then, death alone is irretrievable; later, the king may pardon you; later still, and the action punished to-day may be looked upon as a deed to be rewarded. Then we will return; then nothing need keep us from Bretagne, the cradle of our love, the paradise of our memories. Oh!" continued she, in an accent of mingled love and impatience, "tell me, Gaston, that you share my hopes, that you are content, that you are happy."

"Yes, Helene, I now am happy, indeed; for now—and only now—I know by what an angel I am beloved. Yes, dearest, one hour of such love as yours, and then death would be better than a whole life with the love of any other."

"Well!" exclaimed Helene, her whole mind and soul earnestly fixed on the new future which was opening before her, "what will they do? Will they let me see you again before your departure? When and how shall we meet next? Shall you receive my letters? Can you reply to them? What hour to-morrow may I come?"

"They have almost promised me that our marriage shall take place this evening or to-morrow morning."

"What! here in a prison," said Helene, shuddering involuntarily.

"Wherever it may be, Helene, it will bind us together for the rest of our lives."

"But suppose they do not keep their promise to you; suppose they make you set out before I have seen you?"

"Alas!" said Gaston, with a bursting heart, "that is possible, Helene, and it is that I dread."

"Oh, mon Dieu! do you think your departure is so near?"

"You know, Helene, that prisoners are not their own masters; they may be removed at any moment."

"Oh, let them come—let them come; the sooner you are free, the sooner we shall be reunited. It is not necessary that I should be your wife, in order to follow and join you. Do I not know my Gaston's honor, and from this day I look upon him as my husband before God. Oh, go proudly, Gaston, for while these thick and gloomy walls surround you I tremble for your life. Go, and in a week we shall be reunited; reunited, with no separation to threaten us, no one to act as a spy on us—reunited forever."

The door opened.

"Great Heaven, already!" said Helene.

"Madame," said the lieutenant, "the time has elapsed."

"Helene," said Gaston, seizing the young girl's hand, with a nervous trembling which he could not master.

"What is it?" cried she, watching him with terror. "Good Heaven! you are as pale as marble."

"It is nothing," said he, forcing himself to be calm; "indeed, it is nothing," and he kissed her hand.

"Till to-morrow, Gaston."

"To-morrow—yes."

The duke appeared at the door; Gaston ran to him.

"Monseigneur," said he, "do all in your power to obtain permission for her to become my wife; but if that be impossible, swear to me that she shall be your daughter."

The duke pressed Gaston's hand; he was so affected that he could not speak.

Helene approached. Gaston was silent, fearing she might overhear.

He held out his hand to Helene, who presented her forehead to him, while silent tears rolled down her cheeks; Gaston closed his eyes, that the sight of her tears might not call up his own.

At length they must part. They exchanged one last lingering glance, and the duke pressed Gaston's hand.

How strange was this sympathy between two men, one of whom had come so far for the sole purpose of killing the other.

The door closed, and Gaston sank down on a seat, utterly broken and exhausted.

In ten minutes the governor entered; he came to conduct Gaston back to his own room.

Gaston followed him silently, and when asked if there was anything he wanted, he mournfully shook his head.

At night Mademoiselle de Launay signaled that she had something to communicate.

Gaston opened the window, and received a letter inclosing another.

The first was for himself.

He read:

"DEAR NEIGHBOR—The coverlid was not so contemptible as I supposed; it contained a paper on which was written the word already spoken by Herment —'Hope!' It also inclosed this letter for M. de Richelieu; send it to Dumesnil, who will pass it to the duke.

"Your servant,

"DE LAUNAY."

"Alas!" thought Gaston, "they will miss me when I am gone," and he called Dumesnil, to whom he passed the letter.

CHAPTER XXXI.

STATE AFFAIRS AND FAMILY AFFAIRS.

On leaving the Bastille, the duke took Helene home, promising to come and see her as usual in the evening; a promise which Helene would have estimated all the more highly if she had known that his highness had a bal masque at Monceaux.

On re-entering the Palais Royal the duke asked for Dubois, and was told he was in his study, working. The duke entered without allowing himself to be announced. Dubois was so busy that he did not hear the duke, who advanced and looked over his shoulder, to see what was occupying him so intently.

He was writing down names, with notes by the side of each.

"What are you doing there, abbe?" asked the regent.

"Ah! monseigneur, it is you; pardon; I did not hear you."

"I asked what you were doing?"

"Signing the burial tickets for our Breton friends."

"But their fate is not yet decided, and the sentence of the commission—"

"I know it," said Dubois.

"Is it given, then?"

"No, but I dictated it before they went."

"Do you know that your conduct is odious?"

"Truly, monseigneur, you are insupportable. Manage your family affairs, and leave state affairs to me."

"Family affairs!"

"Ah! as to those, I hope you are satisfied with me, or you would indeed be difficult to please. You recommend to me M. de Chanlay, and on your recommendation I make it a rose-water Bastille to him; sumptuous repasts, a charming governor. I let him pierce holes in your floors, and spoil your walls, all which will cost us a great deal to repair. Since his entrance, it is quite a fete. Dumesnil talks all day through his chimney, Mademoiselle de Launay fishes with a line through her window, Pompadour drinks champagne. There is nothing to be said to all this: these are your family affairs; but in Bretagne you have nothing to see, and I forbid you to look, monseigneur, unless you have a few more unknown daughters there, which is possible."

"Dubois! scoundrel!"

"Ah! you think when you have said 'Dubois,' and added 'scoundrel' to my name, you have done everything. Well, scoundrel as much as you please; meanwhile, but for the scoundrel you would have been assassinated."

"Well, what then?"

"What then! Hear the statesman! Well, then, I should be hanged, perhaps, which is a consideration; then Madame de Maintenon would be regent of France! What a joke! What then, indeed! To think that a philosophic prince should utter such naïvetés! Oh, Marcus Aurelius! was it not he who said, 'Populos esse demum felices si reges philosophi forent, aut philosophi reges?' Here is a sample."

Dubois still wrote on.

"Dubois! you do not know this young man."

"What young man?"

"The chevalier."

"Really! you shall present him to me when he is your son-in-law."

"That will be to-morrow, Dubois."

The abbe looked round in astonishment, and looking at the regent, with his little eyes as wide open as possible—

"Ah, monseigneur, are you mad?" he said.

"No, but he is an honorable man, and you know that they are rare."

"Honorable man! Ah, you have a strange idea of honor."

"Yes; I believe that we differ in our ideas of it."

"What has this honorable man done! Has he poisoned the dagger with which he meant to assassinate you? for then he would be more than an honorable man, he would be a saint. We have already St. Jacques Clement, St. Ravaillac; St. Gaston is wanting in the calendar. Quick, quick, monseigneur! you who will not ask the pope to give a cardinal's hat to your minister, ask him to canonize your assassin; and for the first time in your life you would be logical."

"Dubois, I tell you there are few capable of doing what this young man has done."

"Peste! that is lucky; if there were ten in France I should certainly resign."

"I do not speak of what he wished to do, but of what he has done."

"Well, what has he done? I should like to be edified."

"First, he kept his oath to D'Argenson."

"I doubt it not, he is faithful to his word; and but for me would have kept his word also with Pontcalec, Talhouet, etc."

"Yes, but one was more difficult than the other. He had sworn not to mention his sentence to any one, and he did not speak of it to his mistress."

"Nor to you?"

"He spoke of it to me, because I told him that I knew it. He forbade me to ask anything of the regent, desiring, he said, but one favor."

"And that one?"

"To marry Helene, in order to leave her a fortune and a name."

"Good; he wants to leave your daughter a fortune and a name; he is polite, at least."

"Do you forget that this is a secret from him?"

"Who knows?"

"Dubois, I do not know in what your hands were steeped the day you were born, but I know that you sully everything you touch."

"Except conspirators, monseigneur, for it seems to me that there, on the contrary, I purify. Look at those of Cellamare, how all that affair was cleared out; Dubois here, Dubois there, I hope the apothecary has properly purged France from Spain. Well, it shall be the same with Olivares as with Cellamare. There is now only Bretagne congested; a good dose, and all will be right."

"Dubois, you would joke with the Gospel."

"Pardieu! I began by that."

The regent rose.

"Come, monseigneur, I was wrong; I forgot you were fasting; let us hear the end of this story."

"The end is that I promised to ask this favor from the regent, and that the regent will grant it."

"The regent will commit a folly."

"No, he will only repair a fault."

"Ah, now you find you have a reparation to make to M. de Chanlay."

"Not to him, but to his brother."

"Still better. What have you done to his brother?"

"I took from him the woman he loved."

"Who?"——"Helene's mother."

"Well, that time you were wrong; for if you had let her alone we should not have had all this tiresome affair on our hands."

"But we have it, and must now get out of it as well as possible."

"Just what I am working at: and when is the marriage to take place?"

"To-morrow."

"In the chapel of the Palais Royal? You shall dress in the costume of a knight of the order; you shall extend both hands over your son-in-law's head—one more than he meant to have held over you—it will be very affecting."

"No, abbe, it shall not be thus; they shall be married in the Bastille, and I shall be in the chapel where they cannot see me."

"Well, monseigneur, I should like to be with you. I should like to see the ceremony; I believe these kind of things are very touching."

"No, you would be in the way, and your ugly face would betray my incognito."

"Your handsome face is still more easy to recognize, monseigneur," said Dubois, bowing; "there are portraits of Henry the Fourth and Louis the Fourteenth in the Bastille."

"You flatter me."

"Are you going away, monseigneur?"

"Yes, I have an appointment with De Launay."

"The governor of the Bastille?"

"Yes."

"Go, monseigneur, go."

"Shall I see you to-night at Morceaux?"

"Perhaps."

"Have you a disguise?"

"I have La Jonquière's dress."

"Oh! that is only fit for the Rue du Bac."

223

"Monseigneur forgets the Bastille, where it has had some success."

"Well, adieu, abbe."

"Adieu, monseigneur."

When Dubois was left alone he appeared to take some sudden resolution. He rang the bell, and a servant entered.

"M. de Launay is coming to the regent, watch him, and bring him here afterward."

The servant retired without a reply, and Dubois resumed his work.

Half an hour afterward the door opened, and the servant announced De Launay. Dubois gave him a note.

"Read that," said he; "I give you written instructions, that there may be no pretext for neglecting them."

"Ah, monseigneur," said De Launay, "you would ruin me.".

"How so?"

"To-morrow when it becomes known."

"Who will tell it? will you?"

"No, but monseigneur—"

"Will be enchanted; I answer for him."

"A governor of the Bastille!"

"Do you care to retain the title?"

"Certainly."

"Then do as I tell you."

"'Tis hard, however, to close one's eyes and ears."

"My dear De Launay, go and pay a visit to Dumesnil's chimney and Pompadour's ceiling."

"Is it possible? You tell me of things I was not at all aware of."

"A proof that I know better than you what goes on in the Bastille; and if I were to speak of some things you do know, you would be still more surprised."

"What could you tell me?"

"That a week ago one of the officers of the Bastille, and an important one too, received fifty thousand francs to let two women pass with—"

"Monsieur, they were—"

"I know who they were, what they went for, and what they did. They were Mademoiselle de Valois and Mademoiselle de Charolais; they went to see the Duc de Richelieu, and they eat bon-bons till midnight in the Tour du Coin, where they intend to pay another visit to-morrow, as they have already announced to M. de Richelieu."

De Launay turned pale.

"Well," continued Dubois, "do you think if I told these kind of things to the regent, who is, as you know, greedy of scandal, that a certain M. de Launay would be long governor of the Bastille? But I shall not say a word, for we must help each other."

"I am at your orders, monsieur."

"Then I shall find everythingready?"

"I promise you; but not a word to monseigneur."

"That is right, M. de Launay. Adieu!"

"Good," said Dubois, when he was gone; "and now, monseigneur, when you want to marry your daughter to-morrow there shall be only one thing missing —your son-in-law."

As Gaston passed on the letter to Dumesnil he heard steps in the corridor, and, hastily signing to the chevalier not to speak, he put out the light and began to undress. The governor entered. As it was not his custom to visit his prisoners at this hour, Gaston saw him with alarm, and he noticed that as M. de Launay placed his lamp on the table his hand trembled. The turnkeys withdrew, but the prisoner saw two soldiers at the door.

"Chevalier," said the governor, "you told me to treat you as a man—learn that you were condemned yesterday."

"And you have come to tell me," said Gaston, who always gained courage in the face of danger, "that the hour of my execution is arrived."

"No, monsieur, but itapproaches."

"When will it be?"

"May I tell you the truth, chevalier?"

"I shall be most grateful to you."

"To-morrow, at break of day."

"Where?"

"In the yard of the Bastille."

"Thank you; I had hoped, however, that before I died I might have been the husband of the young girl who was here yesterday."

"Did M. d'Argenson promise you this?"

"No, but he promised to ask the king."

"The king may have refused."

"Does he never grant such favors?"

"'Tis rare, monsieur, but not without a precedent."

"I am a Christian," said Gaston; "I hope I shall be allowed a confessor."

"He is here."

"May I see him?"

"Directly; at present he is with your accomplice!"

"My accomplice! who?"

"La Jonquiere, who will be executed with you."

"And I had suspected him!" said Gaston.

"Chevalier, you are young to die," said the governor.

"Death does not count years: God bids it strike and it obeys."

"But if one can avert the blow, it is almost a crime not to do so."

"What do you mean? I do not understand."

"I told you that M. d'Argenson gave hopes."

"Enough, monsieur, I have nothing to confess."

At this moment the major knocked at the door and exchanged some words with the governor.

"Monsieur," said the latter, "Captain la Jonquiere wishes to see you once more."

"And you refuse it?" said Gaston, with a slight ironical smile.

"On the contrary, I grant it, in the hope that he will be more reasonable than you, and that he wishes to consult you as to making confessions."

"If that be his intention, tell him I refuse to come."

"I know nothing of it, monsieur; perhaps he only wishes once again to see his companion in misfortune."

"In that case, monsieur, I consent."

"Follow me, then."

They found the captain lying on the bed with his clothes in rags.

"I thought the almoner of the Bastille was with you?" said M. de Launay.

"He was, but I sent him away."

"Why so?"

"Because I do not like Jesuits; do you think, morbleu, that I cannot die properly without a priest?"

"To die properly, monsieur, is not to die bravely, but as a Christian."

"If I had wanted a sermon, I would have kept the priest, but I wanted M. de Chanlay."

"He is here, monsieur; I refuse nothing to those who have nothing to hope."

"Ah! chevalier, are you there?" said La Jonquiere, turning round; "you are welcome."

"Explain," said Gaston; "I see with sorrow that you refuse the consolations of religion."

"You also! if you say another word, I declare I will turn Huguenot."

"Pardon, captain, but I thought it my duty to advise you to do what I shall do myself."

"I bear you no ill-will, chevalier; if I were a minister, I would proclaim religious liberty. Now, M. de Launay," continued he, "you understand that as the chevalier and I are about to undertake a long tete-à-tete journey, we have some things to talk over together first."

"I will retire. Chevalier, you have an hour to remain here."

"Thank you, monsieur," said Gaston.

"Well?" said the captain, when they were alone.

"Well," said Gaston, "you were right."

"Yes; but I am exactly like the man who went round Jerusalem crying out 'Woe!' for seven days, and the eighth day a stone thrown from the walls struck him and killed him."

"Yes, I know that we are to die together."

"Which annoys you a little; does it not?"

"Very much, for I had reason to cling to life."

"Every one has."

"But I above all."

"Then I only know one way."

"Make revelations! never."

"No, but fly with me."

"How! fly with you?"

"Yes, I escape."

"But do you know that our execution is fixed for to-morrow?"

"Therefore I decamp to-night."

"Escape, do you say?"

"Certainly."

"How? where?"

"Open the window."

"Well."

"Shake the middle bar."

"Great God!"

"Does it resist?"

"No, it yields!"

"Very good, it has given me trouble enough, Heaven knows."

"It seems like a dream."

"Do you remember asking me if I did not make holes in anything, like all the others?"

"Yes, but you replied—"

"That I would tell you another time; was the answer a good one?"

"Excellent; but how to descend?"

"Help me."

"In what?"

"To search my paillasse."

"A ladder of cord!"

"Exactly."

"But how did you get it?"

"I received it with a file in a lark pie the day of my arrival."

"Certainly, you are decidedly a great man."

"I know it; besides that, I am a good man—for I might escape alone."

"And you have thought of me."

"I asked for you, saying that I wished to say adieu to you. I knew I should entice them to do some act of stupidity."

"Let us make haste, captain."

"On the contrary, let us act slowly and prudently; we have an hour before us."

"And the sentinels?"

"Bah! it is dark."

"But the moat, which is full of water?"

"It is frozen."

"But the wall?"

"When we are there, will be time enough to think about that."

"Must we fasten the ladder?"

"I want to try if it be solid; I have an affection for my spine, such as it is, and do not want to break my neck to save it from another fate."

"You are the first captain of the day, La Jonquiere."

"Bah! I have made plenty of others," said La Jonquiere, tying the last knot in the ladder.

"Is it finished?" asked Gaston.

"Yes."

"Shall I pass first?"

"As you like."

"I like it so."

"Go, then."

"Is it high?"

"Fifteen to eighteen feet."

"A trifle."

"Yes, for you who are young, but it is a different affair for me; be prudent, I beg."

"Do not be afraid."

Gaston went first, slowly and prudently, followed by La Jonquiere, who laughed in his sleeve, and grumbled every time he hurt his fingers, or when the wind shook the cords.

"A nice affair for the successor of Richelieu and Mazarin," he growled to himself. "It is true I am not yet a cardinal; that saves me."

Gaston touched the water, or rather ice, of the fosse; a moment after, La Jonquiere was by his side.

"Now follow me," said the latter. On the other side of the moat a ladder awaited them.

"You have accomplices then?"

"Parbleu! do you think the lark paté came by itself?"

"Who says one cannot escape from the Bastille?" said Gaston joyously.

"My young friend," said Dubois, stopping on the third step, "take my advice; don't get in there again without me; you might not be as fortunate the second time as the first."

They continued to mount the wall, on the platform of which a sentinel walked, but instead of opposing them, he held his hand to La Jonquiere to assist him, and in three minutes they were on the platform, had drawn up the ladder, and placed it on the other side of the wall.

The descent was as safely managed, and they found themselves on another frozen moat.

"Now," said the captain, "we must take away the ladder, that we may not compromise the poor devil who helped us."

"We are then free?"

"Nearly so," said La Jonquiere.

Gaston, strengthened by this news, took up the ladder on his shoulder.

"Peste, chevalier! the late Hercules was nothing to you, I think."

"Bah!" said Gaston, "at this moment I could carry the Bastille itself."

They went on in silence to a lane in the Faubourg St. Antoine; the streets were deserted.

"Now, my dear chevalier," said La Jonquiere, "do me the favor to follow me to the corner of the Faubourg."

"I would follow you to—"

"Not so far, if you please; for safety's sake we will each go our own way."

"What carriage is that?"

"Mine."

"How! yours?"——"Yes."

"Peste! my dear captain: four horses! you travel like a prince!"

"Three horses; one is for you."

"How! you consent?"

"Pardieu! that is not all."

"What?"

"You have no money?"

"It was taken away."

"Here are fifty louis."

"But, captain—"

"Come, it is Spanish money; take it."

Gaston took the purse, while a postilion unharnessed a horse and led it to him.

"Now," said Dubois, "where are you going?"

"To Bretagne, to rejoin my companions."

"You are mad, my dear fellow; they are all condemned and may be executed in two or three days."

"You are right," said Gaston.

"Go to Flanders," said La Jonquiere, "it is a pleasant country; in fifteen or eighteen hours you can reach the frontier."

"Yes," said Gaston gloomily; "thank you, I know where I shall go."

"Well, good luck to you," said Dubois, getting into his carriage.

"The same to you," said Gaston.

They grasped each other's hands, and then each went his own way.

CHAPTER XXXII.

SHOWING THAT WE MUST NOT ALWAYS JUDGE OTHERS BY OURSELVES, ABOVE ALL IF WE ARE CALLED DUBOIS.

The regent, as usual, passed the evening with Helene. He had not missed for four or five days, and the hours he passed with her were his happy hours, but this time he found her very much shaken by her visit to her lover in the Bastille.

"Come," said the regent, "take courage, Helene; to-morrow you shall be his wife."

"To-morrow is distant," replied she.

"Helene, believe in my word, which has never failed you. I tell you that to-morrow shall dawn happily for you and for him."

Helene sighed deeply.

A servant entered and spoke to the regent.

"What is it?" asked Helene, who was alarmed at the slightest thing.

"Nothing, my child," said the duke; "it is only my secretary, who wishes to see me on some pressing business."

"Shall I leave you?"

"Yes; do me that favor for an instant."

Helene withdrew into her room.

At the same time the door opened and Dubois entered, out of breath.

"Where do you come from in such a state?"

"Parbleu! from the Bastille."

"And our prisoner?"

"Well."

"Is everything arranged for the marriage."

"Yes, everything but the hour, which you did not name."

"Let us say eight in the morning."

"At eight in the morning," said Dubois, calculating.

"Yes, what are you calculating?"

"I am thinking where he will be."

"Who?"

"The prisoner."

"What! the prisoner!"

"Yes; at eight o'clock he will be forty leagues from Paris!"

"From Paris!"

"Yes; if he continues to go at the pace at which I saw him set out."

"What do you mean?"

"I mean, monseigneur, that there will be one thing only wanting at the marriage; the husband."

"Gaston?"

"Has escaped from the Bastille half-an-hour ago."

"You lie, abbe; people do not escape from the Bastille."

"I beg your pardon, monseigneur; people escape from any place when they are condemned to death."

"He escaped, knowing that to-morrow he was to wed her whom he loved?"

"Listen, monseigneur, life is a charming thing, and we all cling to it; then your son-in-law has a charming head which he wishes to keep on his shoulders—what more natural?"

"And where is he?"

"Perhaps I may be able to tell you to-morrow evening; at present, all I know is that he is at some distance, and that I will answer for it he will not return."

The regent became deeply thoughtful.

"Really, monseigneur, your naïveté causes me perpetual astonishment; you must be strangely ignorant of the human heart if you suppose that a man condemned to death would remain in prison when he had a chance of escape."

"Oh! Monsieur de Chanlay!" cried the regent.

"Eh, mon Dieu! this chevalier has acted as the commonest workman would have done, and quite right too."

"Dubois! and my daughter?"

"Well, your daughter, monseigneur?"

"It will kill her," said the regent.

"Oh no, monseigneur, not at all; when she finds out what he is, she will be consoled, and you can marry her to some small German or Italian prince—to the Duke of Modena, for instance, whom Mademoiselle de Valois will not have."

"Dubois! and I meant to pardon him."

"He has done it for himself, monseigneur, thinking it safer, and ma foi! I should have done the same."

"Oh you; you are not noble, you had not taken an oath."

"You mistake, monseigneur; I had taken an oath, to prevent your highness from committing a folly, and I have succeeded."

"Well, well, let us speak of it no more, not a word of this before Helene—I will undertake to tell her."

"And I, to get back your son-in-law."

"No, no, he has escaped, let him profit by it."

As the regent spoke these words a noise was heard in the neighboring room, and a servant entering, hurriedly announced—

"Monsieur Gaston de Chanlay."

Dubois turned pale as death, and his face assumed an expression of threatening anger. The regent rose in a transport of joy, which brought a bright color into his face—there was as much pleasure in this face, rendered sublime by confidence, as there was compressed fury in Dubois's sharp and malignant countenance.

THE REGENT.—*Page* 544.

Link to larger image

"Let him enter," said the regent.

"At least, give me time to go," said Dubois.

"Ah! yes, he would recognize you."

Dubois retired with a growling noise, like a hyena disturbed in its feast, or in its lair; he entered the next room. There he sat down by a table on which was every material for writing, and this seemed to suggest some new and terrible idea, for his face suddenly lighted up.

He rang.

"Send for the portfolio which is in my carriage," said he to the servant who appeared.

This order being executed at once, Dubois seized some papers, wrote on them some words with an expression of sinister joy, then, having ordered his carriage, drove to the Palais Royal.

Meanwhile the chevalier was led to the regent, and walked straight up to him.

"How! you here, monsieur!" said the duke, trying to look surprised.

"Yes, monseigneur, a miracle has been worked in my favor by La Jonquiere; he had prepared all for flight, he asked for me under pretense of consulting me as to confessions; then, when we were alone, he told me all and we escaped together and in safety."

"And instead of flying, monsieur, gaining the frontier, and placing yourself in safety, you are here at the peril of your life."

"Monseigneur," said Gaston, blushing, "I must confess that for a moment liberty seemed to me the most precious and the sweetest thing the world could afford. The first breath of air I drew seemed to intoxicate me, but I soon reflected."

"On one thing, monsieur?"

"On two, monseigneur."

"You thought of Helene, whom you were abandoning."

"And of my companions, whom I left under the ax."

"And then you decided?"

"That I was bound to their cause till our projects were accomplished."

"Our projects!"

"Yes, are they not yours as well as mine?"

"Listen, monsieur," said the regent; "I believe that man must keep within the limits of his strength. There are things which God seems to forbid him to execute; there are warnings which tell him to renounce certain projects. I believe that it is sacrilege to despise these warnings, to remain deaf to this voice; our projects have miscarried, monsieur, let us think no more of them."

"On the contrary, monseigneur," said Gaston, sadly shaking his head, "let us think of them more than ever."

"But you are furious, monsieur," said the regent, "to persist in an undertaking which has now become so difficult that it is almost madness."

"I think, monseigneur, of our friends arrested, tried, condemned; M. d'Argenson told me so; of our friends who are destined to the scaffold, and who can be saved only by the death of the regent; of our friends who would say, if I were to leave France, that I purchased my safety by their ruin, and that the gates of the Bastille were opened by my revelations."

"Then, monsieur, to this point of honor you sacrifice everything, even Helene?"

"Monseigneur, if they be still alive I must save them."

"But if they be dead?"

"Then it is another thing," replied Gaston; "then I must revenge them."

"Really, monsieur," said the duke, "this seems to me a somewhat exaggerated idea of heroism. It seems to me that you have, in your own person, already paid your share. Believe me, take the word of a man who is a good judge in affairs of honor; you are absolved in the eyes of the whole world, my dear Brutus."

"I am not in my own, monseigneur."

"Then you persist?"

"More than ever; the regent must die, and," added he in a hollow voice, "die he shall."

"But do you not first wish to see Mademoiselle de Chaverny?" asked the regent.

"Yes, monseigneur, but first I must have your promise to aid me in my project. Remember, monseigneur; there is not an instant to lose; my companions are condemned, as I was. Tell me at once, before I see Helene, that you will not abandon me. Let me make a new engagement with you—I am a man; I love, and therefore I am weak. I shall have to struggle against her tears and against my own weakness; monseigneur, I will only see Helene under the condition that you will enable me to see the regent."

"And if I refuse that condition?"

"Then, monseigneur, I will not see Helene; I am dead to her; it is useless to renew hope in her which she must lose again, it is enough that she must weep for me once."

"And you would still persist?"

"Yes, but with less chance."

"Then what would you do?"

"Wait for the regent wherever he goes, and strike him whenever I can find him."

"Think once more," said the duke.

"By the honor of my name," replied Gaston, "I once more implore your aid, or I declare that I will find means to dispense with it."

"Well, monsieur, go and see Helene, and you shall have my answer on your return."

"Where?"

"In that room."

"And the answer shall be according to my desire?"

"Yes."

Gaston went into Helene's room; she was kneeling before a crucifix, praying that her lover might be restored to her. At the noise which Gaston made in opening the door she turned round.

Believing that God had worked a miracle, and uttering a cry, she held out her arms toward the chevalier, but without the strength to raise herself.

"Oh, mon Dieu! is it himself? is it his shade?"

"It is myself, Helene," said the young man, darting toward her, and grasping her hands.

"But how? a prisoner this morning—free, this evening?"

"I escaped, Helene."

"And then you thought of me, you ran to me, you would not fly without me. Oh! I recognize my Gaston there. Well—I am ready, take me where you will —I am yours—I am—"

"Helene," said Gaston, "you are not the bride of an ordinary man; if I had been only like all other men you would not have loved me."

"Oh, no!"

"Well, Helene, to superior souls superior duties are allotted, and consequently greater trials; before I can be yours I have to accomplish the mission on which I came to Paris; we have both a fatal destiny to fulfill. Our life or death hangs on a single event which must be accomplished to-night."

"What do you mean?" cried the young girl.

"Listen, Helene," replied Gaston, "if in four hours, that is to say, by daybreak, you have no news of me, do not expect me, believe that all that has passed between us is but a dream—and, if you can obtain permission to do so, come again and see me in the Bastille."

Helene trembled, Gaston took her back to her prie-Dieu, where she knelt.

Then, kissing her on the forehead as a brother might have done—"Pray on, Helene;" said he, "for in praying for me you pray also for Bretagne and for France." Then he rushed out of the room.

"Alas! alas!" murmured Helene, "save *him*, my God! and what care I for the rest of the world."

Gaston was met by a servant who gave him a note, telling him the duke was gone.

The note was as follows:

"There is a bal masque to-night at Monceaux; the regent will be there. He generally retires toward one o'clock in the morning into a favorite conservatory, which is situated at the end of the gilded gallery. No one enters there ordinarily but himself, because this habit of his is known and respected. The regent will be dressed in a black velvet domino, on the left arm of which is embroidered a golden bee. He hides this sign in a fold when he wishes to remain incognito. The card I inclose is an ambassador's ticket. With this you will be admitted, not only to the ball, but to this conservatory, where you will appear to seek a private interview. Use it for your encounter with the regent. My carriage is below, in which you will find my own domino. The coachman is at your orders."

On reading this note, which, as it were, brought him face to face with the man he meant to assassinate, a cold perspiration passed over Gaston's forehead, and he was obliged for a moment to lean against a chair for support; but suddenly, as if taking a violent resolution, he darted down the staircase, jumped into the carriage, and cried—

"To Monceaux!"

Scarcely had he quitted the room, when a secret door in the woodwork opened, and the duke entered. He went to Helene's door, who uttered a cry of delight at seeing him.

"Well," said the regent sadly, "are you content, Helene?"

"Oh! it is you, monseigneur?"

"You see, my child, that my predictions are fulfilled—believe me when I say, 'Hope.'"

"Ah! monseigneur, are you then an angel come down to earth to stand to me in the place of the father whom I have lost?"

"Alas," said the regent, smiling. "I am not an angel, my dear Helene; but such as I am, I will indeed be to you a father, and a tender one."

Saying this, the regent took Helene's hand, and was about to kiss it respectfully, but she raised her head and presented her forehead to him.

"I see that you love him truly," said he.

"Monseigneur, I bless you."

"May your blessing bring me happiness," said the regent, then, going down to his carriage—

"To the Palais Royal," said he, "but remember you have only a quarter of an hour to drive to Monceaux."

The horses flew along the road.

As the carriage entered under the peristyle, a courier on horseback was setting out.

Dubois, having seen him start, closed the window and went back to his apartments.

CHAPTER XXXIII.

MONCEAUX.

Meanwhile Gaston went toward Monceaux.

He had found the duke's domino and mask in the carriage. The mask was of black velvet—the domino of violet satin. He put them both on, and suddenly remembered that he was without arms.

He thought, however, he should easily procure some weapon at Monceaux. As he approached, he found it was not a weapon that he needed, but courage. There passed in his mind a terrible contest. Pride and humanity struggled against each other, and, from time to time, he represented to himself his friends in prison, condemned to a cruel and infamous death.

As the carriage entered the courtyard of Monceaux, he murmured, "Already!"

However, the carriage stopped, the door was opened, he must alight. The prince's private carriage and coachman had been recognized, and all the servants overwhelmed him with attentions.

Gaston did not remark it—a kind of mist passed before his eyes—he presented his card.

It was the custom then for both men and women to be masked: but it was more frequently the women than the men who went to these reunions unmasked. At this period women spoke not only freely, but well, and the mask hid neither folly nor inferiority of rank, for the women of that day were all witty, and if they were handsome, they were soon titled: witness, the Duchesse de Chateauroux and the Comtesse Dubarry.

Gaston knew no one, but he felt instinctively that he was among the most select society of the day. Among the men were Novilles, Brancas, Broglie, St. Simon, and Biron. The women might be more mixed, but certainly not less spirituelles, nor less elegant.

No one knew how to organize a fete like the regent. The luxury of good taste, the profusion of flowers, the lights, the princes and ambassadors, the charming and beautiful women who surrounded him, all had their effect on Gaston, who now recognized in the regent, not only a king, but a king at once powerful, gay, amiable, beloved, and above all, popular and national.

Gaston's heart beat when, seeking among these heads the one for which his blows were destined, he saw a black domino.

Without the mask which hid his face and concealed from all eyes its changing expression, he would not have taken four steps through the rooms without some one pointing him out as an assassin.

Gaston could not conceal from himself that there was something cowardly in coming to a prince, his host, to change those brilliant lights into funeral torches, to stain those dazzling tapestries with blood, to arouse the cry of terror amid the joyous tumult of a fete—and at this thought his courage failed him, and he stepped toward the door.

"I will kill him outside," said he, "but not here."

Then he remembered the duke's directions, his card would open to him the isolated conservatory, and he murmured—

"He foresaw that I should be a coward."

He approached a sort of gallery containing buffets where the guests came for refreshment. He went also, not that he was hungry or thirsty, but because he was unarmed. He chose a long, sharp and pointed knife, and put it under his domino, where he was sure no one could see it.

"The likeness to Ravaillac will be complete," said he.

At this moment, as Gaston turned, he heard a well-known voice say—

"You hesitate?"

Gaston opened his domino and showed the duke the knife which it concealed.

"I see the knife glisten, but I also see the hand tremble."

"Yes, monseigneur, it is true," said Gaston; "I hesitated, I trembled, I felt inclined to fly—but thank God you are here."

"And your ferocious courage?" said the duke in a mocking voice.

"It is not that I have lost it."

"What has become of it then?"

"Monseigneur, I am under his roof."

"Yes; but in the conservatory you are not."

"Could you not show him to me first, that I might accustom myself to his presence, that I may be inspired by the hatred I bear him, for I do not know how to find him in this crowd?"

"Just now he was near you."

Gaston shuddered.

"Near me?" said he.

"As near as I am," replied the duke, gravely.

"I will go to the conservatory, monseigneur."

"Go then."

"Yet a moment, monseigneur, that I may recover myself."

"Very well, you know the conservatory is beyond that gallery; stay, the doors are closed."

"Did you not say that with this card the servants would open them to me?"

"Yes; but it would be better to open them yourself—a servant might wait for your exit. If you are thus agitated before you strike the blow, what will it be afterward? Then the regent probably will not fall without defending himself—without a cry; they will all run to him, you will be arrested, and adieu your hope of the future. Think of Helene, who waits for you."

It is impossible to describe what was passing in Gaston's heart during this speech. The duke, however, watched its effect upon his countenance.

"Well," said Gaston, "what shall I do? advise me."

"When you are at the door of the conservatory, the one which opens on to the gallery turning to the left—do you know?"

"Yes."

"Under the lock you will find a carved button—push it, and the door will open, unless it be fastened within. But the regent, who has no suspicion, will not take this precaution. I have been there twenty times for a private audience. If he be not there, wait for him. You will know him, if there, by the black domino and the golden bee."

"Yes, yes; I know," said Gaston; not knowing, however, what he said.

"I do not reckon much on you this evening," replied the duke.

"Ah! monseigneur, the moment approaches which will change my past life into a doubtful future, perhaps of shame, at least of remorse."

"Remorse!" replied the duke. "When we perform an action which we believe to be just, and commanded by conscience, we do not feel remorse. Do you doubt the sanctity of your cause?"

"No, monseigneur, but it is easy for you to speak thus. You have the idea—I, the execution. You are the head, but I am the arm. Believe me, monseigneur," continued he in a hollow voice, and choking with emotion, "it is a terrible thing to kill a man who is before you defenseless—smiling on his murderer. I thought myself courageous and strong; but it must be thus with every conspirator who undertakes what I have done. In a moment of excitement, of pride, of enthusiasm, or of hatred, we take a fatal vow; then there is a vast extent of time between us and our victim; but the oath taken, the fever is calmed, the enthusiasm cools, the hatred diminishes. Every day brings us nearer the end to which we are tending, and then we shudder when we feel what a crime we have undertaken. And yet inexorable time flows on; and at every hour which strikes, we see our victim take another step, until at length the interval between us disappears, and we stand face to face. Believe me, monseigneur, the bravest tremble—for murder is always murder. Then we see that we are not the ministers of our consciences, but the slaves of our oaths. We set out with head erect, saying 'I am the chosen one:' we arrive with head bowed down, saying, 'I am accursed.'"

"There is yet time, monsieur."

"No, no; you well know, monseigneur, that fate urges me onward. I shall accomplish my task, terrible though it be. My heart will shudder, but my hand will still be firm. Yes, I tell you, were it not for my friends, whose lives hang on the blow I am about to strike, were there no Helene, whom I should cover with mourning, if not with blood, oh, I would prefer the scaffold, even the scaffold, with all its shame, for that does not punish, it absolves."

"Come," said the duke, "I see that though you tremble, you will act."

"Do not doubt it, monseigneur; pray for me, for in half an hour all will be over."

The duke gave an involuntary start; however, approving Gaston's determination, he once more mixed with the crowd.

Gaston found an open window with a balcony. He stepped out for a moment to cool the fever in his veins, but it was in vain; the flame which consumed him was not to be extinguished thus.

He heard one o'clock strike.

"Now," he murmured, "the time is come, and I cannot draw back. My God, to thee I recommend my soul—Helene, adieu!"

Then, slowly but firmly, he went to the door, and pressing the button, it opened noiselessly before him.

A mist came before his eyes. He seemed in a new world. The music sounded like a distant and charming melody. Around him breathed the sweetly perfumed flowers, and alabaster lamps half hidden in luxuriant foliage shed a delicious twilight over the scene, while through the interlacing leaves of tropical plants could just be seen the leafless gloomy trees beyond, and the snow covering the earth as with a winding sheet. Even the temperature was changed, and a sudden shiver passed through his veins. The contrast of all this verdure, these magnificent and blossoming orange trees—these magnolias, splendid with the waxy blooms, with the gilded salons he had left, bewildered him. It seemed difficult to connect the thought of murder with this fair-smiling and enchanted scene. The soft gravel yielded to his tread, and plashing fountains murmured forth a plaintive and monotonous harmony.

Gaston was almost afraid to look for a human form. At length he glanced round.

Nothing! he went on.

At length, beneath a broad-leaved palm, surrounded by blooming rhododendrons, he saw the black phantom seated on a bank of moss, his back turned toward the side from whence he was approaching.

The blood rushed to Gaston's cheeks, his hand trembled, and he vainly sought for some support.

The domino did not move.

Gaston involuntarily drew back. All at once he forced his rebellious limbs to move on, and his trembling fingers to grasp the knife they had almost abandoned, and he stepped toward the regent, stifling a sob which was about to escape him.

At this moment the figure moved, and Gaston saw the golden bee, which seemed like a burning gem before his eyes.

The domino turned toward Gaston, and as he did so, the young man's arm grew rigid, the foam rose to his lips, his teeth chattered, for a vague suspicion entered his breast.

Suddenly he uttered a piercing cry. The domino had risen, and was unmasked —his face was that of the Duc d'Olivares.

Gaston, thunderstruck, remained livid and mute. The regent and the duke were one and the same. The regent retained his calm majestic attitude; looked at the hand which held the knife, and the knife fell. Then, looking at his intended murderer with a smile at once sweet and sad, Gaston fell down before him like a tree cut by the ax.

Not a word had been spoken; nothing was heard but Gaston's broken sobs, and the water of the fountains plashing monotonously as it fell.

CHAPTER XXXIV.

THE PARDON.

"Rise, monsieur," said the regent.

"No, monseigneur," cried Gaston, bowing his forehead to the ground, "oh, no, it is at your feet that I should die."

"Die! Gaston! you see that you are pardoned."

"Oh, monseigneur, punish me, in Heaven's name; for you must indeed despise me if you pardon me."

"But have you not guessed?" asked the regent.

"What?"

"The reason why I pardon you."

Gaston cast a retrospective glance upon the past, his sad and solitary youth, his brother's despairing death, his love for Helene, those days that seemed so long away from her, those nights that passed so quickly beneath the convent window, his journey to Paris, the duke's kindness to the young girl, and last, this unexpected clemency; but in all this he beheld nothing, he divined nothing.

"Thank Helene," said the duke, who saw that Gaston vainly sought the cause of what had happened; "thank Helene, for it is she who saves your life."

"Helene! monseigneur."

"I cannot punish my daughter's affianced husband."

"Helene, your daughter! oh, monseigneur, and I would have killed you!"

"Yes, remember what you said just now. We set out the chosen one, we return the murderer. And sometimes you see more than a murderer—a parricide—for I am almost your father," said the duke, holding out his hand to Gaston.

"Monseigneur, have mercy on me."

"You have a noble heart, Gaston."

"And you, monseigneur, are a noble prince. Henceforth, I am yours body and soul. Every drop of my blood for one tear of Helene's, for one wish of your highness's."

"Thanks, Gaston," said the duke, smiling, "I will repay your devotion by your happiness."

"I, happy, through your highness! Ah! monseigneur, God revenges himself in permitting you to return me so much good for the evil I intended you."

The regent smiled at this effusion of simple joy, when the door opened and gave entrance to a green domino.

"Captain la Jonquiere!" cried Gaston.

"Dubois!" murmured the duke, frowning.

"Monseigneur," said Gaston, hiding his face in his hands, pale with affright; "monseigneur, I am lost. It is no longer I who must be saved. I forgot my honor, I forgot my friends."

"Your friends, monsieur?" said the duke, coldly. "I thought you no longer made common cause with such men."

"Monseigneur, you said I had a noble heart; believe me when I say that Pontcalec, Montlouis, Du Couëdic, and Talhouet have hearts as noble as my own."

"Noble!" repeated the duke, contemptuously.

"Yes, monseigneur, I repeat what I said."

"And do you know what they would have done, my poor child? you, who were their blind tool, the arm that they placed at the end of their thoughts. These noble hearts would have delivered their country to the stranger, they would have erased the name of France from the list of sovereign nations. Nobles, they were bound to set an example of courage and loyalty—they have given that of perfidy and cowardice; well, you do not reply—you lower your eyes; if it be your poniard you seek, it is at your feet; take it up, there is yet time."

"Monsieur," said Gaston, clasping his hands, "I renounce my ideas of assassination, I detest them, and I ask your pardon for having entertained them; but if you will not save my friends, I beg of you at least to let me perish with them. If I live when they die, my honor dies with them; think of it, monseigneur, the honor of the name your daughter is to bear."

The regent bent his head as he replied:

"It is impossible, monsieur; they have betrayed France; and they must die."

"Then I die with them!" said Gaston, "for I also have betrayed France, and, moreover, would have murdered your highness."

The regent looked at Dubois; the glance they exchanged did not escape

Gaston. He understood that he had dealt with a false La Jonquiere as well as a false Duc d'Olivares.

"No," said Dubois, addressing Gaston, "you shall not die for that, monsieur; but you must understand that there are crimes which the regent has neither the power nor the right to pardon."

"But he pardoned me!" exclaimed Gaston.——"You are Helene's husband," said the duke.

"You mistake, monseigneur; I am not; and I shall never be; and as such a sacrifice involves the death of him who makes it, I shall die, monseigneur."

"Bah!" said Dubois, "no one dies of love nowadays; it was very well in the time of M. d'Urfe and Mademoiselle de Scuderi."

"Perhaps you are right, monsieur; but in all times men die by the dagger;" and Gaston stopped and picked up the knife with an expression which was not to be mistaken. Dubois did not move.

The regent made a step.

"Throw down that weapon, monsieur," said he, with hauteur.

Gaston placed the point against his breast.

"Throw it down, I say," repeated the regent.

"The life of my friends, monseigneur," said Gaston.

The regent turned again to Dubois, who smiled a sardonic smile.

"'Tis well," said the regent, "they shall live."

"Ah! monsieur," said Gaston, seizing the duke's hand, and trying to raise it to his lips, "you are the image of God on earth."

"Monseigneur, you commit an irreparable fault," said Dubois.

"What!" cried Gaston, astonished, "you are then——"

"The Abbe Dubois, at your service," said the false La Jonquiere, bowing.

"Oh! monseigneur, listen only to your own heart—I implore."

"Monseigneur, sign nothing," said Dubois.

"Sign! monseigneur, sign!" repeated Gaston, "you promised they should live; and I know your promise is sacred."

"Dubois, I shall sign," said the duke.

"Has your highness decided?"

"I have given my word."

"Very well; as you please."

"At once, monseigneur, at once; I know not why, but I am alarmed in spite of myself; monseigneur, their pardon, I implore you."

"Eh! monsieur," said Dubois, "since his highness has promised, what signify five minutes more or less?"

The regent looked uneasily at Dubois.

"Yes, you are right," said he, "this very moment; your portfolio, abbe, and quick, the young man is impatient."

Dubois bowed assent, called a servant, got his portfolio, and presented to the regent a sheet of paper, who wrote an order on it and signed it.

"Now a courier."

"Oh, no! monseigneur, it is useless."

"Why so?"

"A courier would never go quickly enough. I will go myself, if your highness will permit me; every moment I gain will save those unhappy men an age of torture."

Dubois frowned.

"Yes! yes! you are right," said the regent, "go yourself;" and he added in a low voice, "and do not let the order leave your hands."

"But, monseigneur," said Dubois, "you are more impatient than the young man himself; you forget that if he goes thus there is some one in Paris who will think he is dead."

These words struck Gaston, and recalled to him Helene, whom he had left, expecting him from one moment to another, in the fear of some great event, and who would never forgive him should he leave Paris without seeing her. In an instant his resolution was taken; he kissed the duke's hand, took the order, and was going, when the regent said—

"Not a word to Helene of what I told you; the only recompense I ask of you is to leave me the pleasure of telling her she is my child."

"Your highness shall be obeyed," said Gaston, moved to tears, and again bowing, he hastily went out.

"This way," said Dubois; "really, you look as if you had assassinated some one, and you will be arrested; cross this grove, at the end is a path which will lead you to the street."

"Oh, thank you; you understand that delay—"

"Might be fatal. That is why," added he to himself, "I have shown you the longest way—go."

When Gaston had disappeared, Dubois returned to the regent.

"What is the matter, monseigneur?" asked he; "you seem uneasy."

"I am."

"And why?"

"You made no resistance to my performing a good action—this frightened me." Dubois smiled.

"Dubois," said the duke, "you are plotting something."

"No, monseigneur, it is all arranged."

"What have you done?"

"Monseigneur, I know you."

"Well."

"I knew what would happen. That you would never be satisfied till you had signed the pardon of all these fellows."

"Go on."

"Well, I also have sent a courier."

"You!"

"Yes, I; have I not the right to send couriers?"

"Yes; but, in Heaven's name, tell me what order your courier carried."

"An order for their execution."

"And he is gone?"

Dubois took out his watch.

"Two hours ago," said he.

"Wretch!"

"Ah, monseigneur! always big words. Every man to his trade, save M. de Chanlay, if you like; he is your son-in-law; as for me, I save you."

"Yes; but I know De Chanlay. He will arrive before the courier."

"No, monseigneur."

"Two hours are nothing to a man like him; he will soon have made them up."

"Were my courier only two hours in advance," said Dubois, "De Chanlay might overtake him, but he will be three."

"How so?"

"Because the worthy young man is in love; and if I reckon an hour for taking leave of your daughter, I am sure it is not too much."

"Serpent! I understand the meaning of what you said just now."

"He was in an excess of enthusiasm—he might have forgotten his love. You know my principle, monseigneur: distrust first impulses, they are always good."

"It is an infamous principle."

"Monseigneur, either one is a diplomatist or one is not."

"Well," said the regent, stepping toward the door, "I shall go and warn him."

"Monseigneur," said Dubois, stopping the duke with an accent of extreme resolution, and taking a paper out of his portfolio, already prepared, "if you do so, have the kindness in that case to accept my resignation at once. Joke, if you will, but, as Horace said, 'est modus in rebus.' He was a great as well as a courteous man. Come, come, monseigneur, a truce to politics for this evening —go back to the ball, and to-morrow evening all will be settled—France will be rid of four of her worst enemies, and you will retain a son-in-law whom I greatly prefer to M. de Riom, I assure you."

And with these words they returned to the ballroom, Dubois joyous and triumphant, the duke sad and thoughtful, but convinced that his minister was right.

CHAPTER XXXV.

THE LAST INTERVIEW.

Gaston left the conservatory, his heart bounding with joy. The enormous weight which had oppressed him since the commencement of the conspiracy, and which Helene's love had scarcely been able to alleviate, now seemed to disappear as at the touch of an angel.

To dreams of vengeance, dreams both terrible and bloody, succeeded visions of love and glory. Helene was not only a charming and a loving woman, she was also a princess of the blood royal—one of those divinities whose tenderness men would purchase with their hearts' blood, if they did not, being after all weak as mortals, give this inestimable tenderness away.

And Gaston felt revive within his breast the slumbering instinct of ambition. What a brilliant fortune was his—one to be envied by such men as Richelieu and Lauzun. No Louis XIV., imposing, as on Lauzun, exile or the abandonment of his mistress—no irritated father combating the pretensions of a simple gentleman—but, on the contrary, a powerful friend, greedy of love, longing to prove his affection for his pure and noble daughter. A holy emulation between the daughter and the son-in-law to make themselves more worthy of so just a prince, so mild a conqueror.

In a quarter of an hour Gaston had gained the Rue du Bac.

The door opened before him—a cry was heard—Helene, at the window watching for his return, had recognized the carriage, and ran joyously to meet him.

"Saved!" cried Gaston, seeing her; "saved! my friends, I—you—all—saved!"

"Oh, God!" cried Helene, turning pale, "you have killed him, then?"

"No, no; thank God! Oh! Helene, what a heart, what a man is this regent! Oh, love him well, Helene; you will love him, will you not?"

"Explain yourself, Gaston."

"Come, and let us speak of ourselves; I have but a few moments to give you, Helene; but the duke will tell you all."

"One thing before all," said Helene, "what is your fate?"

"The brightest in the world, Helene—your husband, rich and honored. Helene, I am wild with joy."

"And you remain with me at last?"

"No, I leave you, Helene."

"Oh, heavens!"

"But to return."

"Another separation!"

"Three days at the most—three days only. I go to bring blessings on your name, on mine, on that of our protector, our friend."

"Where are you going?"

"To Nantes!"

"To Nantes!"

"Yes. This order is the pardon of Pontcalec, Montlouis, and Talhouet and Du Couëdic. They are condemned to death, and they will owe me their lives. Oh, do not keep me here, Helene; think of what you suffered just now, when you were watching for me."

"And, consequently, what I am to suffer again."

"No, my Helene; for this time there is no fear, no obstacle: this time you are sure of my return."

"Gaston, shall I never see you, but at rare intervals and for a few minutes? Ah! Gaston, I have so much need of happiness."

"You shall be happy, Helene, be assured."

"My heart sinks."

"Ah! when you know all!"

"But tell me at once."

"Helene, the only thing wanting to my happiness is the permission to fall at your feet and tell you all—but I have promised—nay more, I have sworn."

"Always some secret!"

"This, at least, is a joyful one."

"Oh, Gaston, Gaston, I tremble."

"Look at me, Helene; can you fear when you see the joy that sparkles in my eyes?"

"Why do you not take me with you, Gaston?"

"Helene!"

"I beg of you to let us go together."

"Impossible."

"Why?"

"Because, first, I must be at Nantes in twenty hours."

"I will follow you, even should I die with fatigue."

"Then, because you are no longer your own mistress; you have here a protector, to whom you owe respect and obedience."

"The duke?"

"Yes; the duke. Oh, when you know what he has done for me—for us."

"Let us leave a letter for him, and he will forgive us."

"No, no; he will say we are ungrateful; and he would be right. No, Helene; while I go to Bretagne, swift as a saving angel, you shall remain here and hasten the preparations for our marriage. And when I return I shall at once demand my wife; at your feet I shall bless you for the happiness and the honor you bestow on me."

"You leave me, Gaston?" cried Helene, in a voice of distress.

"Oh, not thus, Helene, not thus; I cannot leave you so. Oh, no—be joyous, Helene; smile on me; say to me—in giving me your hand—that hand so pure and faithful—'Go, Gaston—go—for it is your duty.'"

"Yes, my friend," said Helene, "perhaps I ought to speak thus, but I have not the strength. Oh! Gaston, forgive me."

"Oh, Helene, when I am so joyful."

"Gaston, it is beyond my power; remember that you take with you the half of my life."

Gaston heard the clock strike three and started.

"Adieu, Helene," said he.

"Adieu," murmured she.

Once more he pressed her hand and raised it to his lips, then dashed down the staircase toward the door.

But he heard Helene's sobs.

Rapidly he remounted the staircase and ran to her. She was standing at the door of the room he had just left. Gaston clasped her in his arms, and she hung weeping upon his neck.

"Oh, mon Dieu!" cried she, "you leave me again, Gaston; listen to what I say, we shall never meet more."

"My poor Helene," cried the young man, "you are mad."

"Despair has made me so."

And her tears ran down her cheeks.

All at once she seemed to make a violent effort, and pressing her lips on those of her lover, she clasped him tightly to her breast, then quickly repulsing him —

"Now go, Gaston," said she, "now I can die."

Gaston replied by passionate caresses. The clock struck the half hour.

"Another half hour to make up."

"Adieu, adieu, Gaston; you are right, you should already be away."

"Adieu for a time."

"Adieu, Gaston."

And Helene returned to the pavilion. Gaston procured a horse, saddled, mounted, and left Paris by the same gate by which he had entered some days previously.

CHAPTER XXXVI.

NANTES.

The commission named by Dubois was to be permanent. Invested with unlimited powers, which in certain cases means that the decision is settled beforehand, they besieged the earth, supported by strong detachments of troops.

Since the arrest of the four gentlemen, Nantes, terrified at first, had risen in their favor. The whole of Bretagne awaited a revolt, but in the meanwhile was quiet.

However, the trial was approaching. On the eve of the public audience, Pontcalec held a serious conversation with his friends.

"Let us consider," said he, "whether in word or deed we have committed any imprudence."

"No," said the other three.

"Has any one of you imparted our projects to his wife, his brother, a friend? Have you, Montlouis?"

"No, on my honor."

"You, Talhouet?"

"No."

"You, Couëdic?"

"No."

"Then they have neither proof nor accusation against us. No one has surprised us, no one wishes us harm."

"But," said Montlouis, "meanwhile we shall be tried."

"On what grounds?"

"Oh, secret information," said Talhouet, smiling.

"Very secret," said Du Couëdic, "since they do not breathe a word."

"Ah, one fine night they will force us to escape, that they may not be obliged to liberate us some fine day."

"I do not believe it," said Montlouis, who had always been the most desponding, perhaps because he had the most at stake, having a young wife and two children who adored him. "I do not believe it. I have seen Dubois in England. I have talked with him; his face is like a ferret's, licking his lips when thirsty. Dubois is thirsty, and we are taken. Dubois's thirst will be slaked by our blood."

"But," said Du Couëdic, "there is the parliament of Bretagne."

"Yes, to look on, while we lose our heads."

There was only one of the four who smiled; that was Pontcalec.

"My friends," said he, "take courage. If Dubois be thirsty, so much the worse for Dubois. He will go mad, that is all; but this time I answer for it he shall not taste our blood."

And, indeed, from the beginning the task of the commission seemed difficult. No confessions, no proofs, no witnesses. Bretagne laughed in the commissioners' faces, and when she did not laugh, she threatened. The president dispatched a courier to Paris to explain the state of things, and get further instructions.

"Judge by their projects," said Dubois; "they may have done little, because they were prevented, but they intended much, and the intention in matters of rebellion is equivalent to the act."

Armed with this terrible weapon, the commission soon overthrew the hopes of the province. There was a terrible audience, in which the accused commenced with raillery and ended with accusation. On re-entering the prison, Pontcalec congratulated them on the truths they had told the judge.

"Nevertheless," said Montlouis, "it is a bad affair. Bretagne does not revolt."

"She waits our condemnation," said Talhouet.

"Then she will revolt somewhat late," said Montlouis.

"But our condemnation may not take place," said Pontcalec. "Say, frankly, we are guilty, but without proofs who will dare to sentence us? The commission?"

"No, not the commission, but Dubois."

"I have a great mind to do one thing," said Du Couëdic.

"What?"

"At the first audience to cry, 'Bretagne to the rescue!' Each time we have seen faces of friends; we should be delivered or killed, but at least it would be decided. I should prefer death to this suspense."

"But why run the risk of being wounded by some satellite of justice?"

"Because such a wound might be healed; not so the wound the executioner would make."

"Oh!" said Pontcalec, "you will have no more to do with the executioner than I shall."

"Always the prediction," said Montlouis. "You know that I have no faith in it."

"You are wrong."

"This is sure, my friends," said Pontcalec. "We shall be exiled, we shall be forced to embark, and I shall be lost on the way. This is my fate. But yours may be different. Ask to go by a different vessel from me; or there is another chance. I may fall from the deck, or slip on the steps; at least, I shall die by the water. You know that is certain. I might be condemned to death, taken to the very scaffold, but if the scaffold were on dry ground I should be as easy as I am now."

His tone of confidence gave them courage. They even laughed at the rapidity with which the deliberations were carried on. They did not know that Dubois sent courier after courier from Paris to hasten them.

At length the commission declared themselves sufficiently enlightened, and retired to deliberate in secret session.

Never was there a more stormy discussion. History has penetrated the secrets of these deliberations, in which some of the least bold or least ambitious counselors revolted against the idea of condemning these gentlemen on presumptions which were supported solely by the intelligence transmitted to them by Dubois; but the majority were devoted to Dubois, and the committee came to abuse and quarrels, and almost to blows.

At the end of a sitting of eleven hours' duration, the majority declared their decision.

The commissioners associated sixteen others of the contumacious gentlemen with the four chiefs, and declared:

"That the accused, found guilty of criminal projects, of treason, and of felonious intentions, should be beheaded: those present, in person, those absent, in effigy. That the walls and fortifications of their castles should be demolished, their patents of nobility annulled, and their forests cut down to the height of nine feet."

An hour after the delivery of this sentence, an order was given to the usher to announce it to the prisoners.

The sentence had been given after the stormy sitting of which we have spoken, and in which the accused had experienced such lively marks of sympathy from the public. And so, having beaten the judges on all the counts of the indictment, never had they been so full of hope.

They were seated at supper in their common room, calling to mind all the details of the sitting, when suddenly the door opened, and in the shade appeared the pale and stern form of the usher.

The solemn apparition changed, on the instant, into anxious palpitations their pleasant conversation.

The usher advanced slowly, while the jailer remained at the door, and the barrels of muskets were seen shining in the gloom of the corridor.

"What is your will, sir?" asked Pontcalec, "and what signifies this deadly paraphernalia?"

"Gentlemen," said the usher, "I bear the sentence of the tribunal. On your knees and listen."

"How?" said Montlouis, "it is only sentences of death that must be heard kneeling."

"On your knees, gentlemen," replied the usher.

"Let the guilty and the base kneel," said Du Couëdic; "we are gentlemen, and innocent. We will hear our sentences standing."

"As you will, gentlemen; but uncover yourselves, for I speak in the king's name."

Talhouet, who alone had his hat on, removed it. The four gentlemen stood erect and bare-headed, leaning on each other, with pale faces and a smile upon their lips.

The usher read the sentence through, uninterrupted by a murmur, or by a single gesture of surprise.

When he had finished—

"Why was I told," asked Pontcalec, "to declare the designs of Spain against France, and that I should be liberated? Spain was an enemy's country. I declared what I believed I knew of her projects; and, lo! I am condemned. Why is this? Is the commission, then, composed of cowards who spread snares for the accused?"

The usher made no answer.

"But," added Montlouis, "the regent spared all Paris, implicated in the conspiracy of Cellamare; not a drop of blood was shed. Yet those who wished to carry off the regent, perhaps to kill him, were at least as guilty as men against whom no serious accusations even could be made. Are we then chosen to pay for the indulgence shown to the capital?"

The usher made no reply.

"You forget one thing, Montlouis," said Du Couëdic, "the old family hatred against Bretagne; and the regent, to make people believe that he belongs to the family, wishes to prove that he hates us. It is not we, personally, who are struck at; it is a province, which for three hundred years has claimed in vain its privileges and its rights, and which they wish to find guilty in order to have done with it forever."

The usher preserved a religious silence.

"Enough," said Talhouet, "we are condemned. 'Tis well. Now, have we, or have we not, the right of appeal?"

"No, gentlemen," said the usher.

"Then you can retire," said Couëdic.

The usher bowed and withdrew, followed by his escort, and the prison door, heavy and clanging, closed once more upon the four gentlemen.

"Well!" said Montlouis, when they were again alone.

"Well, we are condemned," said Pontcalec. "I never said there would be no sentence; I only said it would not be carried into execution."

"I am of Pontcalec's opinion," said Talhouet. "What they have done is but to terrify the province and test its patience."

"Besides," said Du Couëdic, "they will not execute us without the regent's ratification of the sentence. Now, without an extraordinary courier, it will take two days to reach Paris, one to examine into the affair, and two to return, altogether five days. We have, then, five days before us; and what may not happen in five days? The province will rise on hearing of our doom—"

Montlouis shook his head.

"Besides, there is Gaston," said Pontcalec, "whom you always forget."

"I am much afraid that Gaston has been arrested," said Montlouis. "I know Gaston, and were he at liberty, we should have heard of him ere now."

"Prophet of evil," said Talhouet, "at least you will not deny that we have some days before us."

"Who knows?" said Montlouis.

"And the waters?" said Pontcalec; "the waters? You always forget that I can only perish by the waters."

"Well, then, let us be seated again," said Du Couëdic, "and a last glass to our healths."

"There is no more wine," said Montlouis; "'tis an evil omen."

"Bah! there is more in the cellar," said Pontcalec.

And he called the jailer.

The man, on entering, found the four friends at table; he looked at them in astonishment.

"Well, what is there new, Master Christopher?" said Pontcalec.

Christopher came from Guer, and had a particular respect for Pontcalec, whose uncle Crysogon had been his seigneur.

"Nothing but what you know," he replied.

"Then go and fetch some wine."

"They wish to deaden their feelings," said the jailer to himself; "poor gentlemen."

Montlouis alone heard Christopher's remark, and he smiled sadly.

An instant afterward they heard steps rapidly approaching their room.

The door opened, and Christopher reappeared without any bottle in his hand.

"Well," said Pontcalec, "where is the wine?"

"Good news," cried Christopher, without answering Pontcalec's inquiry, "good news, gentlemen."

"What?" said Montlouis, starting. "Is the regent—dead?"

"And Bretagne in revolt?" asked Du Couëdic.

"No. I could not call that good news."

"Well, what is it then?" said Pontcalec.

"Monsieur de Chateauneuf has just ordered back to their barracks the hundred and fifty men who were under arms in the market-place, which had terrified everybody."

"Ah," said Montlouis, "I begin to believe it will not take place this evening."

At this moment the clock struck six.

"Well," said Pontcalec, "good news is no reason for our remaining thirsty; go and fetch our wine."

Christopher went out, and returned in ten minutes with a bottle.

The friends who were still at table filled their glasses.

"To Gaston's health," said Pontcalec, exchanging a meaning glance with his friends, to whom alone this toast was comprehensible.

And they emptied their glasses, all except Montlouis, who stopped as he was lifting his to his lips.

"Well, what is it?" said Pontcalec.

"The drum," said Montlouis, stretching out his hand in the direction where he heard the sound.

"Well," said Talhouet, "did you not hear what Christopher said? it is the troops returning."

"On the contrary, it is the troops going out; that is not a retreat, but the générale."

"The générale!" said Talhouet, "what on earth can that mean?"

"No good," said Montlouis, shaking his head.

"Christopher!" said Pontcalec, turning to the jailer.

"Yes, gentlemen, I will find out what it is," said he, "and be back in an instant."

He rushed out of the room, but not without carefully shutting the door behind him.

The four friends remained in anxious silence. After a lapse of ten minutes the door opened, and the jailer reappeared, pale with terror.

"A courier has just entered the castle court," said he; "he comes from Paris, he has delivered his dispatches, and immediately the guards were doubled, and the drums beat in all the barracks."

"Oh, oh," said Montlouis, "that concerns us."

"Some one is ascending the stairs," said the jailer, more pale and trembling than those to whom he spoke. In fact, they heard the butt ends of the muskets clanging on the stones of the corridor, and at the same time several voices were heard speaking hastily.

The door opened, and the usher reappeared.

"Gentlemen," said he, "how long do you desire to set your worldly affairs in order, and to undergo your sentence?"

A profound terror froze even the hearers.

"I desire," said Montlouis, "time for the sentence to reach Paris and return, approved by the regent."

"I," said Talhouet, "only desire the time necessary for the commission to repent of its iniquity."

"As for me," said Du Couëdic, "I wish for time for the minister at Paris to commute the sentence into eight days' imprisonment, which we deserve for having acted somewhat thoughtlessly."

"And you," said the usher gravely, to Pontcalec, who was silent, "what do you ask?"

"I," said Pontcalec calmly, "I demand nothing."

"Then, gentlemen," said the usher, "this is the answer of the commission: you have two hours at your disposal to arrange your spiritual and temporal affairs; it is now half-past six, in two hours and a half you must be on the Place du Bouffay, where the execution will take place."

There was a profound silence; the bravest felt fear seizing the very roots of their hair.

The usher retired without any one having made any answer; only the condemned looked at each other, and pressed each other's hands.

They had two hours.

Two hours, in the ordinary course of life, seem sometimes an age, at others two hours are but a moment.

The priests arrived, after them the soldiers, then the executioners.

The situation was appalling. Pontcalec, alone, did not belie himself. Not that the others wanted courage, but they wanted hope; still Pontcalec reassured them by the calmness with which he addressed, not only the priests, but the executioners themselves.

They made the preparations for that terrible process called the toilet of the condemned. The four sufferers must proceed to the scaffold dressed in black cloaks, in order that in the eyes of the people, from whom they always feared some tumult, they might be confounded with the priests who exhorted them.

Then the question of tying their hands was discussed—an important question.

Pontcalec answered with his smile of sublime confidence.

"Oh, leave us at least our hands free; we will go without disturbance."

"That has nothing to do with us," replied the executioner who was attending to Pontcalec; "unless by special order, the rules are the same for all sufferers."

"And who gives these orders?" said Pontcalec, laughing, "the king?"

"No, marquis," answered the executioner, astonished by such unexampled presence of mind, "not the king, but our chief."

"And where is your chief?"

"That is he, talking with the jailer Christopher."

"Call him then," said Pontcalec.

"Ho, Monsieur Waters!" cried the executioner, "please to come this way; there is one of these gentlemen asking for you."

A thunderbolt falling in the midst of them would not have produced a more terrible effect upon the four gentlemen than did this name.

"What did you say?" cried Pontcalec, shaking with affright; "what did you say? What name did you pronounce?"

"Waters, our chief."

Pontcalec, pale and overcome, sank upon a chair, casting an unutterable glance upon his affrighted companions. No one around them understood this sudden despair, which so rapidly succeeded to so high a confidence.

"Well?" asked Montlouis, addressing Pontcalec in a tone of tender reproach.

"Yes, gentlemen, you were right," said Pontcalec; "but I also was right to believe in this prediction, for it will be accomplished, as the others were. Only this time I yield, and confess that we are lost."

And by a spontaneous movement the four gentlemen threw themselves into each other's arms with fervent prayers to Heaven.

"What do you order?" asked the executioner.

"It is useless to tie their hands if they will give their words of honor; they are soldiers and gentlemen."

CHAPTER XXXVII.

THE TRAGEDY OF NANTES.

Meanwhile Gaston posted along the road to Nantes, leaving behind him all postilions, whose place, then as now, was to hold the horses instead of urging them on.

He had already passed Sevres and Versailles, and on arriving at Rambouillet just at daybreak, he saw the innkeeper and some postilions gathered round a horse which had just been bled. The horse was lying stretched on its side, in the middle of the street, breathing with difficulty.

Gaston at first paid no attention to all this; but as he was mounting himself, he heard one of the by-standers say:

"If he goes on at that pace he will kill more than one between this and Nantes."

Gaston was on the point of starting, but struck by a sudden and terrible idea, he stopped and signed to the innkeeper to come to him.

The innkeeper approached.

"Who has passed by here?" asked Gaston, "going at such a pace as to have put that poor animal in such a state?"

"A courier of the minister's," answered the innkeeper.

"A courier of the minister's!" exclaimed Gaston, "and coming from Paris?"

"From Paris."

"How long has he passed, more or less?"

"About two hours."

Gaston uttered a low cry which was like a groan. He knew Dubois—Dubois, who had tricked him under the disguise of La Jonquiere. The good will of the minister recurred to his mind and frightened him. Why this courier dispatched post haste just two hours before himself?

"Oh! I was too happy," thought the young man, "and Helene was right when she told me she had a presentiment of some great misfortune. Oh, I will overtake this courier, and learn the message that he bears, or perish in the attempt."

And he shot off like an arrow.

But with all these doubts and interrogations he had lost ten minutes more, so that on arriving at the first post station he was still two hours behind. This time the courier's horse had held out, and it was Gaston's which was ready to drop. The inn-keeper tried to make some remarks, but Gaston dropped two or three louis and set off again at a gallop.

At the next posting-house he had gained a few minutes, and that was all. The courier who was before him had not slackened his pace. Gaston increased his own; but this frightful rapidity redoubled the young man's fever and mistrust.

"Oh!" said he, "I *will* arrive at the same time that he does, if I am unable to precede him." And he doubled his speed, and spurred on his horse, which, at every station, stopped dripping with blood and sweat, or tumbled down exhausted. At every station he learned that the courier had passed almost as swiftly as himself, but he always gained some few minutes, and that sustained his strength.

Those whom he passed upon the way, leaving them far behind, pitied, in spite of themselves, the beautiful young man, pale faced and haggard, who flew on thus, and took neither rest, nor food, dripping with sweat, despite the bitter cold, and whose parched lips could only frame the words: "A horse! a horse! quick, there, a horse!"

And, in fact, exhausted, with no strength but that supplied him by his heart, and maddened more and more by the rapidity of his course and the feeling of danger, Gaston felt his head turn, his temples throb, and the perspiration of his limbs was tinged with blood.

Choked by the thirst and dryness of his throat, at Ancenis he drank a glass of water: it was the first moment he had lost during sixteen hours, and yet the accursed courier was still an hour and a half in advance. In eighty leagues Gaston had only gained some forty or fifty minutes.

The night was drawing in rapidly, and Gaston, ever expecting to see some object appear on the horizon, tried to pierce the obscurity with his bloodshot glances; on he went, as in a dream, thinking he heard the ringing of bells, the roar of cannon, and the roll of drums. His brain was full of mournful strains and inauspicious sounds; he lived no longer as a man, but his fever kept him up, he flew as it were in the air.

On, and still on. About eight o'clock at night he perceived Nantes at length upon the horizon, like a dark mass from out the midst of which some scattered lights were shining starlike in the gloom.

He tried to breathe, and thinking his cravat was choking him, he tore it off and threw it on the road.

Thus, mounted on his black horse, wrapped in his black cloak, and long ago bareheaded (his hat had fallen off), Gaston was like some fiendish cavalier bound to the witches' Sabbath.

On reaching the gates of Nantes his horse stumbled, but Gaston did not lose his stirrups, pulled him up sharply, and driving the spurs into his sides, he made him recover himself.

The night was dark, no one appeared upon the ramparts, the very sentinels were hidden in the gloom, it seemed like a deserted city.

But as he passed the gate a sentinel said something which Gaston did not even hear.

He held on his way.

At the Rue du Chateau his horse stumbled and fell, this time to rise no more.

What mattered it to Gaston now?—he had arrived. On he went on foot—his limbs were strained and deadened, yet he felt no fatigue, he held the paper crumpled in his hand.

One thing, however, astonished him, and that was meeting no one in so populous a quarter.

As he advanced, however, he heard a sullen murmur coming from the Place de Bouffay, as he passed before a long street which led into that *Place*.

There was a sea of heads, lit up by flaring lights; but Gaston passed on—his business was at the castle—and the sight disappeared.

At last he saw the castle—he saw the door gaping wide before him. The sentinel on guard upon the drawbridge tried to stop him; but Gaston, his order in his hand, pushed him roughly aside and entered the inner door.

Men were talking, and one of them wiping his tears off as he talked.

Gaston understood it all.

"A reprieve!" he cried, "a re—"

The word died upon his lips; but the men had done better than hear, they had seen his despairing gesture.

"Go, go!" they cried, showing him the way, "go! and, perhaps you may yet arrive in time."

And they themselves dispersed in all directions. Gaston pursued his way; he traversed a corridor, then some empty rooms, then the great chamber, and then another corridor.

Far off, through the bars, by the torchlight, he perceived the great crowd of which he had caught a glimpse before.

He had passed right through the castle, and issued on a terrace; thence he perceived the esplanade, a scaffold, men, and all around the crowd.

Gaston tried to cry, but no one heard him, he waved his handkerchief, but no one saw him; another man mounts on the scaffold, and Gaston uttered a cry and threw himself down below.

He had leaped from the top of the rampart to the bottom. A sentinel tried to stop him, but he threw him down, and descended a sort of staircase which led down to the square, and at the bottom was a sort of barricade of wagons. Gaston bent down and glided between the wheels.

Beyond the barricade were all St. Simon's grenadiers—a living hedge; Gaston, with a desperate effort, broke through the line, and found himself inside the ring.

The soldiers, seeing a man, pale and breathless, with a paper in his hand, allowed him to pass.

All of a sudden he stopped, as if struck by lightning. Talhouet!—he saw him! —Talhouet kneeling on the scaffold!

"Stop! stop!" cried Gaston, with all the energy of despair.

But even as he spoke the sword of the executioner flashed like lightning—a dull and heavy blow followed—and a terrible shudder ran through all the crowd.

The young man's shriek was lost in the general cry arising from twenty thousand palpitating breasts at once.

He had arrived a moment too late—Talhouet was dead: and, as he lifted his eyes, he saw in the hand of the headsman the bleeding head of his friend— and then, in the nobility of his heart, he felt that, one being dead, they all should die. That not one of them would accept a pardon which arrived a head too late. He looked around him; Du Couëdic mounted in his turn, clothed with his black mantle, bareheaded and bare-necked.

Gaston remembered that he also had a black mantle, and that his head and neck were bare, and he laughed convulsively.

He saw what remained for him to do, as one sees some wild landscape by the lightning's livid gleam—'tis awful, but grand.

Du Couëdic bends down; but, as he bends, he cries—"See how they recompense the services of faithful soldiers!—see how you keep your promises, oh ye cowards of Bretagne!"

Two assistants force him on his knees; the sword of the executioner whirls round and gleams again, and Du Couëdic lies beside Talhouet.

The executioner takes up the head; shows it to the people; and then places it at one corner of the scaffold, opposite that of Talhouet.

"Who next?" asks Waters.

"It matters little," answers a voice, "provided that Monsieur de Pontcalec be the last, according to his sentence."

"I, then," said Montlouis, "I." And he springs upon the scaffold. But there he stops, his hair bristling; at a window before him he has seen his wife and his children.

"Montlouis! Montlouis!" cries his wife, with the despairing accent of a breaking heart, "Montlouis! look at us!"

At the same moment all eyes were turned toward that window. Soldiers, citizens, priests, and executioners look the same way. Gaston profits by the deathlike silence which reigns around him—springs to the scaffold, and grasps the staircase—and mounts the first steps.

"My wife! my children!" cries Montlouis, wringing his hands in despair; "oh! go, have pity upon me!"

"Montlouis!" cries his wife, holding up afar the youngest of his sons, "Montlouis, bless your children, and one day, perhaps, one of them will avenge you."

"Adieu! my children, my blessing on you!" cries Montlouis, stretching his hands toward the window.

These mournful adieux pierce the night, and reverberate like a terrible echo in the hearts of the spectators.

"Enough," says Waters, "enough." Then turning to his assistants:

"Be quick!" says he, "or the people will not allow us to finish."

"Be easy," says Montlouis; "if the people should rescue me, I would not survive them."

And he pointed with his finger to the heads of his companions.

"Ah, I had estimated them rightly, then," cried Gaston, who heard these words, "Montlouis, martyr, pray for me."

Montlouis turned round, he seemed to have heard a well-known voice; but at the very moment the executioner seized him, and almost instantly a loud cry told Gaston that Montlouis was like the others, and that *his* turn was come.

He leaped up; in a moment he was on the top of the ladder, and he in his turn looked down from the abominable platform upon all that crowd. At three corners of the scaffold were the heads of Talhouet, Du Couëdic, and Montlouis.

But there arose then a strange emotion in the people. The execution of Montlouis, attended by the circumstances we have narrated, had upset the crowd. All the square, heaving and uttering murmurs and imprecations, seemed to Gaston some vast sea with life in every wave. At this moment the idea flashed across him that he might be recognized, and that his name uttered by a single mouth might prevent his carrying out his intention. He fell on his knees, and laid his head himself upon the block.

"Adieu!" he murmured, "adieu, my friends, my tender, dear Helene; thy nuptial kiss has cost me my life, indeed, but not mine honor. Alas! those fifteen minutes wasted in thine arms will have struck down five heads. Adieu! Helene, adieu!"

The sword of the executioner gleamed.

"—And you, my friends, pardon me," added the young man.

The steel fell; the head rolled one way, and the body fell the other.

Then Waters raised the head and showed it to the people.

But then a mighty murmur rose from the crowd; no one had recognized Pontcalec.

The executioner mistook the meaning of this murmur; he placed Gaston's head at the empty corner, and with his foot pushing the body into the tumbril where those of his three companions awaited it, he leaned upon his sword, and cried aloud:

"Justice is done."

"And I, then," cried a voice of thunder, "am I to be forgotten?"

And Pontcalec, in his turn, leaped upon the scaffold.

"You!" cried Waters, recoiling as if he had seen a ghost. "You! who are you?"

"I," said Pontcalec; "come, I am ready."

"But," said the executioner trembling, and looking one after the other at the four corners of the scaffold—"but there are four heads already."

"I am the Baron de Pontcalec, do you hear; I am to die the last—and here I am."

"Count," said Waters, as pale as the baron, pointing with his sword to the four corners.

"Four heads!" exclaimed Pontcalec; "impossible." At this moment he recognized in one of the heads the pale and noble face of Gaston, which seemed to smile upon him even in death.

And he in his turn started back in terror.

"Oh, kill me then quickly!" he cried, groaning with impatience; "would you make me die a thousand times?"

During this interval, one of the commissioners had mounted the ladder, called by the chief executioner. He cast a glance upon Pontcalec.

"It is indeed the Baron de Pontcalec," said the commissioner; "perform your office."

"But," cried the executioner, "there are four heads there already."

"Well, then, his will make five; better too many than too few."

And the commissioner descended the steps, signing to the drums to beat.

Waters reeled upon the boards of his scaffold. The tumult increased. The horror was more than the crowd could bear. A long murmur ran along the square; the lights were put out; the soldiers, driven back, cried "To arms!" there was a moment of noise and confusion, and several voices exclaimed:

"Death to the commissioners! death to the executioners!" Then the guns of the fort, loaded with grape, were pointed toward the people.

"What shall I do?" asked Waters.

"Strike," answered the same voice which had always spoken.

Pontcalec threw himself on his knees; the assistants placed his head upon the block. Then the priests fled in horror, the soldiers trembled in the gloom, and Waters, as he struck, turned away his head lest he should see his victim. Ten minutes afterward the square was empty—the windows closed and dark. The artillery and the fusiliers, encamped around the demolished scaffold, looked in silence on the spots of blood that incarnadined the pavement.

The priests to whom the bodies were delivered recognized that there were indeed, as Waters had said, five bodies instead of four. One of the corpses still held a crumpled paper in his hand.

This paper was the pardon of the other four. Then only was all explained— and the devotion of Gaston, which he had confided to no one, was divined.

The priests wished to perform a mass, but the president, Chateauneuf, fearing some disturbance at Nantes, ordered it to be performed without pomp or ceremony.

The bodies were buried on the Wednesday before Easter. The people were not permitted to enter the chapel where the mutilated bodies reposed, the greater part of which, report says, the quick lime refused to destroy.

And this finished the tragedy of Nantes.

CHAPTER XXXVIII.

THE END.

A fortnight after the events we have just related, a queer carriage, the same which we saw arrive at Paris at the commencement of this history, went out at the same barrier by which it had entered, and proceeded along the road from Paris to Nantes. A young woman, pale and almost dying, was seated in it by the side of an Augustine nun, who uttered a sigh and wiped away a tear every time she looked at her companion.

A man on horseback was watching for the carriage a little beyond Rambouillet. He was wrapped in a large cloak which left nothing visible but his eyes.

Near him was another man also enveloped in a cloak.

When the carriage passed, he heaved a deep sigh, and two silent tears fell from his eyes.

"Adieu!" he murmured, "adieu all my joy, adieu my happiness; adieu Helene, my child, adieu!"

"Monseigneur," said the man beside him, "you must pay for being a great prince; and he who would govern others must first conquer himself. Be strong to the end, monseigneur, and posterity will say that you were great."

"Oh, I shall never forgive you," said the regent, with a sigh so deep it sounded like a groan; "for you have killed my happiness."

"Ah! yes—work for kings," said the companion of this sorrowful man, shrugging his shoulders. "'Noli fidere principibus terræ nec filiis eorum.'"

The two men remained there till the carriage had disappeared, and then returned to Paris.

Eight days afterward the carriage entered the porch of the Augustines at Clisson. On its arrival, all the convent pressed round the suffering traveler— poor floweret! broken by the rough winds of the world.

"Come, my child; come and live with us again," said the superior.

"Not live, my mother," said the young girl, "but die."

"Think only of the Lord, my child," said the good abbess.

"Yes, my mother! Our Lord, who died for the sins of men."

Helene returned to her little cell, from which she had been absent scarcely a month. Everything was still in its place, and exactly as she had left it. She went to the window—the lake was sleeping tranquil and sad, but the ice which had covered it had disappeared beneath the rain, and with it the snow, where, before departing, the young girl had seen the impression of Gaston's footsteps.

Spring came, and everything but Helene began to live once more. The trees around the little lake grew green, the large leaves of the water-lilies floated once more upon the surface, the reeds raised up their heads, and all the families of warbling birds came back to people them again.

Even the barred gate opened to let the sturdy gardener in.

Helene survived the summer, but in September she faded with the waning of the year, and died.

The very morning of her death, the superior received a letter from Paris by a courier. She carried it to the dying girl. It contained only these words:

"My mother—obtain from your daughter her pardon for the regent."

Helene, implored by the superior, grew paler than ever at that name, but she answered:

"Yes, my mother, I forgive him. But it is because I go to rejoin him whom he killed."

At four o'clock in the afternoon she breathed her last.

She asked to be buried at the spot where Gaston used to untie the boat with which he came to visit her; and her last wishes were complied with.

And there she sleeps beneath the sod, pure as the flowers that blossom over her grave: and like them, broken by the cruel gusts that sweep the delicate blossoms so mercilessly down, and wither them with a breath.

END OF "THE REGENT'S DAUGHTER."

Lightning Source UK Ltd.
Milton Keynes UK
UKHW041843100820
367994UK00007BA/344